One Glance
of Your Eyes

One Glance of Your Eyes

A Montana Mercies Romance

MYRA JOHNSON

Paperback ISBN: 978-1-7356107-8-8

You have stolen my heart with one glance of your eyes . . .
—Song of Solomon 4:9, NIV

"Dogs have a way of finding the people who need them and filling an emptiness we didn't even know we had."
—Thom Jones

In memory of "Kitty," our beloved neighborhood cat lady. We miss your cat stories and how you brightened our community breakfasts with fun ways to get acquainted.

Chapter One

It was make-or-break time. The board of directors would either give Carl Anderson's proposal a chance to turn things around, or they'd shut him down before he made it through the first three slides of his PowerPoint presentation.

Pacing in the waiting area outside the conference room, he mentally reviewed each bullet item he planned to cover. Had he left out any crucial details that would help convince the directors? Or would they deem the plan a pointless attempt to prolong the inevitable?

What if he'd labored and prayed over all the brainstorming and prep work for nothing?

"Carl. You're wearing a trench in the carpet." Witt Wittenbauer, his good friend and wingman for today's presentation, gestured toward the padded chair next to his. "Take a breath. This is gonna work."

He plopped down with a groan and ran a finger beneath his too-tight shirt collar. Not many occasions called for a suit and tie these days, but appearing before the board required the attire of a confident and capable professional.

Which, at the moment, he felt anything but. For the past several years, Carl had served as counselor-in-residence at Hope House, a transitional home for men trying to climb out of homelessness. The program was one of Equipped and Empowered Ministries' many outreaches in and around Missoula, Montana, and Carl had experienced mostly positive outcomes.

Over the past year, though, a worrisome number of participants had either dropped out or been expelled from the program and fallen back into street life, two of them from Hope House. Every loss weighed heavily on Carl's heart, causing him to question whether he'd personally done everything in his power to keep them on the right path.

And now, the board was seriously considering ending E and E's transitional housing program entirely.

Carl looked toward his friend and smiled. Witt was one of his most gratifying success stories—although Carl wasn't sure how much credit he could take. Witt's determination to rebuild his shattered life had a lot to do with the combined influences of the faithful canine stretched out on the floor nearby and the amazing woman Witt had married two years ago.

At age forty-five, Carl had pretty much given up on finding a love like Witt and Maddie's. He blamed it on growing up in a series of foster homes and never having learned by example what it took to sustain a lasting relationship. Besides, the men of Hope House had become his family. All the family he needed.

The family he could lose, unless the board granted him leeway to try something unlike anything they'd done in the past, something he hoped would aid his men in finding new meaning and purpose. Something to teach them not only the sacrifices but also the joys of being accountable to someone or something besides themselves.

He needed all this for himself, as well. Even more, he needed renewed affirmation that what he'd devoted his life to actually mattered.

He reached down to give Witt's shepherd mix a scratch behind the ears. "You're a big reason I'm here, boy."

"Don't worry. Ranger will do his part." Witt picked a stray dog hair off his slacks. He didn't look any more comfortable in a coat and tie than Carl felt.

The elevator chime drew their attention. When the doors slid open, a willowy blonde riveted Carl's attention. She blew through like a tornado, only to make a slight stumble when she caught sight of Ranger. Frowning as she gave the dog a wide berth, she jerked to a halt outside the conference room. She took a moment to smooth her short bob into place and straighten the black-and-white hound-stooth blazer she wore over a slim black skirt. Head held high, she adjusted her grip on an expensive-looking black leather tote and strode into the conference room. The door closed firmly behind her.

Carl had the sudden unnerving sense that his plans and hopes were about to go up in smoke. He turned to Witt. "If she's on the board, I'm more nervous than ever."

"Don't let her get to you. Whoever she is, she only has one vote."

"Yes, but how much influence will she have on everybody else?" She'd have to be someone important to march into a closed-door meeting as if she owned the place.

Except in that last instant, Carl was pretty sure he'd detected a slight quiver to her chin. Did she have a few reasons of her own to be nervous?

He could almost feel for her—unless her issues became

his and she decided to derail any chance of getting his proposal approved.

And what was up with her reaction to Ranger? Was she only keeping her distance because of the dog's red "Emotional Support Animal" vest? If she had something against dogs in general, they were really in trouble.

Ten more agonizing minutes passed before the conference room door whispered open. Kitty Davis, executive director Alton Isaacs's silver-haired assistant, smiled in Carl's direction. "We're ready for you."

Witt patted his shoulder as they both stood. Ranger got to his feet as well, giving himself a head-to-tail shake as if to settle his fur into place. Carl wished he could make a quick trip to the men's room to run a comb through his wayward thatch of dark hair. Thus far, he sported only a few strands of gray at his temples—but too many nail-biter days like he'd had recently could change that.

After buttoning his suit coat, he retrieved the navy faux-leather folio containing his notes. He'd already given Kitty the thumb drive containing his PowerPoint presentation, which she'd promised to have loaded and ready to go. Witt would be in charge of advancing the slides on cue. Then later, at the appropriate time, he'd talk a little about himself and Ranger.

As they filed into the room, Kitty handed Carl a small remote. "Your slides are queued up. After introductions, you can push the green button to begin when you're ready."

"Thank you." He passed the remote to Witt and sent up a silent prayer for no technological glitches.

"Good afternoon, Carl." Alton Isaacs came around the table to shake Carl's hand. "Always good to see you." Near

Carl's ear, he added quietly, "Hang in there. I'm rooting for you."

"I appreciate that, sir." He turned slightly toward Witt. "This is my friend and one of our program graduates, Witt Wittenbauer."

"Welcome, Witt. I've heard many good things about you—and this handsome dog of yours." Mr. Isaacs gave Ranger a pat.

The director went on to introduce board chairperson Enid Mason, then each board member in turn. Keeping his smile in place, Carl made silent predictions about which ones he might count on for support. He recognized Ms. Mason and about half the other members from when he'd given his annual reports over the years.

"And I don't believe you've met Rae Caldwell." When Mr. Isaacs gestured toward the flinty blonde in the hound-stooth blazer, Carl's stomach knotted. "Ms. Caldwell will be your new staff liaison, so I asked her to join us today. She's just come on board this week, replacing Joe Fernandez as program director."

This was news to Carl. "I knew Joe was looking toward retirement, but . . ."

"Yes, his decision to move up the date was rather sudden. His daughter in Phoenix has developed some concerning pregnancy complications. Joe and his wife will be moving to Arizona in the next couple of weeks."

"Ah, I hadn't heard." Carl made a mental note to call Joe and wish him and his family well. But the loss of his staunchest advocate within the E and E ranks was a massive blow. Building rapport with the new program director meant starting from scratch—provided the board decided to keep him around long enough to try.

He offered his new supervisor a weak attempt at a smile.

"Welcome to the team, Ms. Caldwell. I look forward to working with you."

She replied with a curt nod.

After a few more words, Mr. Isaacs took his seat and turned the meeting over to the chairperson. Enid Mason nodded for Carl to begin his presentation.

Witt pressed a button, and the opening slide appeared on a large screen at the opposite end of the room. Moving to stand near the screen, Carl quietly cleared his throat while once more taking the measure of his audience. A few wore curious smiles. Others were graciously attentive but clearly reserving judgment.

The one notable exception was Rae Caldwell. Arms crossed, expression rigid, she leaned back in her chair as if daring him to impress her.

One glance of her startling ice-blue eyes told him he didn't stand a chance.

Rae couldn't shake her embarrassment. Arriving late to her first official board meeting? *Way to make a positive impression.*

As if she didn't have enough to overcome after her previous employer had politely asked her to resign—code for *Just go quietly and you won't have to put "fired" on your updated résumé.*

So they'd had some creative differences. The higher-ups apparently didn't appreciate her candor in voicing concerns about the new direction the company had taken. She'd only been keeping an eye on the bottom line, exactly as they'd hired her to do. A year from now, the company's demise would likely be front-page news in the *Missoulian*.

Realizing she'd missed most of the introductions, she gave herself a mental nudge, not that it helped. She could barely concentrate on whatever the guy doing the PowerPoint was talking about. Something about Hope House, one of the transitional homes now under her purview.

And dogs. *Why did it have to be dogs?*

Eyes closed briefly, she pinched the bridge of her nose. Against her will, the image of a sick twelve-year-old girl and a devoted furry black service dog filled her thoughts. The intervening years since her daughter Kellie's death had tempered her grief, but the painful memories persisted.

"What I'm proposing," the man was saying, "is to establish a working relationship with area animal shelters so that we can match abandoned dogs with participants in our transitional housing program. Caring for an animal is a commitment. It nurtures gentleness, kindness, patience, self-control—fruits of the spirit we continually strive to instill in our residents. I firmly believe this program could have a lasting positive effect on both the men and the dogs."

Rae sat straighter in an attempt to corral her wandering thoughts. Opening her planner to the notes section, she ignored the embossed Equipped and Empowered Ministries ballpoint pens scattered around the table and instead took out her Montblanc gold-nibbed fountain pen. Old-school, yes, but she'd come to find serenity in the feel of a fine writing instrument gliding across the page.

The next slide appearing onscreen showed a grinning middle-aged man kneeling beside a big, scruffy dog wearing a service animal vest—the same dog she'd nearly tripped over on her way in. The speaker continued, "This is Witt with his dog, Ranger—the poster kids, if you will, for what I envision with this program. I'll let Witt tell you a little more about himself and the incredible bond he has with Ranger."

Despite her general lack of enthusiasm for the proposal, Rae couldn't help being moved as the man related his descent into homelessness and how a hungry street dog had become his best friend. After Witt developed a serious illness and was hospitalized, he thought he'd never see his dog again. Assigned to Carl's transitional home after he recovered, he began working as a handyman.

Then one snowy day, he was called out to the little town of Elk Valley on a job at Eventide Dog Sanctuary, a refuge for senior and unadoptable dogs. "I never laughed or cried so hard in my life as when this big, beautiful fella charged up those basement stairs and straight into my arms."

When the man grew teary-eyed, Rae had to look away. Hoping to appear preoccupied with note-taking, she scribbled something in her planner.

The dark-haired man—she simply could not remember his name—resumed his presentation. He continued at length, almost pleadingly, it seemed, about the positive effect his idea could have on the morale and self-esteem of the recovering homeless men he counseled, as well as how the ministry could eventually expand its outreach to providing support animals for others in the community.

"For now, we'd focus on basic obedience training," the speaker stated, "although maybe down the road we could look into more specialized service-dog training. But even so, a well-trained and socialized dog can become a faithful companion who listens attentively and loves unconditionally." He nodded toward the man and dog beside him. "Just like Ranger has been for Witt."

The last image on the screen faded to black, and the room went momentarily silent.

Several of the board members responded with brief applause. Ms. Mason sat forward, hands folded on the table. "Thank you, Carl, for bringing forward this intriguing idea. Your presentation has been quite informative." She cast her gaze around the table. "Does anyone have any questions for Carl or Witt?"

Carl. Witt. Rae discreetly jotted the names in her planner. She'd get their last names later.

"Remind me, Carl," the board member at her left began. "How many residents do you currently oversee?"

He appeared only slightly less tense than when he'd begun his talk. "Hope House capacity is twelve, but we have vacancies right now after recent . . ." Lips twitching, he dipped his chin. "Uh, we've had one graduate and two who, unfortunately, were ejected from the program."

Rae had read the files on the two men who had been ejected. One had been caught stealing at his place of employment. The other had repeatedly violated curfew, then became belligerent when confronted. On one occasion, two other residents had to step in to help break up a fight.

The success story, on the other hand, had a happier ending. The man had completed vocational training and accepted a full-time job in the healthcare field. He now shared an apartment with a coworker and thus far appeared to be thriving.

Rae had also seen the financial figures. Each individual they brought into the program required a huge investment, not only monetarily but of staff resources as well. Equipped and Empowered Ministries was funded primarily by grants and donations, which meant that as program director, Rae had a responsibility to ensure those funds were budgeted wisely.

And she refused to be swayed by a slick presentation, much less this dark-haired spokesman's hopeful smile. She raised her hand. "I realize I'm the new kid on the block —Carl, right? But I have a few budget concerns about your dog-training project. Since, as I understand it, the transitional housing program is already on shaky ground, wouldn't it be prudent to limit our funding to more practical initiatives?"

"*Practical?*" The man locked gazes with her. "Ms. . . ."

"Caldwell," she supplied without flinching.

"Ms. Caldwell." Carl's smile flattened. "*Practical* is pretty much all the men and women in our homeless outreach are getting, and honestly, I think that's part of the problem. If we're going to preserve confidence in the program, seems to me it's time to think outside the box."

Rae pulled out the ministry prospectus she'd received the day she'd been hired. Finding the section she was looking for, she ran a finger down the page. "This clearly states that the daily routine at a transitional home includes household chore assignments, vocational counseling, life skills training, spiritual guidance, and group Bible studies. If you're doing your job right, shouldn't that cover everything your residents require for a successful transition?"

Carl's jaw muscles bunched. He looked away briefly, then back again. "Ma'am, were you even listening to anything I said?"

She flinched. "I may have missed something while taking notes." She nonchalantly slid her hand over the mostly blank page.

Ms. Mason sat forward, both palms planted on the

table. With a nod to Mr. Isaacs's assistant, she said, "Kitty, you may distribute Carl's proposal summary now." As Kitty did so, Ms. Mason continued, "Please review this carefully over the next several days. Jot down any additional questions, and we'll discuss them at next week's meeting. Do I have a motion to adjourn?"

Finally. Rae exhaled a controlled sigh of relief. After sliding everything into her tote, she stood and approached the chairperson. "Ms. Mason, once again, I'm sorry for barging in late. It's just that I was rushing here from another meeting across town, and there was an accident on Reserve—"

"Don't fret about it, Rae." The woman's lips quirked briefly as she gathered up her things. "Delays happen."

"Thank you. I hope you know how grateful I am to be part of this inspiring organization." Did she actually almost *curtsy* just then? "I realize I still have much to learn about working here."

"Alton and Kitty will get you up to speed." Ms. Mason slid her purse strap to her shoulder and pivoted toward the exit. "I must run to another meeting now. Good day."

Frozen in place by the brusque dismissal, Rae stared at the chairperson's back as she strode from the room.

"You'll do fine," Mr. Isaacs said, coming up beside her. "We're family here, and we look out for each other. My door is open any time you have questions."

"That's good, because—"

But the man had already bustled out. Seemed everyone had somewhere else to be in a hurry. The only others remaining were Kitty Davis and those two men with the dog. Kitty was handing Carl a thumb drive as the three of them chuckled over some private joke.

Probably at Rae's expense.

She mentally chided herself for being so paranoid, an attitude that really needed to be dealt with—hopefully, before she was "invited" to resign from this job, too.

Chapter Two

More than a week had passed since Carl's presentation to the board, and he was getting anxious for a decision. He tried not to dwell on the fact that the board had met again yesterday—or that he hadn't heard even a hint of where things stood with his proposal.

Putting it out of his mind as best he could, he pulled out a chair at the large, oval dining table and prepared for early-morning prayer and Bible study with the Hope House residents. They'd been working their way through the Old Testament book of First Chronicles and had just read the story of King David turning over plans for building the temple to his son Solomon.

Carl ended their time together by reading aloud David's promise to Solomon—a promise he tried desperately to claim for himself: "*Be strong and courageous, and do the work. Do not be afraid or discouraged, for the Lord God, my God, is with you.*"

Nine men of various ages nodded in agreement. Not everyone entered the program with a solid foundation of faith—if they believed in God at all. But with prayer and the example of their believing housemates, it usually didn't take long before God began working in their hearts. It was no coincidence the transitional home capacity had been set at twelve, the same number as Jesus' disciples. Carl only hoped those three empty seats would soon be filled.

Even more, he prayed the E and E board wouldn't take away these men's best chance for a fresh start and a fulfilling future.

Next on the agenda was seeing the guys off to their various assignments for the day. As residents built up enough savings from their employment earnings, the purchase of a used vehicle marked a big milestone toward their independence. For the men who hadn't reached that point yet, Carl made daily runs in the aging gray passenger van to deliver them to worksites, vocational training, or the Equipped and Empowered offices for specialized counseling.

It was just past 8:45 a.m. when he returned to the empty house. He grabbed another mug of coffee and sat at his desk to catch up on weekly reports.

As he completed a job training update for a resident, his cell phone rang. The display showed a number at the E and E headquarters. He answered with a tentative, "Carl Anderson, Hope House."

"Hello, Mr. Anderson." The stiffly feminine voice made his neck tighten. "This is Rae Caldwell. As you may recall, I've assumed responsibilities as your program director."

"It's just Carl. And yes, I remember you from the meeting last week." How could he not—and for more reasons than the fact that he'd now be reporting directly to her? The ultimate question was whether she'd phoned with good news or bad.

A noisy exhalation sounded in his ear. "Well. I won't beat around the bush."

Bracing for the worst, he shifted his gaze to the window. The expansive fenced yard behind the house would have made an ideal dog training area. "I guess it's too late to—"

"When would be a convenient time for us to discuss the specifics of implementing your plan?"

He jerked upright. "Wh—what?"

"I *said*—"

"I heard you. It's just not what I expected." Dragging a hand down his face, he realigned his thoughts while struggling to hold back a winning touchdown–worthy cheer.

"Mr. Anderson—"

"Carl."

"*Carl.*" She softly cleared her throat. "I must stipulate that approval for your project is provisional, pending the board's review at the end of a three-month trial run."

He wouldn't let the conditional go-ahead dampen his spirits. "I can live with that."

"Please understand, this is not a guarantee that the transitional housing program will continue beyond the three months. The board has yet to make a final decision in that matter."

"I understand." But a lot could change in three months. Besides, as he kept reminding himself, with God all things are possible.

"Again, when would be a good time for us to meet?"

"I'm available today any time before three thirty. That's when I start my afternoon vanpool run."

"Your . . ." She stretched the word out as if refreshing her memory. "Right, your residents will be getting off work, school, and such. In that case, how about this morning, say, in an hour or so?"

"I'll be there."

Ending the call, he hopped from his chair with a grateful shout and a clumsy version of his own end zone celebration. Next, he texted Witt with the news and said he'd give him a full briefing once he'd met with Rae Caldwell. Witt responded with a thumbs-up followed by three praying hands emojis.

Carl hadn't yet shaved, so he took care of that detail, brushed his teeth, and then changed into a baby-blue Oxford shirt and khakis. No reason to go all suit-and-tie this time—or so he hoped. Ms. Caldwell may be his new up-line, but he'd been working for Equipped and Empowered a whole lot longer than she had. Besides, Joe Fernandez never stood on formalities outside the boardroom.

Soon he was marching down the E and E corridor. Passing Kitty Davis's open door, he offered a cheery "Good morning."

"My, aren't you chipper. Guess you got the good news."

He backtracked and slipped inside to stand across the desk from her. Voice lowered, he said, "I know this experiment doesn't come with any guarantees, but after the meeting last week, I was afraid the board wouldn't even give it a chance. Especially after the new program director voiced her opinion."

Kitty's volume matched his. "She wasn't an easy sell, that's for sure."

"And today's the first I've heard from her since my presentation. I'd have thought she'd want to start getting acquainted with the people working under her."

"Joe left behind some pretty big shoes to fill. I'm sure she's still getting her bearings."

Carl snorted. "On top of everything else, I get the feeling she doesn't like dogs." *Or me either, apparently.* On the drive over, he'd been practicing a few things to say that might set a better tone for their working relationship. He didn't have much confidence any of them would succeed.

Kitty stroked one of the many feline figurines adorning her workspace. "I tried to tell you. A therapy *cats* program might have received much quicker approval." She winked. "With cats, all you need is a litter box and a warm lap."

"And fishy-smelling gourmet food—don't forget that." He ignored the executive assistant's smirk. "Seriously, any last-minute tips before I meet with our new program director?"

Lips pursed, she glanced toward the corridor before casting Carl a meaningful smile. "Just be kind. And patient. Beneath Rae's tough-as-nails persona, I sense there are deeper levels to plumb . . . and a softer heart than she might let on."

He'd like to believe it, provided those deeper levels included a commitment to lifting as many unhoused Montanans as possible from the grip and stigma of their situation. To keep Hope House going, he really, really needed her on his side.

With a nod of thanks to Kitty, he continued to Rae Caldwell's office. The door stood slightly ajar. He tapped twice and peeked in. "Ms. Caldwell?"

Backlighting from a bright window haloed her silver-blond hair, but her frown quickly dispelled the ethereal image. "You're twenty minutes late."

He waited a beat before replying. "I didn't realize we'd agreed on an exact time."

"I believe I specified 'an hour or so.' The *or so* has come and gone." She motioned to a smoke-blue upholstered chair on his side of the desk. "Please. Sit."

Biting the inside of his lip, he stifled the automatic *Yes, Your Majesty.* Instead, he sent up a prayer for tact and a big helping of the patience Kitty had recommended. For a man as discerning as Alton Isaacs to have hired Rae Caldwell for this position, she must have a few redeeming qualities besides being drop-dead gorgeous.

And where had *that* thought come from? *Get a grip, Anderson.* There was entirely too much at stake to let himself be distracted by a pretty face. For one thing, she was his immediate supervisor. For another, he'd long ago declared himself immune to womanly wiles.

Which, thus far, Rae Caldwell seemed utterly devoid of.

A copy of his proposal summary lay on the corner of her desk. She used one finger to slide the document closer, then slowly paged through it. "Mm-hmm . . . mm-hmm."

"If you need me to elaborate on anything—"

She shushed him and continued her perusal.

Okay, have it your way. Being treated like a misbehaving adolescent called to the principal's office effectively chilled any feelings of attraction that had made it past his defenses.

Sitting back with arms folded, he allowed his gaze to roam the space. The desk, credenza, bookshelves, and other furnishings were the same as when Joe had occupied the office. Missing were any personal touches, like the family photos and grandkids' artwork Joe always had on display. He'd give her the benefit of the doubt and assume she was still settling in.

She looked up at long last. "In all fairness, you should know I strongly recommended against your proposal. All I see here is a sinkhole for ministry funds that should rightly be directed toward proven avenues benefiting our unhoused clients. Plus, the liability angle must be thoroughly investigated. We can't risk being sued over dog bites, and we certainly don't want our transitional homes turned into flea hotels. Besides all that—"

"Now hang on a minute." Carl sat forward, fingers tightening around the chrome chair arms. "Every single one of those concerns is addressed in my proposal—which I'd assumed you'd have meticulously reviewed prior to this meeting instead of making me sit here in silence while you read it."

"I *have* studied it, Mr. Anderson—"

"Carl."

"*Carl.*" She sniffed. "I was merely reviewing the key points. Due to your late arrival, I had moved on to deal with other responsibilities."

"I was not late by any definition of the word." He forced a calming breath and eased deeper into his chair. *Attraction?* Pfft. "I get that you have reservations, Ms. Caldwell. Believe me, I do respect your concerns. However, I gather the board overruled you, and now you're stuck working with me on this project." So much for the tactful approaches he'd practiced in the car. "Can you at least try to show a little positivity? Courtesy and cooperation would be nice, too."

Glancing away, she pulled her lips between her teeth. "You're right." She tucked a shimmery strand behind one ear. "It's my job to support and facilitate any and all programming the directors vote to implement, and I promise you will have my full cooperation. However . . ."

Here it came, the *but* behind her compliance. Why did she have to make this so hard?

She took a sip from the insulated mug next to her

computer. "However," she repeated, "you should know that I—that dogs—"

He cocked his head. "You're afraid of dogs?"

"No. Not afraid." Her hand trembled slightly as she reached again for the mug. "Never mind. It's my problem, not yours. I won't allow it to interfere."

Something told him she was kidding herself about that last part. How could something dog-related that seemed so clearly upsetting *not* encroach upon her ability to give his project a fair chance?

Kitty had been right about the woman's deeper layers. In place of mounting resentment toward his prickly new boss, Carl allowed a twinge of empathy to take root. He hoped for Rae Caldwell's sake that she had someone close enough to confide in because she obviously needed to deal with her issues.

He started to ask, then bit his tongue. *You barely know the woman, and she isn't exactly welcoming you into her inner circle.*

Better for now to focus on launching the canine project and saving Hope House—hopefully without biting each other's head off.

Rae could see it in the softening of those perceptive brown eyes—for a moment there, Carl had actually felt sorry for her. Which was the absolute *last* thing she wanted or needed from him. From *any* man.

She snatched up her Montblanc and poised it over an empty page in her planner. "Where shall we begin?"

"Begin?" He cast her a blank look.

"Yes," she said, seizing the upper hand once more. "With your project. What's the first step?"

Clearing his throat, he shifted forward in the chair. "Well, choosing our first group of dogs, obviously. I was thinking three to start with. I have a contact at the Elk Valley Animal Shelter."

Rae nodded and wrote down *3 dogs, Elk Valley Animal Shelter*. She asked a few more questions and made notes accordingly. Though she resisted verbally acknowledging Carl's attention to detail, it was evident in every aspect of the steps he described. The more he talked, the more animated he became. She was soon so caught up in his enthusiasm and the warmth of his voice that she forgot to take notes.

He paused at one point. "You're not writing this down. Did I lose you?"

"No, I, um . . . It's clear you have everything firmly in hand, and I'm sure you'll keep me apprised if there's anything in particular I should be involved in."

One brow cocked, he asked, "How involved would you like to be?"

The question threw her for a moment. She capped her pen while mentally chastising herself for reading something entirely different into his remark. "I should probably ask Mr. Isaacs what his expectations are in that regard. I do have other ministry areas to oversee."

"Right. You can get back to me after you talk to him." Carl pressed his hands against the armrests as if preparing to leave. Then he hesitated. "Look, I realize you're dealing with a learning curve coming into a new job and all. But this is an adjustment for me, too. Your predecessor and I were on pretty solid footing."

"Although my professional style may be different from

that of Mr. Fernandez, I assure you my commitment to the mission of Equipped and Empowered Ministries is equally strong." That sounded good, didn't it? She recalled signing something that affirmed her adherence to the organization's beliefs and vision statement. But then, did anyone really take those things literally?

"Good," Carl stated, "because I'm a firm believer in E and E's vision, and I don't think I could work effectively with someone who isn't fully on board."

Eyes averted, Rae softly cleared her throat. "Of course."

This time, Carl made it all the way to his feet. "All right, then. I'll start the ball rolling with a call to the animal shelter."

"Do that. And keep me apprised."

"Yes, ma'am, I will definitely keep you apprised." He looked ready to salute, then coughed into his hand.

Great. He had her completely flustered and now she was repeating herself. She hiked her chin. "Have we covered everything for now?"

"I believe so. Good day, Ms. Caldwell." He took a step toward the door.

"Rae is fine," she murmured, picking up her pen.

He nodded. "All right, then. Rae it is."

As soon as the door closed behind him, she melted into her chair. Her antiperspirant was having to work overtime today. Since her first day on the job, in fact. Why did she feel like such a misfit at E and E?

You know why. These people are genuine believers, and you lost your faith a long time ago.

But why did one have to believe in God in order to do a respectable job, even for a Christian organization? There was nothing particularly spiritual about spreadsheets, profit-and-loss statements, or corporate pie charts.

The buzz of the intercom intruded. It was Kitty Davis. "I was watching for your meeting with Carl to wrap up. Mr. Isaacs would like you to come to his office."

"Be right there." This was as good a time as any to ask for clarification about how hands-on he expected her to be with Carl Anderson's pet project.

She laughed to herself at her mental choice of words.

Twenty minutes later, she wasn't finding her situation the least bit funny. Seemed her boss had decided she should participate as fully as possible with the arrangements and implementation.

She'd tried to convince Mr. Isaacs that it wasn't Carl she had a problem with. It was the whole *dog* thing. She loved dogs, she really did. Or at least she'd loved one dog in particular. Memories of Kellie and her loyal service dog had ruined Rae for every other dog she'd encountered since.

But to explain all that to her boss would have meant revealing her deepest self—the grief and guilt and utter despair that never failed to grab her by the throat the moment she let her guard down.

The best she could hope for was the canine project's quick demise. Surely, once things were underway, Alton Isaacs and the board of directors would see for themselves how impractical the whole idea was. It didn't matter how thoroughly Carl had vetted the plan, something was bound to go wrong eventually. Someone's shoes would get chewed up, or there'd be potty accidents on the carpet, or—worse —a dog wouldn't adapt well and end up biting someone.

Rae would be left to deal with the aftermath, of course. But she'd be proven right, the project would be terminated, and she could put it all behind her and focus on more prudent uses of her time.

Why didn't those prospects make her feel any better?

Chapter Three

Ellis Newman seethed. The infection in his hand meant he could no longer work at his construction job. Which meant he couldn't pay his share of the rent. Which meant he could soon be out on the street.

And all because of a stupid dog bite. Yeah, he'd ventured too close, but what was up with people thinking they needed a vicious animal to guard their stuff?

From people like you, you mean? You know good and well what you'd have done next if that dog hadn't been on the attack.

Too bad he couldn't permanently silence his conscience. Blame it on all those Sunday school classes his holier-than-thou parents had forced him to attend.

The nurse finished wrapping a fresh bandage around Ellis's swollen and throbbing right hand. "Dr. Abernathy has ordered an antibiotic injection. He's also sending you home with a ten-day supply of amoxicillin. You'll need to take it twice a day, every day, and be sure you—"

"Take it until it's gone. I know the drill." Over the past

few years, he'd used the free clinic services more times than he cared to count.

Eying him through her horn-rimmed glasses, the nurse frowned. "You should have come in right away after this happened. Can you be absolutely certain the dog that bit you had a current rabies vaccination?"

"The owner showed me the certificate." While practically begging him not to sue. Good thing the guy had no idea what Ellis had really been up to.

Using his good hand, he bared the upper part of his hip for the hypo. With a pinched smile, he asked, "Any chance of getting something for pain? This sucker really hurts, and the over-the-counter stuff isn't helping."

"I'll mention it to the doctor." It felt like she jammed the needle in about twice as hard as necessary, and he yelped. On her way out, she dropped the hypo into the red sharps receptacle on the wall.

Perched on the exam table, Ellis wondered how long he should wait for her to come back with a no. Doctors were a little too stingy with pain prescriptions these days. Too bad, because those little white pills made the trip to la-la land a lot more enjoyable than the buzz he'd get downing a cheap bottle of wine.

The nurse returned with a visit summary printout and a brown paper bag. "Here are your antibiotics, plus three days' worth of a stronger pain med." She barely concealed a sneer. "Don't get excited. It isn't oxy. It's a potent combo of acetaminophen and ibuprofen, and best taken with food if you want to avoid stomach problems."

He hated the fresh wave of shame that swept through him. *I'm not a druggie,* he felt like shouting. *It's just that my hand hurts and I can't catch a break.*

A few days on oxy would have been a nice vacation

from his current troubles, even knowing he'd wake up to find his situation that much worse. No job, no money, no food on the table—and no table to put it on, since any day now, his roomies would probably kick him out of the apartment. His life was one long, continuous train wreck, and he wanted off.

Leaving the clinic, he wandered aimlessly through downtown Casper, Wyoming. What was the point of returning to the bug-infested digs where he crashed with three other guys on the construction crew? After the dog bite, his housemates had been covering for him as best they could, letting him do fetching and cleanup while they operated the heavy-duty power tools.

But charity among coworkers only went so far, and the foreman was bound to notice sooner rather than later that Ellis had been slacking off.

Maybe he should just blow this burg. He had no ties to Casper, and it was only a few short blocks to the highway. A little farther north just past Buffalo, Interstate 25 became I-90, and then it was a fairly straight shot northwest into Montana. If he could hitch a ride with a long-haul trucker, he could make it to Missoula. Why he wanted to go back there, he wasn't sure. Maybe because the town held the last good memories he could recall.

After a quick detour to the apartment to stuff his razor, toothbrush, and a few items of clothing into a duffel, he trekked toward the highway. If Missoula didn't work out, he could always move on again. The *where* had never mattered much, because he'd learned far too young how completely alone he was in the world. When his parents refused to bail him out after the worst of his teenage drinking binges, his already messed-up life went even farther down the tubes. So he'd wrecked their car. At least nobody'd gotten hurt but himself. He'd even avoided hitting the mangy dog that caused him to swerve in the first place.

"Stupid mutt." Pausing beneath a sign pointing to I-25, he tucked his aching hand against his ribs and heaved an angry sigh.

Dogs. Nothing but trouble.

Chapter Four

Arms folded, Rae stayed well back from the three dogs they'd come to see at the Elk Valley Animal Shelter. Carl had arranged for the staff to narrow down their selection to the most likely candidates.

"It's a win-win situation," Carl told her as they waited for the kennel workers to bring out the dogs. "Besides the benefits and experience our residents will gain, we're freeing up kennel space while socializing and training the dogs to make them better candidates for adoption."

"That's . . . nice." She was glad she'd dressed in flannel-lined jeans and a heavy cable-knit sweater. The spacious indoor play area, floored with bright green artificial turf, was on the chilly side.

Soon, three excited canines burst through a side door into the playroom. It was good that none of them looked anything like Shadow, or she'd have manufactured a reason to skip out.

Witt Wittenbauer, Carl's partner in this venture, knelt nose-to-nose with a lanky, chocolate-brown Labrador retriever. The dog's tail swished wildly as Witt scratched him behind his floppy ears. "Who's a good boy?" Witt laughed when the dog licked his chin. "Who's a good boy?"

Rae swallowed a snicker. Heaven forbid anyone should assume she was amused by the canine antics.

Carl asked the attendant for a leash and slipped it around the neck of a bouncy, black short-haired dog with a white chest and a white stripe down its nose. "Let's see how well you walk, little girl."

"We've named her Zippy." The fiftysomething woman, wearing green scrubs over a turtleneck, stepped out of the way. "She never seems to run out of energy."

"She seems really smart, though—hey, careful, girl!" Carl nearly tripped as the dog darted back and forth in front of his legs.

Rae snorted. "Maybe *you* should be careful."

Shooting her a smirk, he tipped his head toward the third dog, a black, white, and tan husky-shepherd mix. "Go make friends, why don't you?" Doing a double-take, he added, "That fella's eyes are about the same shade of blue as yours."

She'd already taken note of the dog's striking silver-blue eyes . . . and they kind of gave her the creeps. "That's okay. I'll leave the canine encounters to you and your accomplice."

Now he looked annoyed. After another turn about the room with the black-and-white live wire, who'd settled into a semi-compliant prance, he slipped the leash off the dog's neck and moved on to the husky.

The attendant gave the dog an affectionate pat. "We call this one Frankie, as in Frank Sinatra, Ol' Blue Eyes."

Carl laughed. "That's perfect."

While Carl walked Frankie around, Witt ambled over. The tail-wagging Lab plopped down next to his foot.

Rae spared a pat for the cuddly-looking dog as she cast Witt a brief smile. "Looks like you've found a new best friend."

"He's a sweetheart, all right. But Ranger has nothing to worry about."

"That was quite a story you told at the board meeting last week—losing him, finding him again at the rescue kennel . . . then falling head-over-heels in love and marrying the owner." Rae hadn't meant that last part to sound so cynical, but she no longer believed in true love.

Since Kellie died and her marriage had fallen apart, she didn't believe in much of anything.

"I realize it sounds like something out of a sappy romance novel, but it happened just like I said." Witt grinned like a moonstruck teenager. "I thank the Lord every day for bringing Maddie and me together."

"Mmm." Rae had no other reply to such a statement.

"Say, I know some other Caldwells in Missoula. Any chance you're related?"

She shrugged. "It's a fairly common name."

"I've done a few handyman jobs for this real nice couple, David and Alicia Caldwell."

Trying hard not to wince at the prick to her heart, she kept her tone level. "Yes, I know them. They're my ex-husband's parents." Wanting to get the doggy meet-and-greet over with, she blurted, "How much longer is this going to take?"

Carl headed over, still leading the husky. "Everything okay?"

"Fine." Avoiding his frown, along with the animal's disconcerting blue-eyed stare, she firmed her jaw. "Have you made a decision about the dogs?"

"All three have potential. Next, we need to match them

with their trainers. I already have some Hope House residents in mind."

"Good. Then you should get busy on that."

Studying her, he cocked his head. "Are you sure everything's all right?"

"My fault," Witt said. "I think I unknowingly brought up a sensitive topic."

"Oh, please." She flicked her fingers in a dismissive gesture. "I wasn't so messed up by my divorce that I can't handle mention of my former in-laws. Anyway, it was years ago, and we've all moved on." *Mostly.*

Until she got dragged into this whole dog-training thing and all the memories it evoked of Kellie and her devoted black service dog—literally her Shadow. The little guy had never left Kellie's side, even after she'd closed her eyes for the last time. Mark had to lift the whimpering animal off Kellie's bed and clip on his leash in order to coax him from the room.

Before the moment grew any more awkward, she shrugged into her jacket. "Are we done here?"

Carl and Witt exchanged glances, no doubt silently casting aspersions on their mercurial program director. Well, they'd better get over it.

Passing the husky's leash to Witt, Carl aimed a pointed stare toward Rae that made her flinch. "Before this goes any further, I think you and I should iron out a few things."

"Oh?" The squeak in her voice dashed any hope of sounding unruffled.

He turned to Witt. "Would you mind wrapping things up here? We'll talk more later."

After which Rae was certain Witt whispered, "Go easy on her, okay?"

She didn't know whether to feel grateful or insulted,

but at the moment, she definitely liked Carl's partner a whole lot more than she liked him.

They strode through a corridor to the lobby and then out to their vehicles. Stepping around a melting drift from last week's late-spring snowfall, Rae halted next to her car and faced Carl. "Do you prefer to discuss your issues now, or shall we set up a meeting early next week?"

"Well, I . . ." He looked past her, his somber look morphing into an appreciative stare. "This is *your* car?"

Laying a hand atop the roof of her cherry-red Mazda Miata convertible, she savored a moment of self-satisfaction. The Miata was her identity crisis car, purchased a year to the day after her divorce. "It gets me where I need to be."

In the spring and summer, anyway. She'd kept her trusty twelve-year-old Jeep for when Montana winters made travel difficult.

"I noticed it in the parking lot of the ministry building the other day and wondered whose it was."

"Now you know."

"Uh, right." He seemed to have difficulty tearing his gaze away from the shiny red vehicle.

Oddly, that made her feel slightly less antagonistic toward him—an attitude that was ridiculous from day one, because her lack of enthusiasm for his dog-training venture couldn't be blamed on him. Everything she'd learned about Carl Anderson through her predecessor's reports and conversations with other staff members painted him as a hard-working, highly principled man deeply dedicated to the mission of Equipped and Empowered Ministries.

It was actually a shame that his position as a transitional home counselor could end up on the chopping block. Whatever the outcome, he couldn't expect her to take the blame for something already under consideration before she came on staff.

She quirked her lips. "Look, I know we've gotten off to a rough start. That's on me, and I apologize."

"Thank you." His attention fully on her now, he cast her a curious frown. "I admit to being puzzled by your negativity about my proposal."

She stood straighter. "Despite my reservations, I'm not blind to its merits. And I think we both want the same thing—what best serves the clients of Equipped and Empowered Ministries."

His brows drew together. "Of course."

"In that case . . ." She searched her purse for her key fob, which she didn't really need in hand because a press of the door handle had already unlocked the car. "Are we good? Or is there more you wanted to talk about?"

"No, I'm trusting we're on the same page now." The conviction in those soft brown eyes, combined with his nearness, made her fingertips tingle.

The key fob hit the pavement.

"Here, let me."

"No, I've—" She stooped at the same time he did, and they bumped heads.

Scooping up her keys with one hand, he steadied her with the other and helped her to her feet. "Ouch. Sorry about that."

"It's okay." She massaged her forehead, less embarrassed by her klutziness than her sudden acute awareness of him as a man.

A very manly man. Intelligent. Caring. Kind.

Slamming the door on those thoughts, she reclaimed her keys and dropped them into her purse. "All right, then. Why don't we plan to talk again early next week?"

"Good idea. I'll give you a call—"

A riff from her cell phone interrupted him. Her stomach clenched at the sound of her mother's ringtone. Which of Rae's siblings was Mom calling to whine about this time?

That was the trouble with being the eldest of six—even more so since her father had passed away three years ago. Mom continued to rely on Rae to ride herd over her sometimes rebellious, other times distressingly irresponsible brothers and sisters. Worse, they were all adults now—or should be, if they'd only act like it.

The phone continued ringing.

Carl frowned. "Not someone you want to talk to?"

"It's my mother." She gave her head a quick shake and pulled open the car door. "I have to go. Sorry."

Heading to his dark blue Subaru Forester, Carl paused for a glance over his shoulder. Rae sat stiffly inside the little red car, phone to her ear and looking as if her mother wasn't letting her get a word in edgewise.

He winced. Nothing like family issues to throw a person's life out of whack. On the other hand, at least Rae had a family. Bouncing from one foster home to the next, Carl had never felt like he fit in anywhere. His little brother, five years younger and a lot cuter than Carl, had been adopted a year or so after their homeless, mentally ill mother relinquished them to the state. Carl had never seen his mother or his brother again. As for his nameless father, not a clue.

Even so, he counted two good things that had come out of his experiences. One, he'd had to toughen up quickly.

Two, he'd learned compassion for those who, often through no fault of their own, found themselves disadvantaged, disregarded, and generally misunderstood. That had led to a master's degree in social work from the University of Montana and the position he now held with Equipped and Empowered Ministries.

Although, unless his canine project managed to turn things around, he could soon be seeking a position elsewhere. He didn't relish the idea of leaving Missoula, but larger cities meant larger programs and, hopefully, better opportunities to continue the work he'd devoted his life to.

Before climbing into his SUV, he looked again in Rae's direction. Off the phone now, she gripped the steering wheel with both fists and slowly pounded her head against it. He debated whether to go over and ask if he could help somehow, but before he could, she jerked upright, started the engine, and careened from the parking lot.

Kitty Davis was right—Rae had a lot more going on under the surface than anyone knew.

On his way back to Hope House, he stopped at a Missoula pet supply store Witt had suggested as a possible source of donations. A friendly conversation with the owner elicited a commitment of crates, bowls, training leads, and a variety of other essentials, along with a three-month supply of dog food.

Arriving at the house afterward, he checked to see that the residents' usual weekend chore assignments were being handled. He wasn't happy to discover that Glen, one of the men on his list of potential dog handlers, had left a pile of dirty laundry in the middle of the kitchen.

He found him watching TV in the living room. Snatching up the remote, he switched off the set. "Glen. You know television is off limits until chores are done."

"Come on, man." Glen rose in a huff. "I was just taking a break to look for some sports scores."

"Rules are rules. Get busy on that laundry."

Satisfied the man was following through, Carl went to his office. Next on his to-do list was a follow-up call to the certified dog trainer recommended by the Elk Valley Animal Shelter manager. The young man agreed to conduct a complimentary six-session basic obedience class on Saturday mornings beginning the following weekend. They'd use the shelter's indoor playroom for now, then move to the backyard at Hope House as summer neared.

Now he needed to pair the shelter dogs with the three residents he'd carefully screened and selected for the program's trial run. Glen's flouting of house rules could have been a disqualifying factor, but Carl held out hope that the responsibility of caring for a dog would provide Glen strong incentive to develop better habits.

With the list narrowed down to two more residents who could most benefit from the program, all he could do was leave his choices in God's hands. He'd have Witt arrange with the shelter for them to pick up the dogs early next week, and the men could begin bonding with their new companions.

He leaned back in his desk chair with a satisfied sigh. After months of research, strategizing, and plenty of prayers, his vision was coming together. *This is Your doing, Lord. Please bless these efforts with such measurable success that the E and E board can no longer justify closing down Hope House. Bless and guide the men under my care, and above all, let me trust in Your wisdom and not my own.*

As an afterthought, he murmured, "And by the way, if You could continue to smooth things over between Rae and me, it would really help."

Your guard is slipping, Rae.

Bad enough that Carl Anderson had compelled her to admit she had a problem being around dogs. She should never have let him catch her in a moment of weakness the way he had when her mother phoned. The man didn't need any more ammunition he could someday use to get her fired.

Not that he seemed at all like the vengeful type, but she simply could not afford another career reset, because as long as this codependent relationship with her family continued, they'd keep draining her, both financially and emotionally.

Mom's panicked call resulted in Rae's spending the remainder of the weekend helping Sybil, the baby of the family, find another place to live after her landlord evicted her for being three months overdue with her rent.

Rae hefted another box of her sister's things into the trunk of their mom's car. "How on earth did you get so far behind?"

Toting a laundry basket packed with bedding and towels, Sybil gave an evasive shrug. "Oh, you know how bills pile up."

"Don't tell me—you maxed out your credit card again."

"Now, girls, let's not bicker." Their mother dropped a small shopping bag into the back seat. Hard not to notice she'd left the heavy lifting to her daughters.

Conveniently, their brother Reece, who also lived in the area, had other things to do on a Sunday afternoon. Rae could only hope he was home with his wife and not partying with the less-than-reputable friends who repeatedly led him astray.

As they carried out the rest of Sybil's belongings, the

apartment manager came over to inspect the vacated unit for damages. He came back with a long list of issues— carpet and furniture stains, a broken doorknob, grime in the stove burner wells, cabinet door hinges bent . . .

"Sorry, Miss Ogden, but we won't be refunding your security deposit."

"Hey, the carpet was already a mess when I moved in," Sybil whined. "The doorknob was broken, too."

The manager jabbed his finger on the official-looking page attached to his clipboard. "I have your signature right here acknowledging that everything was in good order when you took possession." He held out his hand. "Keys, please. And expect to hear from our attorneys if your back rent isn't paid in full by the end of the month."

Lower lip trembling, Sybil passed him the keys. When the man had gone, she turned to Rae. "How am I ever gonna get that much money—much less find a new place to live that I can afford?"

Rae should have seen this coming. "I'll handle it," she murmured. "Be right back."

Ten minutes later, she'd written a check to the apartment manager covering Sybil's back rent. By the end of the day, she'd forked over the first and last month's deposit on a furnished studio apartment. It was a small price to pay to prevent her spoiled little sister from becoming her permanent housemate. She'd made the mistake once of letting Leo, the younger of her two brothers, move in with her. It had taken eight months and the threat of a bulldozer to get him to leave. Offered a job in Portland shortly afterward, he'd finally begun to get his act together.

Darkness was falling as they piled the last of Sybil's boxes and bags into the new apartment. While Sybil and Mom began unpacking, Rae phoned in a takeout order from a nearby Thai restaurant—at her own expense, naturally. By the time they sat down to eat, Rae was almost too tired to pick up her chopsticks.

When she was ready to head home, Sybil clung to her arm as she trudged out to her car. "Thank you so much, Rae. For everything. I'll pay you back, I promise."

Rae nodded, though she never expected to see a penny. Exhaustion nearly overwhelmed her as she aimed the red Mazda toward her comfortable little house in Elk Valley. *You're such a pushover*, she chided herself.

Over time, her family's freeloading had only gotten worse. A year or so before her father's death, she'd given him the okay to hook up a small travel trailer behind her house. He'd dubbed it his "man cave" and often holed up in it for an entire weekend. He was a quiet, peace-loving guy, so it was hard to blame him for needing regular breaks from the family drama. Rae wished it were so easy for her to do the same.

After Dad passed away, though, the entire Ogden clan seemed to think they could use the trailer at will. Parties, sleepovers, sleep-it-offs . . . Rae hated to think what else. They took it for granted she'd clean up behind them.

Well, *someone* had to be the adult in the family. Why did it always have to be her?

Chapter Five

Ellis hadn't been as quick to get out of Wyoming as he'd hoped. The first driver who'd offered him a ride was only going as far as Ranchester, up near the Wyoming-Montana border, after which he'd be leaving the interstate and heading west to Burgess Junction. By then, dusk had fallen, and the old man was kind enough to drop Ellis at a small church where he could ask for assistance.

Naturally, the white-haired pastor had assumed Ellis was homeless and offered to refer him to a local shelter.

"I'm not homeless." He'd made up a story about his car breaking down some miles back, and he just needed someplace to stay the night until he could catch a ride to Missoula. "I've got a job waiting for me there"—another lie—"and they won't hold it for me more than a couple of days."

That earned a dubious glance at his bandaged hand, along with a measure of sympathy. The pastor agreed to let him sleep in the church's youth center, where at least it was warm. The men's room even had shower facilities. While

Ellis spread borrowed bedding on a sofa, the pastor made a phone call, and soon afterward, another oldish guy delivered a burger, fries, and cola, along with a thermos of coffee and a packaged cinnamon roll for Ellis's breakfast.

The pastor and his cohort stayed overnight in the building as well, "just in case you need anything." In other words, *We're not leaving you to ransack the church for anything you can pawn later for cash.*

He could hardly blame them. A look in the restroom mirror showed an unshaven hitchhiker in a frayed, sweat-stained shirt and grimy jeans with the knees wearing through. Not a picture that inspired much trust.

Four more days and nights on the road, two of which included shivering alone and hungry beneath a highway overpass, and Ellis's latest ride finally rolled into Missoula. It was around noon when the semi driver, a wiry little man named Joe, exited the interstate near the University of Montana and splashed through patches of melting snow lingering along curbs. Vehicles of all types, including an abundance of mud-spattered pickups and SUVs, jammed the city streets.

"Churches are letting out about now," the trucker remarked as he braked for a red light. "It'll be slow going through town."

"It's Sunday already?" Time had begun to lose meaning for Ellis. Regular employment meant he'd had to keep track of what day of the week it was so he wouldn't miss work. Now, with survival his only job, one day was pretty much like the last.

Traffic was moving again. Joe took a right, then a left. "I've got two deliveries here in town, and then I'm headed south through Idaho and on to Salt Lake City. If you change your mind about Missoula, you're welcome to ride along."

"Thanks, but I'll take my chances here." Ellis let his gaze comb the sights along the roadway. He didn't remember much about his childhood years in Missoula, but what he saw now looked inviting. It seemed like a friendly kind of town, bustling but not huge, and he wouldn't mind exploring that sporting goods store they'd just passed.

If he had two nickels to rub together, anyway. More than once, he'd asked himself why he'd been in such a hurry to leave behind what had promised to be steady work on the Casper construction crew. Then his hand would begin to throb, and he'd curse the animal that had sunk its teeth into his flesh.

And all because he'd gotten too close while pondering what could be in the lockbox in the back of that truck. Must be valuable if the owner needed to leave an attack dog on duty, and likely worth a whole lot more than what the construction boss was paying for grunt work.

He tried to tell himself he wouldn't *really* have tried to break in. But if not for that dog . . .

Cradling his aching hand, he blew out slowly and faced forward. "Drop me anywhere," he told the driver. "I'll let you be on your way."

"No prob. My first stop's coming up. Stick around and I'll treat you to lunch before we part ways."

Ellis's stomach growled at the mere suggestion. "That's real kind of you, but—"

"No buts." Joe nodded toward him with an empathetic smile. "I been down and out before. Might still be if I'd refused the kind help of a godly man who once gave me a lift sorta like I done for you. Turned my life right around, he did. So every stranger I meet on the road, I try to do the same."

Ellis slanted him a disbelieving look. "Isn't that kind of risky? I mean, I could have been a serial killer, for all you knew."

"Just as dangerous for you hitching rides from strangers. There's some bad actors out there I sure wouldn't wanna mess with." Scoffing, Joe shook his head. "Truth is, the Lord's blessed me with a sixth sense about people. I can tell when a man's got a good heart. I saw that in you right away."

A feeling Ellis hadn't experienced in too long to remember made his insides quiver. He covered it with a mocking laugh. "Hate to tell you this, Joe, but your antenna must be out of whack."

Joe merely chuckled. Pulling in behind a massive warehouse, he backed the trailer up to an open loading dock and cut the engine. "Sit tight. This shouldn't take long, and then we'll find something to eat."

Alone in the cab, Ellis briefly considered taking off without a goodbye. Joe was a nice guy, but all this talk of the Lord and blessings and seeing the good in others made Ellis downright twitchy. Despite his parents' best efforts to bring him to the Lord, he'd quickly figured out he could linger in the hallway outside his Sunday school class until no one was looking and then skitter out the rear exit and down the alley. The convenience store at the end of the block made for easy pickings. A Milky Way or bag of M&Ms would find its way into his jacket pocket, and he'd sidle out the door while the cashier served an actual paying customer.

His childhood life of crime was soon cut short, thanks to a firm talking-to one Sunday when the store manager caught him red-handed. He swore he'd never do it again if only the man wouldn't rat him out to his parents. "My dad'll kill me," he'd sobbed, knowing it was close to the truth. His backside hurt just thinking about the paddling he'd get.

The manager had taken pity on him. "All right, then, you get on back to Sunday school, young man." He handed him a shiny laminated card with the Ten Commandments printed on one side and the Lord's Prayer on the other. "And remember, Jesus is always watching."

Whether out of guilt or fear of God's wrath, Ellis couldn't say for sure, but he'd carried the card in his wallet all these years since. Lips clamped, he tugged it out and absently ran his fingers over the rough edges. The card wasn't as shiny anymore, the plastic coating scratched and the corners bent.

How many of those commandments had he broken over the years? He'd never killed anybody, that was for certain. But the rest . . .

If Jesus really was always watching, and if there really was a heaven, Ellis had zero chance of getting in.

The driver's door opened, and Joe climbed behind the wheel. "All done. Ready to grab a bite?"

Ellis quietly slid the card back into his wallet. "Sure, sounds good."

Chapter Six

After church on Sunday, Carl dropped the men back at Hope House, then traded the van for his SUV and drove out to Witt and Maddie's. They'd invited him for Sunday dinner, which usually meant Maddie's slow-cooker pot roast and—he hoped—a slice of huckleberry pie made with berries from last summer's preserves.

He wasn't disappointed. After serving them second helpings of huckleberry pie à la mode, Maddie ushered Carl and Witt to the living room with coffee refills.

"You two talk as long as you want," she said. "I'll be in the study completing a few pet sketches."

Shortly after meeting Maddie, Witt had discovered her incredible artistic talent. Selling pet portraits turned out to be the breakthrough she'd needed to supplement funding for Eventide.

Claiming a spot on the sofa, Carl set his mug on an end table. "Hey, Maddie, maybe you'd do portraits of our Hope House dogs with their handlers. I think the guys would really like that."

"Glad to." She smiled over her shoulder before disappearing into another part of the old farmhouse.

Witt made himself comfortable in an easy chair and stretched one leg across the ottoman. He reached down to stroke Ranger, who'd camped out beside the chair. "I think we did good yesterday. I liked all three of those dogs."

"Me, too. I'm excited to get them acquainted with the guys who'll be kicking this off."

"Good choices for the handlers, too." Witt chuckled. "Martin's a real go-getter, the perfect energy match for Zippy. They'll give each other a run for their money."

"And I have a feeling Cocoa's calm affection will help coax Ramón out of his shell."

"I know you had some concerns about Glen. Are you satisfied he's the right choice for Frankie?"

"Frankie came across as the smartest of the three dogs, plus the shelter workers told me he's got a mind of his own. I'm hoping he'll be challenging enough to give Glen something to think about besides himself."

They talked a bit more about connecting the men with their dogs and what had yet to be done before moving the canines to Hope House.

Then Witt changed the subject. "Rae sure seemed edgy yesterday."

The reminder brought a twinge to Carl's gut. "I think she's dealing with some family stuff. While we were in the parking lot, she got an upsetting call from her mother."

"That doesn't sound good." Witt took a thoughtful sip from his mug. "I didn't help matters when I asked if she knew my friends the Caldwells."

"Wait—don't tell me they're the former in-laws she referred to."

"Turns out she used to be married to their son. He's remarried and living in Texas now."

Carl's brow furrowed. "Didn't you mention the Caldwells lost a grandchild a few years ago?"

"Their son's twelve-year-old daughter. She died from a congenital heart condition."

The pang in Carl's belly sharpened. "Then Rae was the girl's mother?"

"The Caldwells only have the one son. I don't see how it could be anyone else."

Losing a child—the closest thing in Carl's experience was when his little brother had been taken away for adoption. He grew silent while he pondered his own loss along with growing empathy for Rae. Even so, he couldn't exactly walk up to her the next time he saw her and blurt out, *I'm sorry about your daughter. I get now why you seem so negative about everything.*

Nope, Rae Caldwell didn't seem the type who needed —much less *wanted*—anyone's sympathy. Best all around would be to keep things professional between them. If and when she felt like opening up more about her personal life, it should be her choice. He wouldn't pry.

Or so he told himself. Those moments in the parking lot yesterday kept playing in his mind . . . the vulnerability she thought she was hiding, his unexpected urge to rush to her rescue.

And the one fact he'd been trying his best to ignore because it was too implausible to admit . . .

After all these years of pretending his Hope House family was all he needed, he was having second thoughts.

Just because icy and aloof Rae Caldwell had invaded his life? That *really* made no sense.

Back at work on Monday and still recovering from her whirlwind weekend, Rae's plan was to maintain a low profile while giving the impression of composure and efficiency. That worked until Alton Isaacs called her to his office, no doubt expecting an update on current programming. She grabbed her top-priority files, then tucked her planner under her arm and started down the corridor.

As she entered the executive assistant's office, Kitty Davis smiled warmly from behind her array of cat figurines. "Good morning, Rae. Mr. Isaacs is finishing up another meeting right now." She motioned past Rae toward the seating area. "Make yourself comfortable. He'll be with you shortly."

The story of her life, always adapting to someone else's needs and schedule. Stifling a sigh, she pivoted, only to find Carl Anderson occupying a corner chair. She barely kept herself from stumbling. "You're waiting to see Mr. Isaacs, too?"

"He phoned this morning asking if the three of us could go over a few things about the canine project." One eye narrowed. "He didn't tell you I'd be here?"

"Actually, no. I thought this would be a more general discussion. Your project isn't the only one on my agenda, after all."

"I'm aware," Carl said stiffly. "Alton has a lot on his plate. I'm sure he didn't mean to keep you in the dark."

She replied with a curt nod, then stepped around the oval glass-top coffee table and perched on the edge of the sofa. Hands clasped atop her planner and stack of folders, she allowed her gaze to settle on a framed print hanging on the wall to her right. The serenity of the mountain scene stood in direct contradiction to her mood.

Carl's quiet cough drew her attention. "Did everything work out okay with your mother on Saturday?"

"What? Yes. Everything's . . . handled." No point in boring him with the messy details. She'd just as soon forget them, herself.

He looked as though he had something else to say, but then merely nodded and gave his attention to his phone screen.

Ten excruciating minutes later, the door to Mr. Isaacs's office opened. Two middle-aged men in suits and clerical collars and another man dressed in jeans and cowboy boots ambled out.

"Great chat, gentlemen," Mr. Isaacs said, bringing up the rear. "We'll get together again soon." He smiled in the direction of Rae and Carl, and with a quick "Give me one moment, please," he retreated to his office.

Halfway between sitting and standing, Rae gave a frustrated snort and dropped back onto the sofa.

Carl rose to shake hands with the man in the boots. "Pastor Peters. Good to see you again."

"No need for formalities. It's just Jim. Witt's been filling me in about this new experiment of yours. Dogs and recovering homeless men—I love it."

"Thanks. I'm praying the board of directors will recognize the potential." He gestured toward Rae. "Jim, have you met E and E's new program director?"

"Haven't had the pleasure."

"Rae Caldwell, meet Jim Peters, pastor of Elk Valley Community of Faith. That's where Witt and his wife, Maddie, go to church."

Shifting her planner and folders onto the coffee table,

she stood and offered her hand. "Nice to meet you, Pastor Peters."

"You, too. Welcome to Equipped and Empowered. Alton was just telling us what an impressive job you're doing so far."

"Really?" She stood a little taller. "That's very encouraging to hear."

"Well, I'd better be on my way. Carl, I hope you'll bring some of your men to worship with us again soon." He returned his attention to Rae. "You're welcome any time, too, Ms. Caldwell."

Her lips twitched in an awkward smile. "I'll keep it in mind."

After the pastor left, Rae glanced toward Mr. Isaacs's closed door. His "one moment" had obviously been a polite exaggeration.

Carl reclaimed his seat, and she did the same. She picked up her planner and flipped to the calendar to peruse the other items on her agenda this week. After another several minutes passed, she checked the time. "Our meeting was supposed to be at nine thirty. It's almost ten already."

"Cut him some slack." Lips pursed, Carl massaged his eyebrow. "He calls home as often as he can to check in with his wife's caregiver."

"Mrs. Isaacs is ill?"

"Cancer," Carl answered, keeping his voice low. "It's terminal."

Rae's stomach clenched. "I had no idea."

"He tries hard not to let it interfere with work, but if Trudy's having an especially bad day . . ." He shrugged and glanced away.

Encroaching memories swept her back to Kellie's hospital room. Bad days . . . worse days . . . the worst day ever in her life. Her little girl had been amazingly brave, right up to the end. Rae would never forget her daughter's parting instructions to her faithful Shadow-dog: *"Daddy isn't nearly as strong as he wants everyone to believe, so after I go to Heaven, he'll need you to take care of him."*

Take care of Daddy. Not *and Mommy, too.* She flinched as the remembered admonition jolted her, just as it had then. Others always expected Rae to be the responsible one, the shoulder to cry on, a tower of strength for them to lean on. Her parents, her siblings, her ex, even her precious daughter—they never seemed to notice how much effort it took to keep everyone else propped up while her metaphorical feet of clay crumbled beneath her.

"Rae? Rae." Carl was tapping her arm. "Mr. Isaacs is ready for us."

She released a shuddering breath. "Sorry, I was . . ."

Concern filled his expression. "Do you need a moment?"

"What? No." She collected her things and stood. "Don't be silly, I'm fine."

She had to be. It was what everyone else expected.

Noticing Rae's distracted state just now, Carl replayed what Witt had told him yesterday—the death of her only child, the collapse of her marriage.

He felt for her, yes. But he couldn't afford to care so much, not with everything he had at stake. He should simply try to get along and do his best to stay in Rae Caldwell's good graces. If he had any hope of convincing the board not to close down Hope House, he needed her on his side.

Going into the meeting with Rae and Mr. Isaacs required some mental gear-shifting, but by the time they wrapped up, the executive director had assured Carl of his full support. Rae also affirmed her commitment, grudging as it seemed, and would do her best to provide oversight and all necessary assistance for the canine project. Leaving Rae and Mr. Isaacs to discuss other items of business, he thanked them and excused himself.

As he offered a quick wave to Kitty on his way out, she signaled him over. "Carl, hold on a sec. I just had a call from Abe Duncan, the pastor at River of Mercy Church. I think you may want to follow up with him."

Carl knew Pastor Duncan in passing but hadn't had any recent dealings with him. "What's this about?"

"A man who just arrived in Missoula yesterday came asking for assistance, which isn't unusual, of course. But when Abe started asking questions, your name slipped out."

"*My* name? Was it someone who used to be in the homeless program?"

"I don't think so. I haven't found any record of him in our system." She handed Carl a square of note paper on which she'd spelled out the person's name in crisp block letters. "Is he familiar to you?"

Ellis Newman? No . . . no, it couldn't be.

Forcing a swallow over his throat gone suddenly dry, he tucked the note into his shirt pocket. "Thanks, Kitty. I'll, uh . . . I'll look into it."

Furrows etched her forehead. "Carl, are you all right?"

"I'm fine." He was pretty sure his attempt at a smile didn't convince her. "Better go. See you again soon." Before she could press him for explanations he didn't have, he strode out.

Reaching the lobby, he collapsed against the wall. The note felt like it was searing a hole through his shirt fabric. *Ellis?* But how? *Why?*

The click of a woman's heels sounded behind him. He straightened as Rae rounded the corner. At the sight of him, she stopped short, surprise widening her ice-blue stare. "Oh," she said. "I thought you'd gone."

"I was talking to Kitty about . . . something." If the name on that slip of paper burned any hotter, he'd need a fire extinguisher. He glanced around with a bizarre urgency to find one.

Rae folded her arms around the ever-present planner. "Excuse me, but you don't look so well."

"I'm *fine!*" Regretting his outburst, he pulled a hand down his face. "Sorry. I just got blindsided with some unexpected news."

"I see. Well, I hope you get it sorted out." She cast a glance toward the exit doors, probably hoping for a quick getaway. Then her entire demeanor changed. She inhaled slowly through her nostrils before locking eyes with him. "Is there anything I can do?"

The question—coming from her, especially—momentarily threw him. "No, but thanks. This is a personal issue."

She gave a knowing smirk. "Family problems?"

"How did you . . ."

"I recognize the signs. Or should, anyway." One shoulder lifted in a shrug. "Family problems are the story of my life."

Hard to forget witnessing her torment Saturday as she'd taken the call from her mother.

At least she had a mother.

And you have a brother.

A brother he hadn't seen or heard from in the thirty-five years since Ellis had been adopted by the Newmans.

It was his turn to glance longingly toward the exit. "Excuse me, but I really need to . . . to . . ."

She cast him a skeptical smile. "Not used to this kind of life interruption, are you? I suppose your family's usually picture-perfect, straight out of a Norman Rockwell painting."

A choked laugh escaped. "You have no idea."

"If you want to play the dysfunctional family comparison game—"

"No. No, I really don't." He lifted both palms. "I should go. Anyway, it looks like you're on your way out, too."

"I am." Huffing, she consulted the pink sticky note poking out from a planner page. "Maybe you can tell me the best route to River of Mercy Church. My phone GPS can't seem to find it."

His chest squeezed. "What's your business there?"

"Not that it's any of *your* business, but Mr. Isaacs arranged for me to meet with the community outreach coordinator about the church's lunch program for children with low food security."

He didn't need the complication, but she'd never find the church on her own. "The road changed names recently, and the mapping systems take time to catch up. That's actually where I'm headed. You're welcome to ride with me."

"Maybe I should follow you in my car. I wouldn't want to keep you if my meeting runs longer than yours."

"I'm in no hurry. Plus, it's a good twenty-minute drive across town. You'd likely lose me in traffic." He motioned toward the door. "Let's go. I'll drop you back here when we're done."

It didn't dawn on him until they reached his Forester that they'd be stuck in close proximity for the next half hour—and again on the return trip. Their interactions thus far had been strained at best.

Before he could do the gentlemanly thing and get the passenger door for her, she was already climbing in. He buckled in behind the steering wheel, and shortly they were headed across town.

Neither seemed in the mood for polite conversation, which was fine with Carl. Even so, the prolonged silence soon grew awkward. At the next traffic light, he glanced over. "How long have you lived in Missoula?"

"All my life, except for my four years at USC." Hands folded atop her planner, she gazed straight ahead. "You?"

"Same. Except I stayed right here for college."

The light changed. Carl went three more blocks and took a left.

Rae cleared her throat. "I actually live in Elk Valley now. I bought a little house there after . . ." She paused, glancing down to pick at a fingernail. "After my divorce."

"That must have been a tough time." He should let her know what he'd learned about her from Witt.

Before he could say anything, she turned toward the window and murmured, "After our daughter died, we just couldn't make it work anymore."

"I'm sorry."

"Thank you." She sniffed and straightened. "Now you know I'm divorced and childless, and you're already aware that I have an exasperating mother. I also have five codependent siblings. That's pretty much everything worth knowing about me."

He thoroughly doubted it. There was certainly much more to a woman as smart, capable and—yes—attractive as Rae Caldwell. Besides, this conversation was conveniently distracting him from thoughts and questions about his brother. After making the next turn, he said, "So far, nothing I know about you explains why you seem uncomfortable around dogs."

She pulled out her phone and scrolled for so long that he began to think she was ignoring his comment. At the next red light, she held her phone where he could see it. "This is my daughter and her service dog, Shadow."

The photo showed a pale, fair-haired girl in a wheelchair, an oxygen tube looped over her ears and an IV bag on a stand beside her. At her feet sat a furry black dog, his attention riveted on the girl and one paw resting on her knee. The only time Carl had witnessed similar canine devotion was with Witt and his dog, Ranger.

A beep sounded behind them, returning Carl's attention to his driving. Realizing the light had changed, he waved an apology and stepped on the gas pedal. When he could find his voice again, he said, "That's a fine-looking dog. Can I ask what happened to him after . . ."

"My ex took him." Rae sighed. "They shared a bond that . . . well, that I didn't. Besides, seeing Shadow every day would have been too painful a reminder."

Carl let her words sink in. "And now every dog is a reminder?"

"Pretty much." She released a sad, self-deprecating laugh as she tucked away her phone. "I'm glad Shadow is with Mark. They've been good for each other."

Carl slid a glance her way. "And what about you?" he asked softly. "Have you had someone to lean on, too?"

"Me? Are you kidding? I'm everyone else's port in a

storm." Her tone became harsh. "Need something? A listening ear, a loan, a place to crash for a few weeks or a year? Sure, just call Rae."

He winced, sorry he'd opened that can of worms.

She covered her eyes with both hands. "Please pardon my embarrassing display of self-pity. It's been a difficult few days."

"Anything to do with Saturday's call from your mother?"

"Unfortunately, yes." She lowered her hands and interlaced them atop her planner. "But you really don't want to hear my sob story, and I really don't want to talk about it anymore. Your turn. Tell me all about whatever family issues have you so tense this morning—if you want to, that is. I certainly don't mean to pry—"

"It's my brother," he blurted. "I haven't seen him since he was five, and I just found out he's here in Missoula."

Chapter Seven

Rae spent the next few seconds in stunned silence. She wasn't sure what she'd expected Carl to share with her, but certainly not that. He'd made a career of helping others build new lives. That he hadn't been in touch with his own brother since their childhood seemed incomprehensible.

True, there were plenty of times when Rae longed to put some distance between herself and her siblings. But family was family, and no matter how used or frustrated or downright furious they made her feel, she couldn't imagine turning her back on them.

Carl flexed his fingers around the steering wheel. "Didn't mean to dump that on you. Guess I'm still in shock."

"This is the reason for your trip to River of Mercy?"

He explained briefly about the message Kitty had given him. "I've tried to convince myself it has to be a different Ellis Newman, but it isn't a terribly common name."

"Newman? But your last name is Anderson."

They'd arrived at the church. Carl pulled into a parking

space near a side door labeled "Office" and cut the engine. "Ellis and I were in foster care. At five, he was young enough and cute enough to find an adoptive family. I was a moody, trouble-making ten-year-old. I bounced around in the system until I aged out. By then, I'd realized if I didn't create my own best life, it wasn't going to happen."

Rae found her gaze fixed on the man's profile—firm jaw, broad forehead, his hairline forming two peaks over intense, deep-set brown eyes. With a mental shake, she looked away. "It certainly seems to me that you've succeeded."

"Thanks for that. I've tried to make a difference, but . . ." He roughly cleared his throat. "If this person does turn out to be my brother, what does it say about me that I never once reached out to him in all this time?"

"What it says to me is that you were a kid dealing with some bad breaks."

"Maybe." He snorted. "It isn't much of an excuse, but I figured Ellis's life had to have turned out way better than mine. Even if he remembered me at all, I couldn't imagine he'd want to be reminded of our lousy beginnings." Expression crumpling, he slowly turned to face her. "But what if I was wrong? What if he's needed me all this time? What if—"

She gripped his forearm. "What-ifs are useless—believe me, I know. You can't fix a problem until you know what the problem is. Besides, you still don't know if it's him. Is there reason to believe he'd even be in Missoula?"

"All I know is, not long after the Newmans adopted Ellis, they relocated to Denver."

"So go find out if it's him." She nodded toward the church office. "If it is, then you can figure out what to do next."

A smile slowly formed. Not a happy smile, more an acknowledgment of being heard and understood. It warmed Rae's chest to realize she'd helped in some way.

Drawing a quick breath, she reached for the door handle. "I should get to my meeting. And you should get those answers."

As they walked toward the building, she thanked him for the ride. "But don't worry about getting me back to the office, I can call an Uber or something."

He hesitated briefly. "How about we play it by ear?"

After their mutual disclosures of such deeply personal details, she'd expected he might prefer to be rid of her company for the return trip. "All right, if you're sure."

"I am." He arched a brow. "You're actually pretty easy to talk to when you're not shooting annoyed glances at me from behind a desk or in a board meeting."

Guess she deserved as much. "Thank you . . . I think."

That evoked a wry chuckle. He held the door for her, and after they announced their presence at the reception desk, Carl was shown to the pastor's study, while Rae followed directions down the corridor to her meeting.

Thoughts lingering with Carl and his concerns about his brother, she struggled to carry on an intelligent conversation with the community outreach coordinator. Several minutes into their discussion, the woman asked if there was some problem.

"My apologies," Rae said. "A . . . a colleague just shared a personal struggle." She'd started to say *friend*, but could she call him that, really? "I'm afraid my mind is still on that."

"Is it Carl? I saw you walk in with him."

Now she regretted saying anything at all, although her

frown toward the door likely confirmed the director's assumptions. "It isn't my place to comment."

"I understand. I'll be praying it's nothing too serious. All of us here at River of Mercy are fond of Carl. He's a wonderful man, and you're very blessed to be working with him."

"Yes, I'm looking forward to getting better acquainted." Surprisingly, she meant it.

Half an hour later, Rae's meeting concluded. The receptionist told her Carl had gone to wait in the sanctuary and pointed her toward double doors at the end of a wide corridor.

Peering through a glass panel into the darkened auditorium, Rae scanned the rows of empty pews. She spotted Carl down near the chancel. He sat slumped forward, hands clasped and resting on the back of the next pew in a posture of prayer.

She hesitated to disturb him, but she did have other business to attend to. Plus, she'd missed breakfast this morning, no thanks to another frantic call from her mother. This time, it was to referee an argument between the twins, Deena and Dawn, who couldn't agree on where to hold their thirtieth birthday party. Rae had finally told them to toss all their ideas into a hat, then pick one at random and live with it.

Now her stomach was pleading for her to grab lunch somewhere—and soon!

As she slipped into the sanctuary, her tummy emitted what echoed like a volcanic eruption in the quiet space. She winced and pressed one hand against her abdomen.

No reaction from Carl. Maybe the sound had only seemed loud to her ears. She tiptoed down the aisle, stopping at Carl's pew. "Excuse me . . ."

He startled. "Is your meeting done?"

"Yes, a few minutes ago." She fingered her purse strap. "How was your discussion?"

Sinking against the pew, he groaned. "It was definitely my brother. From what little Ellis told the pastor, I gather his life didn't go quite as well as I'd imagined. And now he's injured his hand somehow and can't work. He hitchhiked here all the way from Casper, Wyoming."

"Carl, I'm so sorry." She scooted onto the seat next to him. "What will you do?"

"I have no idea. As soon as Ellis realized Pastor Duncan knew me, he clammed up. He stayed only long enough to accept a change of clothes and some meal vouchers, and then he took off."

"He must have been embarrassed for you to find out how bad off he is. You should look for him." She was ready to drag Carl out to his SUV and get him to drive around town until they found his brother. Rising, she stepped into the aisle. "You know the most likely places where the homeless and transients hang out. Let's pick up some fast food and start looking."

He stared at her like she'd grown another head. "Right now?"

"Yes. Now." Her glance lifted to the stained-glass window at the far end of Carl's pew, where the figure of Jesus smiled down at her with arms extended. An angry shudder rippled through her. *Like You're of any use.*

Jaw firm, she faced Carl. "If you really want to do your brother some good, then stop praying and start acting."

She marched toward the exit doors and hoped he'd

follow because the fast food suggestion was mainly for her benefit. If she didn't get some lunch in the next ten minutes, she'd likely pass out from starvation.

By the time she reached the corridor, Carl had caught up. "Rae. Hold on. Explain to me what that look on your face was all about."

Her shoulders tensed. She kept walking. "What look?"

"The one when you told me to stop praying and start acting. You don't believe in prayer?"

Careful how you answer, Rae. She'd likely lose her job if the truth came out. "It's just—you know. The Lord helps those who help themselves."

They'd reached the exit. Carl pushed through and held the door for her. "You do know the Bible doesn't say that anywhere."

She winced. "Maybe not, but don't you think God appreciates it when we quit sitting on our hands and get out there and do something?"

"Only after we've prayed for God's direction. Which is what I was doing in the sanctuary just now."

Bite your tongue, Rae. Just bite your tongue.

Epic failure. "And did God answer you and tell you what to do about your brother? I'm guessing not, or I wouldn't have found you still sitting there."

"What's the deal with you?" They'd reached his SUV. "Don't you have enough family issues of your own without assuming charge of mine?"

"I wasn't—I didn't mean to—" She couldn't explain why, but she almost relished the idea of dealing with someone else's sibling issues instead of her own. Giving a huff, she circled around to the passenger side and scooted in, then faced straight ahead while Carl got behind the wheel. In a subdued tone, she added, "I was just trying to help."

He pursed his lips. "It isn't that I don't appreciate it, and I apologize for lashing out. But there's no reason for you to get involved." After buckling his seat belt, he started the engine. "I'll drop you back at the ministry center—"

Her stomach let loose with a growl likely heard all the way to Canada.

"—after we stop and get you something to eat," Carl finished with a snicker.

Grimacing, she hugged her planner against her abdomen. "Thanks. I hated to ask."

He cast her a curious frown. "You charge into my personal business like an angry mama bison, but you're too insecure to admit you're hungry? Wow."

She glared. "That is just rude."

"What's your pleasure, ma'am?" He steered the car onto the road. "Burger? Pizza? Mexican? Asian?"

Honestly, the man was incorrigible. "I'd settle for a candy bar from the nearest convenience store."

He scoffed. "Somehow, you don't strike me as the candy bar type."

"When my blood sugar drops this low, I cease being picky." She thought a moment, then narrowed one eye at him. "I'm afraid to ask what *type* you think I am."

"Hmm, filet mignon? Chateaubriand? Lobster tails? Shrimp scampi?" He shot her a sudden worried stare. "Wait—are you diabetic? Is this an insulin emergency?"

"No. Nothing like that. I was running late and skipped breakfast, and now I'm seriously regretting it. That's all."

He whistled out a breath and returned his attention to the road. "Okay, then. We'll stop somewhere for lunch. There's a Five on Black a few blocks away. Work for you?"

"I love Five on Black."

Shortly, Carl parked outside the restaurant. The deliciously health-conscious Brazilian-style cuisine never failed to delight Rae's taste buds, and the quick service meant she'd be sitting down to eat within minutes. At the counter, she opted for a greens-and-rice bowl with churrasco chicken, black beans, and mango barbecue sauce.

By the time Carl joined her with his feijoada Brazilian stew over rice, she'd selected a tall table near the window and had already begun eating. When Carl bowed his head to murmur a blessing over the meal, heat raced up her neck. She paused until he finished, then said, "You must think I'm awful."

He smiled and picked up his fork. "You were hungry. God understands."

She wasn't convinced. Not that it mattered, since she had no use for God anymore.

True, she'd grown up in a church-going family. Learned the standard prayers and memorized a few Bible verses in Sunday school class. But church had always seemed more of a social club to her parents. She hadn't really come to *believe* until a college friend invited her to join a campus Christian association. There, in the fellowship of other believers, she'd experienced a closeness with God she hadn't known was possible.

Then, as career, marriage, and motherhood—not to mention the ongoing demands of her birth family—claimed more and more of her focus, her relationship with God took a backseat.

The day Kellie died, she completely shut Him out.

Shoving the memories aside, she took another bite, then noticed Carl wasn't eating. "Something wrong with your food?"

"I can't stop thinking about Ellis." He stabbed a chunk of stew and stared at it. "I keep asking myself what must have happened in his life that he'd find himself in this position. Alone. On the road. Needing handouts just to get by."

The reminder effectively curtailed her appetite. She took a sip of iced tea, then dabbed her lips with a paper napkin. "I still think you should look for him." She reached into her purse for her phone. "I have numbers in my directory for several of the homeless shelters. Maybe he went to one of those. Let me make some calls."

He massaged one eyebrow with his fingertip. "Okay, but it can wait till you return to the office. And don't mention my name. If he's dead set on me not knowing about him, he may decide to leave town in a hurry." A hint of a smile forming, he nodded toward her bowl. "Now finish your lunch. I don't want you biting anyone's head off because you went back to work hangry."

At his warmly teasing tone, her heart tripped. She picked up her fork and jabbed it in his direction. "Same goes for you, mister. Don't forget, you're about to launch a Hail Mary pass with this canine project, so you'd better keep up your energy."

The look he cast her—pleasant surprise mixed with a huge dose of gratitude—turned her heart flutter into a seismic tremor. Without a word, he scooped up a forkful of rice and Brazilian stew, popped it into his mouth, and chewed with gusto.

She tried to follow suit with her own meal, but a tumble of feelings she couldn't begin to name, much less comprehend, made it difficult to swallow. She'd never been good at forming workplace alliances, which likely contributed once or twice to her being "encouraged" to move on to other employment.

Doesn't play well with others, she recalled teachers marking on her elementary school report cards a few times. *Rae must learn to curb her superior attitude toward classmates.*

Yet here she sat sharing a meal with an undeniably attractive man—a man she'd been in opposition with from the first time they'd met—and she found herself actually *liking* him.

Even more disconcerting, she desperately wanted him to like *her.*

Carl hesitated to admit it, but he was actually beginning to like Rae Caldwell. He was stunned at how easily he'd opened up to her about his brother. In fact, he couldn't remember the last time he'd told anyone he even had a brother, much less their painful childhood history.

After returning Rae to the office, he headed back to Hope House. With details of the canine project to iron out in addition to his usual daily routine, he had plenty to keep himself busy this week. If he sat around waiting to learn if Rae's phone calls turned up any new information about Ellis, he risked doing himself permanent emotional harm.

It was probably already too late. The damage had begun the first time he'd come home from school to find his mother in an opioid-induced stupor and his little brother screaming from his crib because his diaper hadn't been changed all day. Similarly disturbing incidents, repeated again and again until a teacher had sensed something was off and called Social Services, were permanently etched in his brain. For most of his life, he'd managed to lock the memories away into the farthest corners of his mind . . .

Until today.

Now, he wasn't completely sure he wanted Rae to find his brother. He'd constructed a good life for himself. He'd believed all these years that Ellis had done the same. He wanted Ellis to get the help he needed, but with all that had happened—both good and bad—in the intervening years, maybe it'd be better for both of them if they didn't reconnect. Less embarrassing for Ellis, and for Carl, less . . . what? Inconvenient?

He pushed away from his desk and pressed his palms against his eye sockets. *I'm sorry, God. I know that's a terrible way to think about my baby brother.*

But it was true. He remained fully committed to assuring the wellbeing of the men in his charge, and that included establishing the canine program he hoped would save both Hope House and the career he'd devoted his life to.

There was no room in the picture for a destitute brother.

For a brother who should have had more advantages. Structure and consistency. The best schools. Shoes and clothes that actually fit and didn't come handed down who knew how many times. Most of all, a loving family who'd always be there for him.

No doubt about it, Ellis should have had a better life in every respect.

On Wednesday afternoon, as Carl toiled over end-of-the-month reports and spreadsheets, his phone buzzed. The screen displayed Witt's name and number. "Hey. What's up?"

"I thought we were meeting to pick up the dogs at the Elk Valley shelter this afternoon. I've been waiting for you since two o'clock."

Stomach plummeting, he saw it was already two thirty. "Sorry, I lost track of time."

A pause. "Everything okay?"

"Yeah, sure. I'm on my way. The crates are already in the back of the van."

He made the typical thirty-five-minute drive from Hope House in just under half an hour, screeching to a halt in the animal shelter parking lot. Witt met him at the entrance and thankfully had already completed the necessary paperwork. With the help of two attendants, they soon had Cocoa, Frankie, and Zippy secured in the crates.

"How about I follow you to the house and help get these pups settled?" Witt offered.

"That'd be great. I'll have to head out soon afterward for the evening vanpool run."

After they arrived at Hope House and brought the dogs inside, Carl texted the men to let them know he'd be running late. Leaving Witt to keep an eye on the dogs until he got back, he hit the road again.

His last stop was Equipped and Empowered Ministries, where the two newest residents had spent the day in employment counseling sessions. Pulling under the portico near the doors, he glimpsed Rae's little red Mazda in the staff parking area. It surprised him that she'd be working this late.

It surprised him even more when she walked out with his two residents. As they climbed in alongside the men he'd already picked up, Rae came around to his door.

He lowered the window and tried not to pounce on her

immediately to ask if she'd had any word about Ellis. "Hi. Thought you'd have headed home by now."

"Not much waiting for me there. Anyway, I had some paperwork to finish up." Stepping closer, she lowered her voice. "I'm afraid I still don't have any news for you."

"It's okay. He could be miles from here by now." He tamped down a confusing mixture of relief and disappointment. "I've got plenty on my plate as it is. Witt and I picked up the dogs this afternoon."

From the seat behind Carl's, Martin leaned forward and slapped him on the shoulder. "My dog's here? Hey, let's go. I can't wait to meet him!"

He chuckled at the young man's enthusiasm. "Patience, fella. All in good time."

Smirking, Rae arched a brow. "One of your designated handlers, I presume?"

"That's Martin. Witt and I decided his energy's the right match for Zippy, the feisty black-and-white one."

"I remember him well." She peered past Carl toward the man behind him. "Martin, you're going to have your hands full."

"I'm ready!"

Ignoring the guy's impromptu drum roll on the seat back, Carl propped his forearm in the open window and cast Rae a tentative smile. "If you're really not in a hurry to head home, you could come by and watch the fun at Hope House."

"I'm sure it'd be a lot more entertaining than whatever I can find on Netflix, but . . ." She inched back a step. "I don't think so."

"Another time, then. Will you be at our first training class on Saturday?"

"It's on my calendar." With a brusque nod, she pivoted and marched toward her car.

As Carl raised his window, Martin whistled. "Ms. Caldwell's got a thing for you, man."

The other guys in the van murmured their agreement.

Face warming, Carl harrumphed. "We work together. That's all."

"Uh-huh," came a chorus of replies.

"Knock it off, you guys." He checked the rearview mirror to make sure everyone was buckled in, then aimed the van toward the road.

Rae? A thing for him? They had to be joking. Besides, as much as his world had tilted lately, he didn't need one more complication.

By the time he arrived back at Hope House, the residents with their own vehicles or who shared rides were home from school and jobs—including Ramón and Glen, who were already making friends with their new charges, Cocoa and Frankie.

The instant Carl stopped the van in the driveway, Martin shoved out the door and made a beeline through the back gate. Seconds later, he and Zippy were play-wrestling in the grass, with Martin on the losing end as the frisky pup pinned him down and slathered his face with a wet tongue.

Carl laughed as he stepped into the yard. "Try to remember who's boss," he chided, to no avail. Oh, well, discipline could come later—and certainly would when the dog-training class began.

Witt ambled over. "You're in for fun times ahead."

"Tell me about it."

"I left the dog-care instruction sheet on the fridge. You should go over it again with the guys once things settle down a bit." He chewed his lip. "And keep a close eye on Glen. His attention span isn't the greatest."

"As I'm well aware." Carl heaved a sigh and fought off the fatigue that was rapidly setting in. "I should see how the supper crew's coming along."

"And I should get home to Maddie and our menagerie. Ranger wasn't real happy I left him behind this afternoon, but I figured there'd be excitement enough."

"No doubt about that." Carl stepped aside to keep from being bowled over by Zippy and Cocoa playing chase.

Chuckling, Witt pulled his keys from his pocket. He gently tossed them a few times as his expression grew thoughtful. "Sure there isn't anything else you need to talk about? You haven't seemed quite yourself this week."

Carl heaved a breath. He'd like nothing better than to sit down for a quiet heart-to-heart with one of the most perceptive and faith-filled men he'd had the privilege of knowing. "Another time, okay? I'm still mulling over a few things."

"Whenever you're ready, you know where to find me."

"I do indeed." Carl cast his friend a grateful smile. "See you Saturday if not before."

Chapter Eight

Mentioning Carl's name to that pastor had been a big mistake. Ellis never expected the man would actually know Carl. All things considered, he was surprised to learn his brother had stuck around Missoula.

Ellis didn't remember much about living here as a kid. Memories of life before his adoption were pretty much a blur, which in many ways was a good thing. He could never honestly say he missed his real mom and all her issues, but he'd missed Carl something terrible. That first year, he'd pleaded with his new parents numerous times to find his brother and adopt him, too.

"We only have room in our hearts for one little boy," they'd reasoned, *"and that little boy is you."*

It didn't make sense, though. Most of the kids he'd met at his new elementary school in Denver had at least one brother or sister, and some had several. Sure, there were the usual complaints about the baby of the family getting spoiled rotten, or older siblings getting privileges the younger ones weren't allowed. But Ellis couldn't recall a single one of those kids ever worrying that their parents didn't have enough love to go around.

Not to say the Newmans were bad parents—depending on your definition of *bad*, of course. They dressed him well, fed him healthy meals, got him into a prestigious private Christian school, and took him to church every Sunday. He didn't grow up thinking his parents' strictness was mistreatment—not the kind that got people arrested, anyway—but he did wonder sometimes if spankings and Bible-thumping diatribes were normal for other kids who occasionally misbehaved.

By the time he'd reached adolescence, he'd come to believe he could do absolutely nothing right in his parents' eyes, so he figured it was pointless to try. Hence the acting out, disobedience, more than one thwarted attempt to run away from home, and eventually attempting to numb his discontent with drugs and alcohol.

He could use a drink right about now, except the two burly guys passing a bottle back and forth didn't look inclined to share. He'd been watching them from a safe distance in the alley where he'd taken refuge the last couple of nights while contemplating his next steps. Seeking help at any of the homeless shelters the pastor had recommended risked too great a chance word would get back to his big brother, and he couldn't bear for Carl to find out what a mess he'd made of his life.

Their final goodbye still haunted him.

"It's gonna be great, I promise." Carl hugged him hard, then backed away, his lower lip trembling. *"You're getting a real forever home with parents who'll love you and watch over you every single day."*

"But why can't you come, too?" Ellis didn't even try to

wipe away the tears streaming down his face. "They have a big house. They have room."

Carl firmly shook his head. "It doesn't work that way, kiddo. But I'll be okay, don't you worry. You will, too. You're gonna have the best life ever." His reassuring grin wobbled as he tweaked Ellis's chin. "Hey, you could even grow up to become president someday."

"But I don't wanna be president." The sobs came harder and messier. "I just want to stay with you!"

"Son, you're making a scene." Mr. Newman gripped Ellis's shoulder and nudged him toward the big, fancy car parked in the driveway. "It's time to go. Stop embarrassing yourself."

Years later, Ellis realized it was his adoptive father who'd been embarrassed. Harold Newman did not tolerate *scenes*. Which was why Ellis had come to take such pleasure in finding new ways to create them. At church, in front of business acquaintances, or during one of Mother's regular dinner parties, turning his father's face red with rage was sweet compensation for whatever punishment would follow.

Catching a threatening glance from the guy currently holding the bottle, he slunk behind a garbage bin. Fetid odors of rotting food assailed him as he sank to his haunches. He despised himself for even considering foraging through the garbage for anything halfway edible.

President. Like that was ever happening. He should hike over to the interstate and flag down another trucker. Why he'd thought Missoula would be a good jumping-off point, he'd never know. The sooner he shook the dust of this burg off his feet, the sooner he could try again to put the memories behind him.

Chapter Nine

"No, Reece. Just no." Rae could *not* believe her brother would show up just after seven on a Saturday morning with such an impossible request.

"C'mon, sis." Panic edged his tone. He appeared to have dressed in a hurry—in yesterday's shirt and slacks. "If Heather finds out, she'll kill me. It'll be the end of our marriage."

"Maybe it should be." Carrying her coffee mug to the breakfast table, Rae aimed for the nearest chair. Being asked to cover for her brother's night of infidelity was not the ideal beginning to her weekend.

Reece sagged against the kitchen counter with a groan. "It was a stupid lapse in judgment. But it shouldn't have to ruin my life. Or Heather's."

"You're right about one thing—it was stupid." Insides shaking with anger and disappointment, she pressed one hand against her forehead. "How could you, Reece? Your wife is finally pregnant with the baby you've waited six years for."

"Maybe that's exactly why. Do you have any idea the strain trying to get pregnant put on our marriage?" He scoffed. "Of course you don't. You and Mark didn't have any trouble making a baby, after which you decided one kid was all you could handle. I'm not sure you even wanted Kellie."

His words ripped open the wound in Rae's heart that would never fully heal. Her throat closed over a stifled sob.

"I'm sorry, I'm sorry." Reece moved closer, hands uplifted. "I'm just . . . I can't think straight, Rae. I'm desperate. Please, if you care about me at all, you've gotta help me fix this."

She stood and faced him. "Didn't you hear me? I am not going to lie for you."

"Rae—"

"Not one more word, Reece. Just go." She jammed an index finger in the direction of the front door.

A whole spectrum of emotions played across his face—surprise, disbelief, anger, defeat. With one final intake of breath, he snatched up his sports coat and stormed out.

He hadn't been gone five minutes when her phone rang. Seeing Heather's name on the display, she nearly choked. If she didn't answer, her sister-in-law would leave a message, and eventually she'd have to return the call. Better to get it over with—and hope she could sidestep any direct questions about her errant brother.

She forced a smile and willed it into her voice. "Hi, Heather."

"Rae, I'm scared. Reece was supposed to meet some coworkers for drinks after work last night, but when I woke up this morning, I realized he never came home."

"Oh, um . . ." Rae grimaced. *You will owe me for this forever, Reece.* "He's fine, Heather. He spent the night here.

He . . . he had too many beers and didn't want to drive himself home or drag you out of bed, so he called me. I'm sure he meant to let you know, but he must have fallen right to sleep."

Silence. Then, "None of that's true, is it?"

"Heather—" The tone in her ear announced another call coming in. Lowering the phone briefly to read the display, she saw the name of a downtown homeless shelter she'd contacted yesterday asking about Carl's brother. "Can we talk later, Heather? I have an important call coming in."

"Oh, sure, cover for your brother like you always do." A series of beeps indicated her sister-in-law had hung up on her.

Which was almost a relief, even knowing she'd eventually have to face her sister-in-law's wrath. Inhaling a calming breath, she tapped the phone screen and switched over to the other caller. "This is Rae Caldwell."

The shelter director identified himself. "Hope I'm not calling too early, but you seemed anxious to find out about the man you were looking for. Fortyish, just got into town, you said."

"Yes, that's right." Her grip tightened on the phone. "Have you learned something?"

"A new guy just went through the breakfast line. He acted like he was trying to be inconspicuous, but I heard him asking about the best place to pick up a ride going west."

"Did you get his name?"

"No, sorry. But I'm looking right at him. Average height, on the thin side, with thick brown hair. Tan, with squint lines around his eyes like he's been working outdoors. Oh, and he has a bandage on his hand."

Carl had mentioned the hand injury. "That could be him. Any chance you can keep him there a little longer?"

"Wait—you said he wasn't in any kind of trouble."

"Not as far as I know. I'm reaching out on behalf of a family member who's been concerned for him." Rae grabbed a pen and paper. "What's the address there, please?"

The director's tone changed from helpful to annoyed. "I thought this involved an Equipped and Empowered client. We have a strict confidentiality policy regarding the people we serve."

"I completely understand. But there's a chance the man may be Carl Anderson's long-lost brother."

The mention of Carl's name altered the man's demeanor once again. "I had no idea Carl had a brother."

"They were very young when they got separated." Briefly, Rae explained that Ellis might be ashamed for Carl to know he'd fallen on hard times. "Until Carl can get there, it would be better if you didn't say anything."

The director exhaled sharply. "Okay, then. Short of lying, I'll do what I can to encourage him to stick around."

Rae cringed at the reminder of how, only minutes ago, she'd lied to Heather about Reece. Her sister-in-law deserved better. And Reece . . . well, she wasn't sure what he deserved, but it certainly was *not* a free pass. She'd figure out how to deal with him later. In the meantime, she needed to make sure Carl had a chance to reconnect with his brother.

Today's dog-training session would begin in just over an hour, which would be her opportunity to convince Carl to go with her to the shelter. In case his brother needed some convincing to see him, she'd be on hand to run interference. She'd certainly had plenty of practice mediating her own siblings' messes.

Dressed in jeans, a turtleneck and a quilted vest, she filled a travel mug with coffee and headed to the Elk Valley Animal Shelter. An attendant led her to the indoor play area, where she found Carl and Witt watching from the sidelines as three men romped with the dogs from the shelter.

Carl noticed her and ambled over. "I was afraid you might change your mind about coming."

She wouldn't admit she'd seriously thought about it, right up until the shelter director had called. "I have some news."

His tight expression said he'd read her meaning. He motioned toward the door she'd come through. "Let's talk inside."

Facing him in a quiet hallway off the main corridor, she summarized what she'd learned. "They'll try to keep Ellis at the shelter as long as possible. If we wait until your class finishes, it might be too late. Can Witt supervise so we can go right now?"

Carl fisted his hips. "This program was my idea—my responsibility. I have a lot riding on it. I can't just leave."

She gaped at him. "But this could be your best chance to find your brother."

"I appreciate everything you've done to help locate him. The thing is . . ." Turning toward the wall, he straightened a framed poster of a happy dog licking a little boy's face. His voice dropped to barely a whisper. "I'm not sure if seeing Ellis again is the right thing to do."

"But he's your brother. How can you even think that?"

"I can't—" Loud voices and a dog's excited bark interrupted him. Carl peered around the corner toward the playroom. "The trainer's here. We'll have to finish this later."

Stunned, Rae followed him to the playroom. She

snagged his elbow as they stepped through the door. "*Finishing this later* isn't an option, unless you want to risk losing track of your brother again."

"Didn't you hear me? I'm not doing this right now." Carl shook his arm free and marched across the room toward a young guy with a border collie.

She could only stare openmouthed at the man's stiff back. She'd been coerced into lying for her infuriatingly self-centered sibling, but Carl Anderson wouldn't break free to reconnect with the brother he hadn't seen in thirty-five years?

What is wrong with this picture?

Pasting on a smile he didn't feel, Carl introduced dog trainer Luke Daniels to his new students. While they spent a few minutes getting acquainted, Carl decided he owed Rae an apology and turned to look for her.

Too late. The glass door swung shut as she disappeared inside the building. He hoped she'd only stepped away for a moment to simmer down. Or had she already forgotten her commitment to attend the class? Certainly, she possessed some level of common sense and wasn't, at this moment, rushing off to find Ellis on her own.

On the other hand, there could be some advantages to having Rae serve as a go-between. Maybe she could encourage Ellis to apply for temporary housing and aid, or at least get him to a free clinic where his injured hand could get proper attention. Pastor Duncan had described the dirty bandage covering a red, angry wound. While Ellis was there, the pastor had phoned a church member who was a retired nurse, and she'd come over to apply antibiotic ointment and a fresh dressing. Even so, it sounded like further treatment would be necessary.

It bothered Carl that Rae seemed this miffed at him for not dropping everything to go after his brother. It wasn't that he didn't care about reconnecting with Ellis. He'd always hoped they would . . . someday. But the timing was all wrong. For now, Hope House and the men he'd committed to serve needed his undivided attention.

Pinching the bridge of his nose, he squeezed his eyes shut. Trusting God in every situation used to come easily. Why, all of a sudden, did God seem so far away?

He'd have to puzzle over that question later. Making a conscious effort, he dialed back in to the class.

Luke had brought along his own dog, an eagerly attentive border collie named Fletch. Using Fletch as an example, Luke demonstrated what the men could expect with regular class participation and consistent practice.

As Luke began a lesson on how to teach the "sit" command, Witt ambled over next to Carl. "Rae sure left in a hurry. I thought she was going to observe the class."

"She's annoyed with me. As usual." Carl collapsed onto a nearby bench and massaged his temples.

Joining him on the bench, Witt snorted. "Any particular reason?"

He had yet to mention Ellis's arrival in town, let alone admit he even had a brother, but this was neither the time nor the place. He couldn't say exactly why he hadn't confided in his friend. If anyone could relate to what Ellis was going through and offer some perspective, it'd be Witt.

Carl expelled a lengthy sigh. "I'll explain everything later, I promise. Right now, this class is my priority."

"Interesting, because ever since you walked through

that door, it's clear your mind's been everywhere *but* on this class."

"You think I don't know that?" Carl stood abruptly, then grimaced and hung his head. "I'm trying, okay? All I can handle for now is getting through the next hour."

By the time class ended, both the dogs and their handlers were dragging, but with the kind of exhaustion that came from putting forth concerted effort and seeing measurable results. Even Glen had shown more attentiveness than usual, exactly as Carl had been counting on. If the canine program proved successful for one of Hope House's more problematic residents, it would go a long way toward swaying the board of directors in Carl's favor.

Most of his own fatigue stemmed from something else entirely. He could hardly wait to get back to Hope House and sink into his favorite chair with a steaming mug of hot chocolate and some peaceful, meditative music playing on the sound system.

It wasn't meant to be. Once he and Witt had helped Ramón, Martin, and Glen load their dogs into the crates in the back of the van, Witt drew him aside. "I'm following you to the house, and then we're going to have that talk you promised."

His friend's tone left no room for dispute. At the house, Carl sent the three dog handlers to tend to their charges and then set the teakettle on to boil. The other residents were excited to hear about the training class, so those conversations would keep everyone occupied for a while.

When the kettle whistled, Carl prepared two mugs of hot cocoa mix. Handing one to Witt, he led the way to the office. He nudged the door closed with his heel and gestured for Witt to take the easy chair near the window.

Carl settled into his recliner and took a deep breath.

"For any of this to make sense, I need to start way back at the beginning."

"I'm listening."

He let his eyes fall shut as images beginning forty-plus years ago played through his mind like a movie on fast-forward. With a slow sigh, he met Witt's gaze. "I have a younger brother. His name is Ellis. I haven't seen him since I was ten years old."

If the revelation surprised his friend, he did a good job of not showing it. "What happened?"

"Our mother had a serious drug problem. I was eight and Ellis was three when Social Services intervened and put us in our first foster home."

"Man, I'm sorry. Where was your dad through all this?"

"I have no idea who our father even was, and I'm not even sure Ellis and I share the same father." Carl took a thoughtful sip from his mug. "Anyway, we got shuffled around between foster homes for the next couple of years, but at least they kept us together. Then Ellis got adopted. He'd just turned five. His new family moved to Denver, and I haven't seen him since."

"But you continued in foster care?"

Carl nodded.

Witt sadly shook his head. "I had no idea."

"It isn't something I talk about, or even care to think about. Except now I have to. This is where it gets interesting." He swallowed hard before recounting what he'd learned about Ellis over the last several days, ending with the news that Rae had gotten a call from the shelter director early that morning.

"Wow. So he's here in Missoula now." Setting his mug on a side table, Witt leaned forward. "Carl, you should have gone to find him as soon as Rae told you. I could have handled everything with the training class."

"I know." He took another swallow of cocoa in hopes it would wash down the bitter taste of guilt. It didn't. "I'm ashamed to admit it, but there's a part of me that just wants this to go away. A part of me wishes Ellis had never come back."

Witt remained silent for several moments, his expression inscrutable. "You're angry that he ended up this way. You're disappointed. Confused. You want to know what went wrong. Where *he* went wrong."

"Yes. All those things. Because he was supposed to have every advantage I didn't." Carl's stomach churned. He beat a fist against his thigh. "I struggled all my life to get to where I am today. There was nobody cheering me on, nobody paying my way. Nobody who—" His voice cracked. "Who loved and cared and fought for me."

Witt scoffed. "So God deserted you, too, huh?"

The mockery in his friend's tone caused Carl to blink several times. "Of course not. I just meant—"

"I know what you meant." Gentling his tone, Witt continued, "No matter how much we trust the Lord, we can't escape our longing—our very real *need*—to be seen, loved, and valued by another human being. That's what you did for me, Carl. Same with my sweet wife. When I needed someone to believe in me, someone to help me make a fresh start, first you and then Maddie became my Jesus with skin on."

Hands wrapped around his mug, Carl stared into the froth. "Hearing you say that means a lot," he murmured. "It's one of the best, most rewarding parts of my job here at Hope House. It's why I can't let anything—even my own brother—jeopardize its future."

Witt slowly stood. "You should think on things, so I'll head home now." At the door, he paused and turned with a sagacious half-smile. "Just a suggestion while you're cogitating. Make a list of all those people you've conveniently forgotten about who at various times were there to show you the hands and heart of Jesus. Because without them, no way you'd have become the generous, compassionate, God-loving man you are today."

Long after Witt's departure, his words played through Carl's thoughts. The man was right, of course. Over the years, countless teachers, mentors, pastors, friends, and even the best of his foster families had guided Carl and helped to mold his character. To doubt God's hand in it all was pure arrogance.

The realization ought to make it easier to reach out to his brother, but it didn't. Not yet, anyway. Carl's emotions were still too scattered and confused. When—*if*—he did see Ellis again, he didn't want the first words out of his mouth to be an accusatory *You had a family. You had everything. Why did you throw it all away?*

Chapter Ten

Rae tucked her elbows close to her sides and her hands in her lap. On her left, a pregnant woman holding a drooling toddler kept flipping her long, oily hair, barely missing Rae's face. A snoring gray-haired man with a scraggly beard sprawled on the chair to her right. Every once in a while, he'd bark out a phlegmy cough that made Rae wish she'd picked up a disposable mask from the sanitation stand at the clinic entrance. To get up now would mean losing her chair to one of several seedy-looking patients leaning against the wall.

Although giving up her seat might not be such a bad idea. She could just as easily wait outside until they finished treating Ellis's wound. A nurse had called him back half an hour ago. Surely he'd be out soon. Unless gangrene had set in and they were talking amputation—

Get a grip, Rae. She'd fallen into the habit of worst-case-scenario thinking, no thanks to her mother and problem-atic siblings.

The inner door creaked open, and Ellis appeared. His right hand sported a royal blue stretchy gauze wrap covering a thick, white bandage. While he stopped at the front desk to sign out and collect his paperwork, Rae made her way to the exit.

As he approached, she noted once again his strong resemblance to Carl. He had the same thick, dark hair and the same solid build. Even their walk was similar, though Ellis was probably an inch or two shorter. He had a more weathered look, too, as if aged by his hard life. If she hadn't known better, she'd think he was the elder brother, not Carl.

With a quick smile, she pulled open the door. "All set?"

"Yeah, thanks." He halted on the sidewalk near her car. "I appreciate you bringing me to the clinic, but you don't need to stick around. I can take care of myself from here on."

She cast him a doubtful frown. "Are you sure about that?"

"I got myself this far, didn't I? I'm doing just fine."

"You have a bad hand injury, you're out of work, you hitchhiked across two states, and you've been hanging out in a homeless encampment. Tell me how any of that falls into the category of *just fine*."

The man looked away briefly, his shoulders drooping. "Okay, I've had some tough breaks. What I don't get is why you singled me out at the free meal center. And don't tell me it's because of my hand, because I saw plenty of other guys there who looked a lot worse off than me."

"As I explained, I work for an organization that provides assistance to unhoused people."

"Yeah, you said that. Come on, lady, what's the real story?"

In deference to Carl's ambivalence, she'd tried her best

not to say more than necessary, but Ellis wasn't making it easy. Frankly, she could understand why he'd be suspicious.

"All right," she said, carefully choosing her words. "I learned about you from someone at River of Mercy Church, and since the pastor there seemed quite concerned about your hand injury, I checked with my shelter contacts to ask if any had seen you."

One eye narrowed. "That's it?"

"That's it." Or as much as she was prepared to reveal at the moment. She unlocked her car. "Where can I take you? The shelter where I picked you up has an excellent temporary housing program. I can get you registered with just a few quick steps."

"Not so fast, okay? I haven't decided if I'm staying in Missoula." His throat muscles worked. Glancing away, he gave a weak shrug. "The only reason I'm here at all is . . ."

The discouragement shading his whole demeanor squeezed Rae's heart. "Is it because some part of you hoped you'd find your family?"

"*Family*?" He released a disparaging laugh. "I could not possibly be more alone in the world."

Her next words flew out before she could stop them. "You know that isn't true. You have a brother. Right here in Missoula."

He gaped at her. "How do you know about my brother?"

Now she'd done it. Would Carl ever forgive her? Chin lowered, she said, "Carl and I work together at Equipped and Empowered Ministries."

"I never should have given his name to that pastor." Something like panic flashed in Ellis's eyes. Glancing around, he murmured, "I never should have come here at all."

Sensing he was ready to bolt, she gently took hold of his wrist. "Don't run. It won't solve anything." Something she wished she could say to Carl, since he seemed intent on running from the fact that his brother needed him.

"You don't understand," he said, his voice cracking. "*He* wouldn't understand."

"I get it. Somewhere along the way, your life fell apart, and you're afraid of how Carl will see you now."

"Does he already know about me?" Ellis's tone sharpened. "Does he know I'm in town?"

Rae winced. "He found out the day after you visited River of Mercy Church."

Pressing his good hand to his forehead, he spun away. "I have to get out of here. I have to—"

"Stop. Listen to me, Ellis. You can start over. You can rebuild a relationship with the brother you lost all those years ago. Give Carl a chance. Give *yourself* a chance."

"Why do you even care? I'm nobody to you."

"I care because . . ." She clenched her fists. "Because I don't believe in turning your back on family. No matter how difficult the relationships are or how bad things get."

Lips skewed, Ellis studied her. "If Carl has known about me all week, where is he? How come you're here and not him?"

It was the one question she'd hoped he wouldn't ask. "Truthfully? I think he's as scared as you are. Thirty-five years is a long time. He's probably equally worried about what you'll think of him."

There was much more to it, she had no doubt. For now, she had to make sure Ellis stuck around long enough for Carl to come to his senses.

She latched arms with the man and propelled him around the car. He seemed too surprised by the gesture to resist. "Just get in. If you don't want to go to the shelter, you can crash at my place for a few days."

He cast her a doubtful look. "Not sure that's such a good idea."

"It won't be a problem. You can sleep in my dad's old travel trailer that's parked behind my house." Giving Ellis a nudge into the passenger seat, she snorted. "Actually, you'd be doing me a huge favor. The trailer's only used when one of my freeloading siblings needs a place to crash. If it's occupied, they'll have to buck up and fend for themselves."

Claiming a headache, Carl skipped church on Sunday. Truth was, he'd been striving all weekend to put his brother out of his mind and didn't care to contend with the Holy Spirit's pokes to his conscience.

As if he could ever hide from God. Adam and Eve couldn't do it. Jonah couldn't do it. Elijah couldn't do it. Seemed the Good Lord should make an exception and let an average guy like Carl Anderson off the hook.

Carl knew better.

He tried to convince himself he merely needed time to figure out how to negotiate having Ellis back in his life. But given the circumstances, both his and his brother's, nothing would make their reunion any less complicated.

Monday morning, after dropping off residents for jobs and other appointments, Carl went to let the three dogs out for a run in the yard. The dogs slept in crates next to their handlers' beds, and during the day, they hung out with Carl in his office. When he left the house, usually no more than two to three hours at a time, the dogs were returned to their crates and seemed to have adapted well to the daily routine.

Hearing scratching and whimpering coming from the room Glen shared with three housemates, Carl went first to get Frankie. He immediately noticed the disarray in Glen's corner of the bedroom. Muddy sneakers peeked out from beneath the bed. The sheets and blanket were tossed back, half covering a pile of dirty laundry.

"Aw, Glen, what am I going to do with you?" Grumbling, he strode over to release Frankie.

When he unlatched the door, the dog bolted out and dashed toward the kitchen. Carl made a quick trip to the other bedrooms for Zippy and Cocoa, then hurried after Frankie, who was pawing frantically at the back door.

"Okay, okay, I'll let you out." He'd barely cracked the door when the dog pushed through and raced down the deck steps to relieve himself.

Carl scratched his head. The men were supposed to let their dogs out to the yard first thing every morning and then feed them. How had he missed that Glen hadn't taken care of Frankie today?

The dog was already at the back door anxious to come inside. When Carl let him in, Frankie went directly to the feeding station and sat down at his empty bowl. He aimed those piercing blue eyes at Carl, his gaze anxious and expectant.

"Breakfast, coming right up. Sorry, boy."

Cocoa and Zippy weren't going to be satisfied to watch Frankie eat, so Carl dropped a handful of treats into each of their bowls.

While the dogs chowed down, he decided he'd better make sure Frankie hadn't had an accident in his crate. The bedding was dry, but the poor dog had chewed big chunks out of his blanket and left several toenail marks on the inside of the crate. Poor guy.

Glen had just begun a new job. It was understandable if he was still adjusting to the schedule. However, these kinds of slip-ups were habitual, and if he wanted to stay in the program, they couldn't continue. Carl needed to have a sit-down talk with the guy this evening and get the situation under control—for Glen's sake as well as for Frankie's, who deserved a master who didn't ignore him in favor of more "important" matters.

Once Frankie had finished his breakfast, Carl took all the dogs outside for a romp. Chuckling at their antics, he sank onto a step at the foot of the deck and tilted his head to catch a ray of warm sunshine. If the spring weather stayed this nice, they could start holding the Saturday training sessions here, which would be easier than transporting everyone to the animal shelter. So far, the program was working as intended—*mostly*—but this three-month trial would be critical.

A car in the driveway drew the dogs' attention. All three bounded to the side gate, their tails wagging a mile a minute as they peered through the slats. By the time Carl pushed to his feet, a familiar blond head appeared on the other side of the fence. It never failed to astound him how his pulse rate went a little haywire each time he saw her. Whatever the reaction meant—and he refused to admit it could be attraction—he'd better get it under control.

"Hello, Carl." Rae remained several steps back, her fretful gaze darting between him and the dogs. "I was hoping we could talk."

The fact that she'd driven over instead of calling from her office couldn't mean anything good, especially as serious as she looked.

His stomach plummeted. This likely concerned his brother.

He should at least listen to what more she knew. He didn't feel like catering to her dog issues, though, no matter how sympathetic he was toward her reasons. Edging between the dogs and the gate, he opened it far enough for her to slip through, then motioned toward the deck. "It's a nice morning. Mind if we sit outside?"

"Fine." She barely glanced at the dogs sniffing at her heels as she marched up the four steps to the deck.

He pulled out a chair for her at the round wrought-iron table. "Coffee?"

"No, thanks." When Cocoa, the chocolate Lab, kept nudging her leg, she gave him a perfunctory pat and then used the hand signal for *sit*. Amazingly, he did just that. "Good dog."

"Impressive." Carl gave an appreciative snort. "Maybe you should be teaching the dog-training class."

"Not a chance."

He lowered himself into the chair opposite hers. Might as well get to the point. "You've obviously got something on your mind. I'm guessing it's about my brother?"

She sat a little straighter and cleared her throat. "You won't like this, but that's too bad. After I left the animal shelter on Saturday, I went to the meal center hoping Ellis would still be there."

Carl had figured as much. He gave a curt nod. "Was he?"

"Yes, thankfully. I introduced myself as a staff member from Equipped and Empowered and said I wanted to help. I could see his hand was in bad shape, so I drove him to an emergency clinic."

A bitter blend of annoyance and guilt tightened Carl's throat. "I wish you hadn't gotten involved."

"Well, someone had to, seeing as how you don't seem to care."

"I *do* care." He had to look away from her icy glare. "This is just bad timing, that's all."

"*Bad timing?* Since when do you put family on a schedule?" She gestured toward the dogs playing chase in the yard. "If one of them got sick or injured, would you wait to take them to the vet until it was *convenient*?"

"It isn't the same. Those animals depend on us for everything." A point he needed to drive home with Glen. "My brother's a grown man. He should be able to fend for himself."

Rae's jaw dropped. "Tell me you're not this condescending and judgmental with the Hope House residents. Because I thought I was speaking with the same Carl Anderson who devoted his adult life to helping the disadvantaged reclaim their lives."

Her words sliced straight through his heart. Rising abruptly, he strode to the deck railing. *Way to go, God. But couldn't You have picked someone a little less exasperating to hit me where it hurts?*

"Point taken," he murmured at last. "You're right, I have been using a double standard."

"Humph, big of you to admit it."

Turning with a resigned sigh, he felt in his pocket for his car keys. "Where did you take Ellis after he got his hand tended to? Is he still in town somewhere?"

"Well . . . yes, and no." Now Rae was acting evasive. "I couldn't talk him into going to an overnight shelter, so I, um . . ." She met his gaze with a sharp stare. "I took him home with me."

He literally staggered. "Didn't your parents ever warn

you about the risks of taking in strays, canine or otherwise? You have no idea what he might be capable of."

"Neither do you, apparently. Anyway, he isn't sleeping *in* my house. I have a small travel trailer hooked up out back. So far, it's been a mutually beneficial arrangement. Ellis has fixed my leaky bathroom faucet, cooked dinner for me *and* cleaned the kitchen afterward, helped with laundry, and dust-mopped my wood floors—all this, mind you, with a badly injured hand."

Frankie, the blue-eyed husky mix, trotted up the steps and parked himself at Carl's feet. Head tilted, the dog emitted a soft whine. When Carl ignored him, Frankie began pawing at his pants leg.

Rae snorted. "He's obviously trying to tell you something."

Whatever the dog was attempting to communicate, Carl wasn't getting the message. He nudged the dog with his knee, but Frankie didn't budge. "And I suppose you know what that something is."

"It's perfectly clear to me. He's saying you're a sanctimonious nincompoop who needs to get off his high horse and do the right thing."

At her ludicrous retort, he laughed in spite of himself. "Wow. I don't recall anyone ever calling me a nincompoop before. In fact, I can't remember the last time I heard that word used by anyone under *any* circumstances."

Chin hiked, she crossed her arms. "If the epithet fits . . ."

He lowered to his haunches. Nose to nose with Frankie, he gave the dog a rub behind both ears. "She thinks I'm a nincompoop, huh? And a sanctimonious one, at that."

Frankie replied with a wet tongue across his cheek.

Carl groaned and pushed to his feet. "No use arguing

when it's two against one." Not to mention both of them were nailing him with their wintry blue-eyed gazes. "Do you think Ellis is ready to see me?"

"I think he'd have no place to run if you should happen to show up unannounced."

"Fine, if it'll get you off my case. When would you suggest?"

Rae pushed her lips to one side in a thoughtful look. "How about this evening? Come to my house for supper."

He was sure to regret this. "Text me your address and let me know what time."

She already had her phone out, her thumbs dancing across the digital keyboard. "Let's plan on six thirty."

Claiming she had another meeting to get to, she marched out to her car, once again deftly avoiding the dogs. Carl watched her drive away, then called the dogs inside. It would take the entire day to prepare himself to see his brother again after all these years. He desperately needed that prep time, both emotionally and spiritually.

Because Rae was right—where his brother was concerned, he'd lost all perspective.

Please, Lord, help me get my head in the right place before tonight. Most of all, smooth away these calluses on my heart, because I don't want to be the judgmental, condemning person Rae pegged me for.

Chapter Eleven

E llis had felt weird all day. How could Rae simply trust him the way she did—enough to give a perfect stranger free access to her home? Inviting him in for breakfast that morning, she'd said there was no reason for him to stay cooped up in the travel trailer all day. He should make himself comfortable in the house and take a break from all the odd jobs he'd found to do for her over the weekend and allow his hand time to heal.

But he just couldn't do it. His conscience—which he'd suddenly seemed to develop for no reason he could fathom —wouldn't let him loll on her sofa watching hour after hour of TV game shows, talk shows, or old movies while stuffing himself with the chips, cookies, and fruit she'd set out on the kitchen counter.

Before she'd left for work, she'd taken something from the freezer and set it in the fridge to thaw. The label pictured a chicken Alfredo casserole, with baking instructions in the bottom right corner: *Preheat oven to 400°F, then place on a baking sheet and cook for 35-40 minutes until interior temperature reaches 165°F.*

Sounded easy enough. Ellis checked her produce drawer to see if she had any salad fixings to go with the meal. All he found was a half-empty bag of greens that were starting to look like a bad science project. They'd passed a small grocery mart on the way into Elk Valley. Rae's house was only a few blocks from there, easily within walking distance. He could go pick something up and have supper on the table by the time she got home.

Except he had a slight cash flow problem. Fishing in his pockets, he came up with a measly $4.73 in bills and change. That should be enough for a head of lettuce and a tomato or two.

The sun warmed his back as he set out for Elk Valley's one and only shopping area, a mini mall on the corner where two main roads crossed. A vague memory surfaced of briefly living in Elk Valley with one of his and Carl's foster families, but he didn't recall much else about the town. Even so, it didn't look like it had grown much since then.

Arriving at the grocery mart and with no reason to hurry, he browsed the aisles while trying not to look like a shoplifter casing the joint. No reason to draw unwanted attention from management.

Too late. A skinny older guy wearing a crisply ironed baby-blue shirt and crooked bowtie strode toward him. "May I help you, sir?"

"Just picking up something for supper." There was something familiar about the man's voice. Something that made Ellis's gut twist. He read the man's badge—*J. Beedles, Asst. Mgr.*—and felt like he should recognize the name, but it wasn't coming to him. He stuck on a stiff smile. "Maybe you could point me to the produce aisle?"

"That way, other side of the store." The man gestured with the ballpoint pen he'd been obsessively clicking.

"Thanks." He started past.

"Haven't seen you in here before," Mr. Beedles called after him. "New in town?"

Without turning, he waved over his shoulder. "Just visiting."

No sooner had he rounded the corner than recognition dawned. *The bowtie.* Beedles had been at least thirty-five years younger the last time Ellis had seen him. The past came rushing back as he remembered fixing his eyes on the perfect square knot in the center of the tie while the man harangued him about one thing or another. Could have been for leaving his dirty socks and underwear beside the bathtub, or not finishing his peas, or forgetting to wipe his feet when he came in from the yard.

And he couldn't in a million years forget the *thwack* of a big, fat wooden spoon across his backside.

Carl had been his savior then, coming between him and Beedles. *"Stop, please! I'll make sure he doesn't do it again."*

"Be sure you do, or you'll be next in line for a whippin'. You're both more trouble than you're worth."

"Ol' Beady Eyes," Carl had nicknamed him. He and his mousy wife were the last of Ellis's brief series of foster parents. He'd been living there when the Newmans adopted him.

He'd worried for years about where Carl ended up. How much longer had his big brother endured Beedles's short fuse and lightning-quick punishments? How many more foster homes before Carl had aged out of the system? Had it scarred him for life the way becoming a Newman had damaged Ellis? Which of them had *really* gotten the bad end of the stick?

Examining a ripe tomato, Ellis scoffed. Himself, obviously, since by all accounts his brother had survived childhood, gone on to college, and was now a respected employee of some kind of outreach ministry organization. Ellis couldn't remember the name Rae had mentioned, only that they helped homeless people.

How many times did he have to keep repeating he wasn't homeless? He preferred to classify his situation as a temporary setback. Between jobs. Starting over. Whatever.

"Find what you were looking for?" Beedles again, sneaking up as if he was hoping to catch Ellis in the act of shoplifting.

"Yeah. Thanks." Like he could tuck a baseball-size tomato into his jacket pocket and walk out without looking suspicious. He tore off a plastic produce bag for the tomato and then couldn't get the stupid bag to open. He cursed under his breath.

"Let me." Beedles snatched the bag from him. "These things are buggers, even for folks with two good hands." Employing what must be a classified secret known only to produce managers, the man peeled the bag open and held it for Ellis to drop the tomato inside.

He looked askance at his former nemesis. "Thanks," he said again, this time almost meaning it.

"Anything else I can help you with?"

Offering a pinched smile, Ellis shook his head. "Just gonna pick up some salad greens and I'll be on my way."

Ten minutes later, he let himself into Rae's house through the back door. He set the groceries in the fridge, then leaned against the kitchen counter while he caught his breath. It wasn't so much the walk that had tired him, but the blast from his past when he'd run into Ol' Beady Eyes. He hated to think how many kids' fragile spirits the man may have shattered over the years.

He hated to think how many more of his and Carl's

former foster families were still in the area. Had Carl run into any of them? Either way, seeing as how his brother had stuck around Missoula, it must say something about his ability to forgive and forget.

But forgiving and forgetting wasn't in Ellis's makeup. He doubted it ever would be.

Chapter Twelve

"Jordy, I'm leaving you in charge of the supper crew tonight." Carl pulled the Hope House van to a stop in the driveway. "Pork chops are thawing in the fridge, and I've already scrubbed the potatoes. You just have to peel and boil—"

"Got it covered," Jordy said from the passenger seat. In the early days of his rehabilitation, he'd discovered a knack for cooking and now worked the day shift at a local restaurant. "You just go enjoy your dinner date with the pretty lady from the office."

Jordy's comment brought a round of chuckles from the other guys in the van. Carl glared into the rearview mirror. "I told you, it isn't a date."

None of the conversations any of the men had witnessed between him and Rae could possibly have left that impression . . . could they? In any case, tonight definitely didn't qualify.

Glen slid open the side door and scooted out. "What is it, then?" He turned to peer at Carl between the front seats.

"I mean, you and Ms. Caldwell sure spend a lot of time together."

"It's ministry business. That's all." He wasn't ready to say anything yet about his brother. Maybe never, depending on how the evening went. "And by the way, Glen, you and I need to have a serious talk later. Right now, I expect you to see to Frankie before you do anything else. Understood?"

The man winced. "Will do."

"The rest of you, check your evening chore list. Then get cleaned up and help Jordy get supper on the table."

"Yes, sir," and, "You got it," came the chorus of replies as the men piled from the van.

Jordy turned as he stepped onto the driveway. "Didn't mean to kid you, Carl. Thing is, we'd all like to see you happy, and it sure seems like there's some sparks in the air when you and Ms. Caldwell are together."

Carl scoffed. "The only sparks you're seeing between us are from the clash of our extremely different personalities."

"You know what they say. Opposites attract."

"Yeah, well, *they* aren't always right." Exiting the van, Carl followed the men into the kitchen and continued on to his room. He'd showered and shaved earlier, but it wouldn't hurt to brush his teeth again and splash some water on his face before heading over to Rae's. He'd argued with himself all day about whether to go through with these dinner plans. Did Ellis know he was coming? Did he even want to see Carl again?

And what would they say to each other after all these years? He'd practiced a few things in his head, lame remarks like *Long time no see*, or *What have you been up to for the last thirty-five years?*

Where was Witt when he needed him? Was it too late to call and invite his wingman along?

Except he could predict exactly what Witt would say: *He's your brother, Carl. You need to face this on your own.*

Too bad he didn't have a script to follow, or maybe even a PowerPoint presentation covering the intervening years. He could only hope God would give him the right words at the right time.

As he stared into the bathroom mirror, all he could see was Ellis's tear-streaked face minutes before the Newmans took him away.

"It's gonna be great, I promise," Carl had insisted, *forcing a smile he didn't feel. "You're getting a real forever home with parents who'll love you and watch over you every single day."*

"But why can't you come, too? They have a big house. They have room."

"It doesn't work that way, kiddo. But I'll be okay, don't you worry. You will, too. You're gonna have the best life ever."

And he should have. The Newmans could get Ellis into the best schools. They could provide resources and opportunities the likes of which he could never hope for in the foster system.

Out of nowhere, another memory surfaced.

"Son, you're making a scene." Mr. Newman's hand *clamped down on Ellis's shoulder, and his voice grew hard. "It's time to go. Stop embarrassing yourself."*

The emotional gut punch doubled Carl over. Had he conveniently forgotten that part? Had he purposely ignored indications that perhaps the Newmans weren't the loving parents he'd tried to convince his scared-to-death baby brother they'd be?

Even if he had seen the signs, at barely ten years old himself, what could he have done?

Nothing. Absolutely nothing.

Moments after Rae parked in her garage, the tempting aroma of chicken Alfredo met her senses. Entering the kitchen, she saw that the breakfast table had been set for two, with frosty water glasses waiting near each plate.

She set her briefcase on the built-in desk near the door. "Ellis?"

"Right here." He strode in from the living room. "Sorry, I was watching something on the news. I put dinner in the oven. Hope that was okay."

"Yes. I appreciate it. Except . . ." Lips pinched, she considered how best to explain it wouldn't be just the two of them.

"Did I start it too early? You're probably used to eating later. I should have asked first."

"No, it's fine," she said quickly. "Really. It's just that I, um . . . I'm expecting a dinner guest."

"Ah." Ellis's brows lifted in a knowing look. "Time for me to do a quick vanishing act."

He'd clearly gotten the wrong idea. "No, please don't. I thought we'd all have dinner together."

"Look, you've been too nice to me already. You don't need me cramping your style."

"You wouldn't be. The thing is, I've arranged for— for—"

"It's okay, I get it," he said with a dismissive laugh. "Seriously, I'm perfectly capable of fending for myself."

"Ellis, you're not listening." Rae pressed a palm to her forehead. "And I'm not explaining very well either."

He stared at her for a long moment. "Then maybe try harder. Because I'm pretty confused right now."

Afraid he'd bolt once he knew the identity of her guest, she squeezed her eyes shut briefly. "Just stay. Please."

Giving a reluctant shrug, he nodded. "All right, if you say so."

"Great. Then if you wouldn't mind moving everything to the dining room and adding another place setting . . ." She was already taking a plate from the cupboard.

"Wait. You didn't invite *him*, did you? Please don't tell me it's my *brother*."

Before she could reply, he was halfway out the back door. Speaking in the voice she typically reserved for her intractable siblings, she ordered, "Ellis Newman, you stop right there!"

Sneakers screeching on the tile, he jerked to a halt but didn't turn around.

Using the same tone, she continued "You are not running away this time. You and Carl need to talk things out. He's your family. You need each other, even if neither of you wants to admit it."

He rotated his head just enough that she could see his partial profile. "So I was right. He's been avoiding me, too."

"He's as nervous about this reunion as you are." She only hoped Carl hadn't spent the day dwelling on his doubts. Would he be texting her any minute now to cancel?

Ellis's shoulders drooped. He pulled a hand across his face and heaved a long, slow sigh. "I should never have come to Missoula. This is only stirring up bad memories for both of us."

"Believe me, I know all about painful memories." Rae slid her gaze toward a mahogany étagère, where a photo of her precious Kellie peeked out from behind a row of elegant china teacups. "The memories never go away, but you learn to live with them. You can only try with every ounce of strength you possess to keep moving forward, one day at a time."

Ellis closed the door and slowly turned to face her. "Guess things can't get any worse, huh? If this doesn't go well, I can always move on to the next town and start over. Again."

"Or stay put and fight for the life you want." She shoved the plate and a handful of flatware toward him and nodded toward the dining room. "Starting right now."

Rinsing off a cutting board in the sink, Rae glimpsed Carl's blue SUV turn into her driveway. The antique chime clock in the living room had just tolled six thirty.

"He's here," she called to Ellis as he carried the salad bowl to the table.

He'd adamantly refused her offer to reimburse him for what he'd spent at the grocery mart, insisting he'd hold on to what little pride he had left. She wished her siblings would show even a modicum of such resolve.

The oven timer beeped. After shutting it off, she donned quilted mitts and set the baking dish on the range top. Realizing Ellis hadn't come back for the water glasses she'd filled, she went to check on him.

He stood stock still in the middle of the living room, his gaze glued to the front picture window.

Slipping off the oven mitts, she came up beside him. "Take a breath. It's going to be all right."

"How can you be so sure?"

"I have five younger brothers and sisters. If we can find a way past all our differences"—which, technically, they didn't always, but she wouldn't admit it to Ellis—"you and Carl certainly can."

He didn't look convinced, but at least he wasn't running for the hills. While the chicken Alfredo baked, he'd even gone out to the trailer to clean up a bit. Rae had a collection of clothes her siblings had left behind at various times. Leo, the youngest of her brothers, was about the same size as Ellis, so she'd offered him Leo's navy blue henley and a pair of jeans. Unfortunately, she couldn't do much about Ellis's dirt-stained sneakers with holes wearing through the toes.

Carl passed the front window, and seconds later the doorbell rang. Rae inhaled deeply before answering. "Hi. I was hoping you hadn't decided to chicken out."

"And incur your unending wrath? *Pffft.*"

His attempt at humor wasn't fooling her. "Come on in," she said with the brightest smile she could muster. "We'll be sitting down to dinner momentarily. Let me take your jacket."

Carl stepped cautiously into the entryway and shrugged out of his jacket, his gaze drifted toward the living room. He made a small choking sound in his throat. "Ellis?"

Rae hung the jacket in the hall closet, then patted his arm. "I'll finish getting dinner on the table while you two get reacquainted."

"I . . . I don't think I can do this." Carl backpedaled toward the door.

She grabbed his hand before he could reach for the knob. Standing on tiptoe and nose-to-nose with him, she spoke through gritted teeth. "You *can*, and you *will*. Now get in there and say hello to your brother."

After giving him a not-so-gentle shove, she waited long enough to confirm his forward momentum, then scurried down the hallway to the kitchen. It was easy enough to stay out of sight and eavesdrop, which she'd intended to do only long enough to make sure they were actually talking.

But once she heard their first few words, she couldn't tear herself away.

Carl halted a few steps into the living room. Heaving a shrug, he stuffed his hands into his pockets. "So. Here we are."

"Guess we weren't gonna get out of this." Ellis tipped his head toward the dining room. "She seems like she's used to having things her way."

"As I'm learning."

"You look good, man." Ellis's crooked smile revealed a mixture of wariness and admiration.

"Thanks." Carl wasn't sure he could say the same for his brother. He blew out slowly. "Look, I'm sorry, but after all these years, I don't know how we're supposed to do this."

"Same here." Several seconds of strained silence followed. "For starters, you probably have a bunch of questions."

"I do. But why don't we keep it simple for now?" Carl gestured toward his brother's bandaged hand. "How'd that happen?"

Ellis glanced away with a snort. "Let's just say it was a construction accident."

"Which implies there's more to it than that. You've obviously gotten yourself into some serious trouble." Carl's barely controlled frustration bubbled to the surface. "Why can't you just be honest with me about it?"

"I haven't lied to you. I was—"

"And what about how you're taking advantage of Rae?" Now that the cage door had been pried open, Carl could no longer restrain the questions and doubts circling his brain like a flock of vultures. "What trumped-up tales did you weave to get her to take you into her home? Or did you win her over with one of your 'homeless puppy' looks?"

Ellis's jaw dropped. "Where did *that* come from?"

"Isn't that how you persuaded the Newmans to adopt you?" The barrage of ridiculous accusations had flown from Carl's mouth before common sense could censor his words. Now there was no taking them back.

Barking a disbelieving laugh, Ellis turned away. "If that's what you believe, then shame on me for thinking there was any chance at all of reconnecting with the brother I once looked up to."

"Honestly, you two." Brandishing a large serving spoon, Rae burst in from the dining room. "This isn't elementary school and this isn't a playground fight. Stop acting like bratty kids and be civil."

"I was trying," Ellis said. "Until he basically accused me of lying."

Carl flung his hand in Ellis's direction. "It's pretty clear you aren't telling us the whole story. What are you even doing here? Were you hoping your big brother would bail you out of whatever mess you've gotten yourself into?"

"*I said stop!*" Stepping forward, Rae thrust out her arms between them, the serving spoon halting inches from Carl's face.

Recoiling, he blinked several times. What was wrong with him, anyway? He'd thought he'd prepared himself for this meeting. Clearly, he was mistaken. Had he lost every trace of objectivity—of *compassion*—where his brother was concerned?

"This isn't at all the way I hoped tonight would go," he muttered, backing away. "I shouldn't have said those things."

Ellis snorted. "Yeah, but now I know how you really feel about me. Apparently, how you've always felt." He looked toward Rae. "I told you this was a bad idea."

"Take a breath, okay?" Rae lowered her arms. "This is new territory for both of you. Please, let's go sit down to dinner while it's hot. There'll be plenty of time later to sort things out."

Carl's appetite had fled long before he'd left Hope House for the drive over. After several shaky breaths in an attempt to regain his equilibrium, he followed Rae to the dining room. Ellis had certainly nailed it when he said Rae was used to getting her own way. If this was how she kept her siblings in line, he couldn't imagine they'd ever think of crossing her.

Positioning herself at the head of the table, Rae motioned for Carl and Ellis to take the seats opposite each other. She served a moderate portion of pasta covered in a thick, creamy sauce onto Carl's plate. "I hope you like chicken Alfredo."

He usually did, but the way his stomach was churning, he wasn't sure he could swallow. Sitting stiffly while Rae serve Ellis and then herself, he hoped she wouldn't ask him to offer grace.

"Carl, I know it's your custom to pray before meals. Perhaps you'd do the honors."

He glanced at his brother, who'd already bowed his head. Silently drawing air between his teeth, he folded his hands and closed his eyes. "Lord, we ask You to bless this food to the nourishment of our bodies. Amen."

"That was short and sweet." Sarcasm tinged Rae's words, as well as the twisted smile she cast his way. She spread her napkin across her lap. "Which salad dressing would you prefer? Italian or ranch?"

"Italian, please."

"Ranch for me." Ellis's tone implied he'd have chosen the exact opposite no matter what Carl had requested.

With their salads suitably dressed, table talk faded, which made the sounds of forks clicking on plates and ice swirling in water glasses all the more noticeable. Carl would probably need a handful of antacids once he got home later, but for the sake of politeness, he forced down as much of his meal as he could manage.

The side benefit of the awkward mealtime silence was the chance to reflect on how, exactly, he'd let himself go off the rails earlier. Why had he automatically assumed Ellis was hiding something? Rae had mentioned learning that Ellis had been working in construction before his injury sidelined him. She'd never once implied Ellis had played on her sympathies about needing a place to stay. Just the opposite, in fact.

Yep, that was pure Rae, the "big sister" who acted as if her siblings' success in life rested solely on her shoulders. Later, he intended to remind her yet again that she was in no way responsible for him and his brother.

When it became apparent that they'd each eaten their fill, Rae rose and began stacking plates.

"Let me help," Ellis said, jumping up.

"I've got it. You and Carl can go talk in the living room. I'll start some decaf."

Carl stayed seated while his brother trudged out, then

followed Rae to the kitchen. Keeping his voice low, he pleaded, "Why don't we just call it a night? I've already humiliated myself enough."

"Glad you can admit it." Casting him an arch frown, she set the plates in the sink. "And no, I'm not letting you off the hook. Go in there and talk to your brother. And this time, *really* talk. Better yet, *listen*."

He released a huff. "Why is my relationship with my brother such a big deal with you, anyway? Seems like your own family issues keep you plenty busy."

Her smug expression faltered briefly. "Your sibling issues seem fixable. Mine tend to be . . . more complicated."

"More complicated than two former foster kids who got separated in childhood and then one of them ends up injured, unemployed, and homeless?"

"In some ways, yes." She busied herself rinsing plates. "And I don't want to talk about it."

"Of course you don't." Striding toward the back door, Carl said over his shoulder, "Good night, Rae."

Chapter Thirteen

Seething inside, Rae carried two mugs of decaf to the living room. She set one on the coffee table within Ellis's reach, then trudged to the chair across from him and sat down with a thud. Hot coffee splashed over the rim and onto her hand. She cursed under her breath.

Ellis hurried to the dining room and grabbed a napkin from the table. Returning, he carefully dabbed at Rae's hand. "You should run that under cold water so it doesn't blister."

"I'm okay. It wasn't that hot." She set her mug on an end table, then took the napkin from him. After wiping more coffee off her fingers, she swiped at the droplets that had spattered her slacks. "Thank you."

Back on the sofa, Ellis sat forward and gingerly sipped from his mug. "I take it Carl left?"

"I'm sorry. Yes."

"You tried."

"Well, *he* certainly didn't." A growl escaped her throat. "I cannot believe his insensitivity. His—his—*immaturity*."

Ellis set down his mug and leaned back with a sigh.

"Can't really blame him. I mean, look at me. I'm a dead-beat. A disappointment. An embarrassment."

"You're a guy who's faced hard times. Carl has no right to judge you for that, especially considering he helps people like you for a living."

"Yeah, but those guys aren't his brothers. They haven't—"

Her cell phone jangled from where she'd left it in her bedroom. Recognizing the all-too-familiar ringtone, she winced but didn't bother getting up.

"Shouldn't you get that?" Ellis asked.

"It's my mother. She'll call back. Or leave a message."

He stood. "You go talk to your mom and I'll clean up the kitchen. It's the least I can do."

Before she could argue, he scuttled through the dining room.

The phone ceased ringing, then seconds later started up again. Her mother must be desperate. Rolling her eyes, Rae slogged to her room and grabbed the phone off the dresser. "I'm here, Mom," she answered tiredly. "What is it?"

"Oh, honey, you won't believe this!" Mom spoke in her typical all-exclamation-points mode. "Heather kicked Reece out! You've *got* to do something!"

"Like what, Mom?" She sank onto the end of the bed. "Isn't it about time he learned his lesson?"

"But she's saying he *cheated* on her! I simply can't believe my son—"

"Believe it. It's true."

Her mother grew momentarily silent. "H-how can you say such an awful thing? Reece would *never*—"

"He's already admitted it to me." The clatter of dishes reached her from the kitchen. Ellis Newman was in there doing his best to be helpful while his brother and Rae's siblings—even her mother—acted out like spoiled children.

"Well, if it's true," her mother sputtered, "then Heather probably deserved it, the way she's been treating him. If she hadn't been so consumed with this pregnancy, she could have been the wife to him that he needed."

"Mom, do you hear yourself? Who's been laying on the pressure—the guilt trips—about wanting a grandchild?" Hand to her forehead, Rae paced to the window and gazed across the lamplit backyard. If her brother dared to come crawling to her door, begging to move into the travel trailer, she now had a ready excuse to say no.

"I think you should let Reece have the trailer for a few weeks," her mother went on. "Just till he and Heather have a chance to work things out."

Right on cue, Mom. She snorted a laugh. "Sorry, it's occupied."

"Really? Who's staying there? One of your sisters?"

"No." *Thank goodness!* "Just . . . a friend."

Again, her mother grew silent. "Rae Anne Ogden, are you entertaining a man?"

Leave it to her mother to haul out her full maiden name. "It isn't like that. He's a coworker's relative who needed a place to stay."

"And a coworker's family takes precedence over your own?"

She turned at the sound of Ellis clearing his throat in the hallway. "Rae? Kitchen's clean. Good night."

Covering the mouthpiece, she spoke just loudly enough for Ellis to hear. "Thanks. See you in the morning."

Her mother yelled in her ear, "He's in your *house*?"

"What of it? It's my house, and I'm an adult. I'll do whatever I want in my own home."

"Rae, I'm your mother. You can't talk to me like that."

"I just did. Now I'm hanging up." She lowered the phone and stabbed the red disconnect icon.

Her heart hammered as she dropped the phone onto the dresser. How long had it been since she'd taken a firm stand with her mother and siblings? How long had she been letting them take advantage, using her to mediate their squabbles, listen to their troubles, provide a safe place to land when—in their opinion—the world turned against them? It was long past time they left her out of their problems and took responsibility for themselves.

The phone rang—her mother again, no surprise. She punched the button that would decline the call and silence the ringing. Then she did something she never did. She turned the phone completely off.

"I blew it, Witt. I blew it bad." Carl hunched over his friend's kitchen table. For the last half hour, Witt had listened patiently while Carl confessed the total fiasco he'd made of his encounter with Ellis.

After a thoughtful silence, Witt spoke. "Now that you've had time to think about it, why do you suppose you reacted like that?"

"Annoyance. Anger. Fear." He lifted his head tiredly. "All of the above?"

"No doubt." Stretching out one leg, Witt rubbed his chin. "Let's start with what annoyed you the most this evening."

"It's mainly that I haven't had time to fully process the idea of having my brother back in my life. It feels like we're being pushed toward some big, happy reconciliation that neither of us is ready for."

"So your anger is partly toward Rae?"

"Absolutely." Carl snorted. "I can't see how this is any of her business."

"You can't deny there's some part of you that wanted to see Ellis again."

"Of course. But in some ways, it was easier *not* knowing what happened to him."

"I can sort of understand that." Witt's tone remained even. "So you went. You tried to talk. What else frustrated you?"

In his mind's eye, Carl saw Ellis standing in Rae's living room across from him. "That I didn't know what to say to my own brother. That he's a complete stranger to me."

"A lot has happened in both your lives since you were separated. You have thirty-five years of catching up to do, and that's going to take time." Witt paused to shift positions. "Let's dig a little deeper. What else are you angry about?"

"I'm angry that my brother squandered every advantage the Newmans were supposed to give him." He scoffed. "Construction work? Come on! I didn't have one-tenth of the breaks Ellis had, but I still put myself through college and graduate school. I worked hard to put my past behind me and make something of myself."

"And you've helped a great many people, me included, to do the same."

"I've tried. It's all I've ever aspired to." Chest deflating, he cast his friend a desperate look.

He waited for Witt to state the obvious, that a man in Carl's position certainly should be able to offer his own brother the empathy and compassion afforded daily to the Hope House residents.

Instead, Witt asked softly, "What are you afraid of, Carl?"

The fear gnawing at his insides was as strong now as it had been when he'd first set foot in Rae's living room and faced his brother. He massaged his eye sockets. "My biggest fear is exactly what happened, that I'd let emotion take over instead of letting Ellis tell me his side of the story."

"Instead of listening and loving him."

Carl nodded, his eyes filling, his heart on the edge of bursting. "I keep replaying the last time I saw my little brother. When the Newmans came for him, he didn't fully understand what was happening. He was crying so hard. I tried to be strong and tell him everything would be okay. All I could do was stand there and smile while his new dad practically had to shove him into the car."

Giving Carl's forearm a firm squeeze, Witt rose silently. He brought back a handful of tissues and placed them near Carl's hand.

He sniffed hard and pressed the entire wad against his leaking eyes. "Thanks," he murmured. "Thank you for being the patient listener I should have been for my brother."

"It isn't too late," his friend said with an encouraging lilt. "It's barely past nine o'clock, and you're less than ten minutes away."

"Maybe I should give it time." Carl blew his nose. "Give us both more time."

"It's been thirty-five years already." Witt's tone softened to a gentle plea. "Isn't that long enough?"

It was probably a good thing Carl hadn't allowed himself to think too hard about Witt's suggestion. Otherwise, he'd have driven straight home to Hope House instead of standing on Rae's front porch ringing her doorbell.

He punched the bell twice more before a yellow porch light blinked on and Rae peeked through a slit. "Carl?" The door opened wider. "What are you doing here?"

"I came to apologize. To Ellis, and to you."

She tightened the sash of a ratty pink chenille bathrobe. "I think he's already turned in for the night. I was about to do the same."

"Sorry, I know it's getting late. I just . . ." He roughly cleared his throat. "Never mind. I shouldn't have bothered you."

"Wait," she said, halting the quick retreat he'd hoped to make. "Do you want to come in?"

He swallowed the metallic taste in his mouth. If he didn't face up to all those emotions he'd confessed to Witt, they'd continue to eat him alive. "Okay," he said. "If you're sure."

She stepped aside to admit him. Her slicked-back hair looked freshly washed. In the overhead light of the entry, her makeup-free face glowed like alabaster. It took a moment to reconcile this version of Rae to her typically stylish, put-together daytime look. He realized he liked the change, and the perplexing thud of his heart made him suck in a breath.

Inviting him into the living room, she said over her shoulder, "I haven't rinsed out the coffeepot yet. There's enough for another cup if you'd like some."

"No, thanks."

"Sit anywhere." She motioned toward the cozy furniture arrangement he'd barely noticed during his earlier visit. "I'll see if Ellis is willing to try again."

He opted for a wing chair at one end of the sofa. Behind him, he listened to the fading scuff of her slippers, then the back door opening and closing. It was all he could do to keep his lungs working as he waited.

An eternity later, the back door clicked again, and two sets of footsteps drew closer. He stood and turned, schooling his features into what he hoped conveyed both remorse and openness.

Ellis struck a stiff pose a few feet away. "Rae said you came to apologize?"

"I did." Trying not to be obvious, Carl dried his sweaty palms on his khakis. "I was a selfish fool and a coward to skip out like I did. I'm hoping you'll give me another chance."

"Give me one good reason."

"Ellis . . ." Rae's quiet use of his name held a warning. "Hear him out."

"Like he did me earlier?" Arms crossed, Ellis angled away.

Carl dared a step forward. "You're right, I wasn't ready to listen then. But I am now." He extended both hands, palms facing up. "Please."

For a tense few seconds, Ellis didn't move. Then, with a noisy exhalation, he marched to a chair matching Carl's at the opposite end of the sofa and sat down heavily. As Carl returned to his seat, he noticed Rae silently slip from the room. He almost wished she'd stay, in case things took another turn for the worse.

He sat forward, forearms braced on his thighs. "Before I ask you to be honest with me, I need to be honest with you."

Ellis snorted. "I thought you made yourself pretty clear before."

"That was my . . . my frustration and fear speaking." He mentally thanked Witt for helping him clarify his emotions. "I'll do my best not to let them get in the way again, but you have a right to know where my feelings were coming from."

Haltingly, he repeated much of what he'd confessed to Witt. While keeping the focus on himself—his feelings and perceptions, his automatic rush to judgment—he didn't hold back as he described his ongoing struggles in the foster care system, the effort it had taken to rise above his past, and everything that had gone through his mind when he'd first learned Ellis was in Missoula.

"So I was angry," he concluded, "because you were supposed to have every advantage I didn't, and I couldn't comprehend how or why you'd ended up like . . . like this."

The air in the room practically vibrated with the stony silence that followed. Carl's new fear was that his blatant honesty would firmly shut the door on whatever chance remained to set things right.

"Now it's my turn," Ellis began slowly, stiffly. "And believe me, when I'm done, you'll probably thank your lucky stars—or God, or whatever higher power you claim— that you *didn't* get adopted. At least not by the Newmans. They definitely weren't the picture-perfect, two-parent American family."

Not ten minutes into his brother's story of growing up as a Newman, Carl found himself quietly weeping. The pressure to be a good little boy—obedient, compliant, never reflecting badly on his parents—and the consequences every time he failed. Then the drinking, drugs, shoplifting, fights.

Running away, only to be hauled back. More punishments. Feeling trapped.

"I turned eighteen one month before I was supposed to graduate from high school," Ellis went on, his face wet with tears. "That morning, I left the house as usual, but instead of going to school, I grabbed the duffel I'd stashed behind a bush and walked away. Three days of hitchhiking put Denver and the Newmans permanently in my rearview mirror. I'd have legally changed my name, too, if not for all the red tape. By then, I was too tired and beaten down to bother."

"If I'd known what kind of people they were," Carl murmured. "If I'd had any idea—"

"What, you'd have come to my rescue?" Ellis's gaze softened into undeserved mercy. "You were only a kid, too. Trapped in your life, just like I was trapped in mine. I don't blame you, Carl. I never did."

"But you didn't look for me either. All these years since, you could have found me any time you wanted." A realization hit him, something he'd never admitted until this moment. "I think it's why I never left Missoula. In case you ever did come back, I wanted to be here."

Ellis released a harsh laugh. "Aren't we a pair? I wanted so bad to see my big brother again, but I couldn't stand the thought of you finding out how I'd wasted my life. Turns out you were avoiding me for that very reason."

"Which was wrong on so many levels." Carl rose and took a few tentative steps toward his brother. "I'm really sorry. Please, can we try again?"

Chapter Fourteen

What else could Ellis do but meet his brother halfway? Choking on a sob, he stumbled into Carl's outstretched arms, only to flinch when Carl accidentally bumped his bandaged right hand.

"Oops, sorry." Carl adjusted his position for a more cautious hug.

"Don't worry about it." Ignoring the twinge of pain, he thumped Carl's back. "Man, I've missed you, big bro!"

"You, too." Carl's voice sounded raspy with emotion. After a few manly pats to Ellis's shoulders, he took a step back and gingerly lifted Ellis's bandaged hand. "Seriously, how bad is it?"

"It's healing." Especially after Rae had told him about Carl's program that paired recovering homeless guys with shelter dogs, he couldn't bring himself to confess the source of his injury.

Worse, he hadn't exactly been innocent in the encounter. How many times had he teased that guard dog as he'd walked past the pickup day after day? For weeks, he'd played guessing games about the contents of the lock-box, even contemplated luring the dog away with a piece of raw meat so he could sneak into the truck bed, pry open the lock, and maybe find something valuable enough to fence. He'd been ready to do almost anything to quit working those stinkin' backbreaking construction jobs.

At the memory of how desperate he'd been, shame filled him. Jaw clenched, he withdrew his hand and turned away.

"You should let me take you to see my doctor," Carl said. "Just to be sure—"

"No." He cringed at the snappiness in his tone and inhaled sharply. "Really, it's gonna be fine. The doc at the free clinic gave me a new antibiotic. It seems to be working."

"That's good." After a moment's hesitation, Carl asked softly, "You're being careful with pain meds, I hope?"

Ellis barely suppressed an indignant glare. "Ibuprofen is as strong as it gets."

"I didn't mean to imply anything, but I know how some of the men I've counseled have struggled with addiction."

"I get it, and I can't say I wasn't tempted." Heaving a shaky sigh, Ellis pivoted and sank hard onto the sofa. "I haven't been a good person, Carl. You *should* be disappointed in me. I'm disappointed in myself."

"Let's not go there again." Carl sat down next to him. With one arm around his shoulders, he pulled him firmly against his side. "You're my brother, and I love you. No matter what went on before, no matter how many mistakes we've both made, we can start fresh. Right now."

Ellis couldn't recall the last time he'd felt the warmth of a genuine human hug. Well, he could, actually. It was the day thirty-five years ago when he'd clung to his brother for dear life in the minutes before the Newmans dragged him away. Choking on an upswell of emotion, he gulped back a torrent of sobs. "I love you, too. I love you, too."

Chapter Fifteen

P ropped up in bed with a magazine, Rae had been trying hard not to eavesdrop, though she'd badly wanted to. Even so, solid walls and her closed bedroom door couldn't completely muffle the muted voices and the rough, ragged sounds of male tears being shed. Those, she remembered all too well from long days and nights with Mark as they'd stood watch at Kellie's bedside, then in the months of unabated grief that followed.

When the thrum of quiet laughter penetrated the walls, she pressed her hand to her swelling heart. Before she could quell the thought, the words *Thank You, God!* rose in her mind. Which was ridiculous because she'd given up on prayer years ago as Kellie's heart condition had slowly—yet all too quickly—stolen her away. God could have healed their precious daughter if He'd wanted to, but He didn't. Rae had never forgiven Him.

Tonight, though, grief over her personal loss couldn't dampen her happiness for Carl and Ellis. Nor could she resist taking most of the credit. If she hadn't pushed them, no telling when, or if, either of them would have taken the first step toward each other.

Men could be so stubborn.

Soon, the rattle of the front door told her Carl must have left.

Then Ellis spoke softly from the entry. "I'm pretty sure you're not asleep, Rae," he said with a light laugh. "Just wanted to say thanks, and I'll see you in the morning."

"Wait," she called, throwing on her robe. Barefoot, she caught up with Ellis as he was turning out lights in the living room. "You had a good talk?"

"Yeah, we cleared the air about a number of things."

"What happens next?"

"Not sure." He gave a tired shrug. "We can't exactly pick up where we left off as kids."

"Obviously. Still, I thought maybe he'd want you to move in with him."

"The subject came up, but he told me that isn't an option at the transitional home. But hey, if you need me to clear out—"

"That isn't what I meant." She rolled her eyes. "I didn't think about him living full-time at Hope House. You're welcome to stay in my trailer for as long as you want."

Mouth flattening, Ellis glanced away. "I don't feel right about mooching off of you indefinitely. Sleeping in your trailer. Eating your food." He snorted. "Sitting on your sofa and watching your TV all day while you're out making a living."

"Oh, please. You've done more around my place in the past three days than any of my good-for-nothing siblings ever did when they needed me to put them up for a while. And they usually stuck around *mooching* for weeks or even months."

"I really appreciate everything you've done for me, Rae." He heaved a sigh. "But if I'm gonna stick around these parts, I've gotta find work."

"What about your hand?"

"It's getting better. I'm using it a little more every day."

"Not too much, I hope. You should wait to look for work until after your follow-up at the clinic."

"That isn't until Friday. Not sure I should put it off that long."

Rae put a finger to her chin. "I have a long list of contacts we use for finding jobs for our ministry clients. Let me put out some feelers for you."

"That'd be great." He drew a hand across his reddened eyes. "And now I'm wiped out. Can we talk more about this later?"

"Of course. Go get some sleep." She covered a yawn. "I'll be leaving for the office early tomorrow to prepare for a meeting. If I'm gone before you're up, help yourself to coffee and breakfast."

With a smile of thanks, he told her good night and headed out the back door.

The stress of the day taking its toll, she wasted no time climbing into bed. But instead of falling straight to sleep, she kept replaying the evening's events.

Especially the happy resolution.

It felt wonderfully freeing to focus her attention on helping someone other than her continually embattled brothers and sisters. Someone who seemed to actually want to improve his life. Even during her short time at Equipped and Empowered Ministries, she'd come across clients who clearly were there only for a handout, with no motivation for climbing out of the holes they'd dug for themselves.

Judgmental much? Rolling onto her back with a groan,

she recalled that several hours ago she'd accused Carl of the same attitude.

So what was she doing working for a community outreach organization—a Christian one, at that? She wasn't even particularly a people person, much preferring to work independently instead of attending the requisite weekly board meetings and scuttling all over town to touch base with E and E's ministry partners.

She'd certainly inflated her résumé when she'd applied for the job. Not regarding her education or previous work experience—she had no reason to stretch the truth about those. But she hadn't been entirely factual about her spiritual beliefs. Not that she didn't believe in God. Oh, she believed, all right. She believed He was sitting up there on His heavenly judgment seat, playing favorites, and deciding who was or wasn't deserving of answered prayer.

Rae, apparently, was not.

Carl's last stop on his morning vanpool run was the ministry offices. Two of his Hope House residents had counseling appointments, and he'd been asked to present an update about the canine project at the weekly board meeting.

He hoped he could speak halfway coherently. Convincing his brain to shut down after his time with Ellis last night had been nearly impossible. His 6:00 a.m. alarm had startled him out of barely four hours of sound sleep, after which he'd needed several mugs of full-strength coffee to get himself in gear. Somehow, he'd gotten through breakfast, devotions, and making sure the guys—Glen, in particular—took care of their dogs before leaving for the day. He still owed Glen that one-on-one. Maybe this evening.

He hoped for a few private moments with Rae before the meeting began. As he exited the elevator, conversational chatter drifted from the conference room. When he peeked inside but didn't see Rae, he returned to the waiting area to watch for her.

Minutes later, the elevator chimed its arrival, and she stepped off. Her gaze locking with Carl's, she smiled, probably the sincerest smile he'd seen on her face in the entire three weeks he'd known her. "Hi," she said, sidling over to where he stood by the window. "I understand you and Ellis had a good talk."

"Very good." He tucked in his chin. "You were right to call me out for passing judgment without knowing the whole story."

Her lips quirked, erasing the smile he was just getting used to . . . and liking more than he cared to admit. "I've done my share of judging, too," she murmured. "It's a hard habit to break."

He sensed something deeper beneath her words and nodded in understanding. "Well, thank you for nudging— no, *shoving*—me in the right direction."

"You're welcome."

Kitty Davis stepped out from the conference room. She shifted her glance between Carl and Rae, her brows lifting briefly. "We're about to get started. Better find your seats."

No doubt the woman had already formed her own opinions about whatever was going on between him and Rae. Since he was too sleep-deprived to be a hundred percent clear on the matter, himself, he'd let Kitty think whatever she wanted. For now.

With everyone assembled, Enid Mason called the

meeting to order. After covering some routine business, she invited Carl to give his report.

"The canine project is going well so far." He peeked at the notes he'd jotted earlier in case he lost his train of thought. "We've paired three dogs from a local shelter with three Hope House residents, and we held our first class with the dog trainer last Saturday."

He went on to list the donations he'd obtained from the pet supply store. "Witt Wittenbauer is also developing plans to construct kennels in the Hope House basement. Those would give the dogs free access to the fenced yard so they wouldn't have to be confined to their crates when no one is home."

"Let's not get ahead of ourselves," Ms. Mason cautioned. "We can't approve such alterations to the premises until—and *unless*—the board agrees the program should continue."

Left unspoken was whether there'd even be a Hope House if the canine project washed out.

He cleared his throat and continued, describing how the residents were adapting to the routine of daily dog care and training. He skimmed past Glen's mishaps, which he hoped to address quickly and quietly. Wrapping up his report, he fielded a few questions. Everyone seemed satisfied with his answers—or at least no one raised any immediate concerns.

Mr. Isaacs turned to Rae. "What's your take on the project thus far?"

Softly clearing her throat, she cast Carl a quick glance. "I'm duly impressed with Carl's diligence, as well as the commitment and responsibility I've observed in the dog handlers. I'm hopeful the program will soon prove its merits."

High praise, coming from the woman Carl had once assumed would be his most vocal detractor. He inclined his head and offered a grateful smile.

With his reporting complete, Ms. Mason excused him. He'd like to stick around to wait for Rae—only to thank her for sticking up for him, he tried to convince himself—but there was no telling how much longer the meeting would run. Latching onto an idea, he took the elevator to the ground floor and strode down the corridor to Rae's office. He found the door unlocked and slipped inside. Spying a pad of sticky notes next to a pen holder, he borrowed one of each and jotted a quick message:

Thanks for the vote of confidence at the staff meeting. Free for lunch later? Hoping we could talk some more. Give me a call.

—Carl

While he waited to hear from her, he had a few errands to run. First stop, Walmart. Amazing how much food, laundry detergent, and paper products a bunch of grown men living under one roof could consume. He'd just about worked through his shopping list when his cell phone buzzed.

When he read Rae's name on the lock screen, his heart did a little flip. He took a deliberate breath before answering. "Hi. You found my note?"

"Hard to miss, since you stuck it smack in the center of my computer monitor."

He could no more stop the silly grin spreading across his face than he could have ignored his pesky wake-up alarm that morning. As for ignoring whatever these new feelings were for Rae, it was getting harder every time he saw her. "So. How about lunch?"

"I could break away around twelve thirty."

He checked his watch. "Great. I'm finishing up a grocery run. That'll give me time to unload everything at Hope House. Hungry for anything in particular?"

"I'm always up for Five on Black."

"How about I meet you at the same location as before?"

"I'll be there."

With the details agreed upon, Carl rushed through the rest of his shopping and hurried home to put everything away. After letting the dogs out for a potty break and brief run around the backyard, he hopped into his SUV and headed for Five on Black.

Pulling into the lot, he glimpsed Rae's red Mazda Miata and parked next to it. In the restaurant, he found her standing off to one side as she perused the menu board.

"Hope you haven't been waiting long," he said.

"Nope, you're right on time." When she tucked a strand of silver-blond hair behind her ear, he imagined the silky feel between his fingers. "I know what I want," she said with a nod. "Do you need a minute?"

"Whatever you're having will be fine with me."

They joined the queue, and a few minutes later picked up their heaping bowls of churrasco chicken over black beans and rice. Rae claimed an out-of-the-way table while Carl filled their drink cups with guarana soda.

Returning as Rae stifled a huge yawn, he snickered. "Looks like you got about as much sleep last night as I did. I wasn't sure I'd make it through my report."

She took a sip of her drink. "I'm glad you didn't have to stay and listen to my updates. I barely stumbled through them."

"I doubt anyone noticed." Spreading a napkin on his lap, he met her gaze. "Thanks again for what you said about the project."

"Just being honest." Blushing slightly, she sniffed and folded her hands. "Go ahead and offer a blessing so we can eat. I'm starved."

Suppressing a snort, he bowed his head and began with his usual table prayer, then continued earnestly, "Also, Lord, thank You for the return of my brother, and for everything Rae did to bring us together. Forgive my stubbornness, and guide each of us as we navigate the path ahead. Amen."

"That was . . . nice." Looking slightly flustered, Rae picked up her fork. "I'm not very good with prayer."

"I had to get used to praying aloud. It can feel awkward at first."

"Actually, I meant praying at all." She spoke so softly that he barely heard her over the hum of other conversations.

"If it's a struggle with faith, I can relate." Wrestling with his reaction to his brother's return had been the farthest he'd felt from God in a long time. He gave in to the impulse to reach across for her arm. "Is there something you'd like to talk about?"

She slid her hand into her lap and released a brusque laugh. "I thought you asked me to lunch because of something *you* wanted to talk about."

The bite of food he'd just taken caught in his throat. He swallowed and coughed before replying. "There was. I mean, sort of." How could he feel this awkward with her all of a sudden? Or maybe it wasn't sudden at all. "I guess after sitting down with Ellis last night, I needed to . . . I don't know . . ."

"Decompress? Vent? Sort out your feelings?"

"All of the above." He stabbed a piece of chicken and stared at it. "Like I said in my prayer, I'm going to need wisdom and direction to figure out where my brother and I go from here."

"Well, for now, things can go on the way they are, can't they? I told him he can stay in my trailer as long as necessary. I also said I'd reach out to a few of my contacts to help him find work after his hand heals."

At the mention of Ellis's injury, Carl's lingering questions resurfaced. "Has he ever told you exactly how he got hurt?"

Rae finished chewing and swallowing, then used her napkin to dab her lips. "Only that it happened on his construction job. You know as much as I do."

Though he'd tried to let it go, his brother's evasiveness —more accurately, *defensiveness*—about the injury still bothered him. "I can't help feeling like he's hiding something."

"Like what?"

"That's the thing. I have no idea." Letting his thoughts wander, he downed more of his meal, then took a long drink of soda. "I'm probably reading too much into it."

"You definitely have some trust issues to work out. Both of you."

She wasn't wrong. With a quiet sigh, he scraped up the remnants left in his bowl.

"You should take him to his follow-up appointment at the clinic on Friday," Rae suggested between bites. "Maybe he'll tell you more about it then."

"Good idea. I'd like to see him again before then, too, if I can work it out."

"I'm sure he'd welcome a visit any time." She washed down the last of her meal with several sips of soda, then scooted off the seat and gathered up her trash. "I'd better run. I have a few in-person calls to make this afternoon."

"Rae—" His shoulders sagged as he watched her march to the door and out to her car.

He hadn't intended their lunch date—if he could even call it a date—to be all about him and Ellis. He really wanted to get to know Rae better, but it seemed they were both horribly out of practice with relationships. With what little he knew of Rae's past—the loss of her daughter, then the breakup of her marriage—he could understand why she'd closed off that part of her heart.

As for himself, he'd invested the last twenty-plus years in building a career he could be proud of. There were trying times, yes—more than he cared for lately—but helping other men overcome whatever messes lay in the wake of their troubled lives had truly become a ministry.

Observing Witt's happiness with Maddie, though, along with the close ties Witt had re-established with his son and daughter, had awakened in Carl a deep sense of missing out. Did he really want to spend the rest of his life serving as a father figure for a houseful of grown men? Was it already too late to hope for true love and the chance to create a family of his own?

Leaving the restaurant, Rae didn't dare let herself think too much about her conversation with Carl. Not if she wanted to keep her head on straight this afternoon. Had she actually almost admitted to an E and E colleague that she wasn't *quite* as strong in her faith as she'd implied in her résumé and interviews? If Alton Isaacs ever found out, she could well find herself looking for new employment.

She made it through her scheduled meetings, but as she drove home at the end of the day, her thoughts caught up with her. Discussions with two pastors and the director of a church-based donations center only served to remind her what a phony she'd become in the faith department.

If there was anyone who seemed remotely like the kind of person she could admit her faith struggles to, it was Carl. She was growing to like and trust him more than she ever expected. If she hadn't been so quick during lunch to don her mask of professional detachment, perhaps they could have shared something genuine. Something honest. Something that truly mattered.

Not that her job didn't matter. It did. She knew E and E did good things and helped so many people, and she was grateful to be a part of it. In some weirdly comforting way, it made up for the fact that she seemed utterly powerless to make a difference in her own family.

Maybe that explained why she'd taken a personal interest in Ellis, not only to help him get back on his feet but to mend his relationship with Carl. Clearly, both men wanted things to be better between them, unlike her siblings, who seemed bent on repeating old mistakes while finding new ways to ruin their lives and hers.

Turning in at home, she was so preoccupied with her musings that she almost didn't see her mother's Honda hatchback parked in the driveway. She slammed on the brakes and muttered an ugly word or two. On top of everything else, she did *not* need another confrontation with Mom.

It took some doing, but she managed to ease around her mother's car and park in the garage. Good thing, because it was just beginning to rain, and as threatening as the clouds looked, they could be in for a noisy night of spring storms.

Thunderclouds were no match for the storm waiting for her as she entered the kitchen.

"How dare you block my calls!" her mother raged. "I've been trying to reach you all day."

"How dare *you* let yourself into my home uninvited." Brushing past, Rae dropped her purse and briefcase on a kitchen chair.

"I *dare* because you let a perfect stranger move into your dad's trailer. I'm telling you, I won't have it."

As Rae swung around to respond to her mother's rant, it was all she could do to keep her voice level. "You're right, it was Dad's trailer. And you know perfectly well why he chose to set it up on *my* property, not yours."

Her mother flinched, her lower lip trembling. "How dare you—"

"Mom, you're repeating yourself." Rae's stomach growled. She crossed the kitchen to check the freezer for something to warm up for supper.

Most everyone in the family assumed Sid Ogden's introversion was the reason he'd turned the old travel trailer into his private retreat. That was a huge part of it, yes. But Rae had her suspicions about why he'd needed it to be as far away as possible from his own backyard, and she would forever blame her mother for the stroke that ended her dad's life.

"You're just cruel," Mom whimpered. She collapsed into a chair and rifled through her purse for a wad of tissues.

It was raining in earnest now, with rumbles of thunder vibrating the house. Finding two frozen entrées in the freezer, Rae scanned the heating directions. She hoped Ellis liked Swedish meatballs.

It occurred to her suddenly that she hadn't seen any sign of him since she'd gotten home. He'd spoiled her so thoroughly in the short time he'd lived out back that she'd half expected he'd already have something cooking.

At the back door, she pulled aside the muslin curtain and peered through the rain toward the trailer.

The windows were dark.

"Mom?" She glared at the woman at the table. "Where is Ellis?"

The woman loudly blew her nose. "Who cares?"

"Did you . . . Mother, please don't tell me you sent him away!"

"What if I did?" Defiance darkened her mother's tone. "Good riddance."

Fists clenched, Rae pivoted toward the window. Her breath came in short, angry bursts as she pictured Ellis wet and shivering beneath an overpass. She had to find him somehow, find him and bring him back before everything she'd done to reunite him and Carl turned out to be for nothing.

Carl. She'd get Carl to help look for him. She grabbed her phone from her purse and scrolled the directory until she found his number.

He answered with a note of surprise in his voice. Men's voices and the clatter of tableware sounded in the background. "Hi, Rae. Everything okay?"

"Ellis is gone."

Chapter Sixteen

Ellis knew he was in trouble the minute someone started hammering on the trailer door. The woman claiming to be Rae's mother had given him ten minutes to pack up and leave before she called the cops.

He'd made it almost to the Elk Valley Mini Mall before the sky opened up, and now his clothes were drenched. Wouldn't be long before the rain soaked through his duffel and waterlogged every last thing he owned.

Splashing through potholes and puddles, he crossed the parking lot and ducked beneath the awning outside the grocery mart. An iron bench sat a few feet beyond the entrance. He plopped down to catch his breath and strip off his wet sneakers and socks.

A fiftyish guy in a baseball cap exited the grocery mart. Glancing in Ellis's direction, he paused. "Hey, bud, need some help?"

He gave a dismissive wave, but the man was already striding his way.

Along with a big, scary-looking dog that looked a whole lot like the beast he'd tangled with back in Casper.

Tensing, Ellis slid farther down the bench. "No, I'm okay." He almost had to yell to be heard over the pounding rain. "But thanks."

The man and his dog stopped in front of him. "You sure? You're pretty soaked." His gaze dipped to Ellis's duffel. "If you need a lift somewhere—"

"I said I'm fine." The dog was sniffing him now. He was too terrified to move. "Could you, uh . . . I mean, the dog . . ."

"Oh, sorry. Ranger, sit."

The dog obeyed. It wore a red vest bearing the words *Emotional Support Animal.* Was his owner psycho or something? Even more reason to be nervous.

"He's friendly, just curious." The man sure didn't look or sound like a nutcase. His gaze fell to Ellis's bandaged hand, and he quirked a brow. "You aren't by chance Carl Anderson's brother?"

"You know Carl?"

"I know him well." The man laughed and thrust out his right arm. "Witt Wittenbauer. Great to meet you, Ellis."

What could he do but return the handshake? But awkwardly, using his left hand. "I'm guessing you know a lot more about me than I know about you."

Witt grew solemn. "Carl's told me about your difficulties. I hear you're staying at Rae Caldwell's place for now."

"I was, but . . ." Jaw clenched, he looked back in the direction he'd come. "It wasn't working out."

"Sorry to hear that. Does Carl know?"

"This is a recent development. As in, twenty minutes ago."

"I see." Witt's mouth twisted as he absently rubbed his dog's ear. "In that case, why don't you come home with me while you figure out what happens next?"

Ellis gave the dog a side-eye. "Uh, I don't think so."

"I mean it. You need some dry clothes, a hot meal, and a place to stay. For tonight at least. My wife and I live just a couple miles from here."

"I couldn't."

"No use arguing." Witt motioned toward a small white pickup a few feet away. "Rain's letting up. Better go while we can."

Ellis was too stunned by the offer to do anything but accept. When the dog climbed into the pickup cab and perched on the seat next to him, he froze and stared straight ahead. Witt made a phone call, and soon they pulled up next to a sprawling white farmhouse. Witt's wife met them in the cozy kitchen, where she threw a towel around Ellis's shoulders, then directed him to the table and set a steaming mug of hot cocoa at his place.

Witt excused himself to find some dry clothes Ellis could borrow. Thankfully, the dog went with him.

Returning with the clothes, including socks, an old pair of sneakers, and more towels, Witt placed them on an empty chair. "The room over our barn is vacant right now," he said. "You're welcome to sleep up there tonight. It's got heat and plumbing and a pretty good mattress. I lived there myself for a while before Maddie and I got married."

"That's real nice of you." Ellis did his best to ignore the dog as he savored the warmth of the cocoa sliding down his throat. The chocolatey aroma, combined with smells from whatever Witt's wife had going in her slow-cooker, had revved up his appetite. Before Rae's mother had thrown him out, he'd planned to grill the chicken breasts he'd found in Rae's freezer and have dinner ready when she got home from work.

Maddie carried plates and flatware to the table. "Go on up to the loft and take a hot shower and get into something dry. We'll have supper as soon as you come down."

Ellis hardly knew how to respond to such kindness. If Carl could claim friends like these, he was definitely the one who'd gotten the better deal in life.

He drained his mug and pushed away from the table. But when he opened his mouth to say thank-you, the words jammed in his throat.

"It's okay, it's okay." Eyes filled with understanding, Witt gripped his shoulder. "I've been where you are . . . and worse. But the Lord, in His great mercy, brought me through. He'll do the same for you."

Ellis scoffed. "Not sure God even remembers who I am."

"Oh, believe me, He does." Wearing an expression of deep and utter *knowing*, Witt spoke words that sounded like something from the Bible: "'You have searched me, Lord, and you know me. You know when I sit and when I rise; you perceive my thoughts from afar. You discern my going out and my lying down; you are familiar with all my ways.'"

"If that's all true," Ellis murmured, an ache in his chest, "then God must surely despise me."

"On the contrary." Gentle laughter filled Witt's voice. "The Lord loves you more than you can possibly comprehend. He longs to bring you into His family and to show you exactly how much He cherishes you."

Cherish? Ellis had only ever heard the word used in old-timey wedding vows. Could God *really* love him like that?

Love him beyond measure, despite every bad choice he'd made, every horrible thing he'd ever done?

Keeping his gaze averted, he gathered up the items Witt had loaned him and edged toward the back door. "Think I'll take you up on that hot shower and dry clothes now."

Chapter Seventeen

C arl was speeding toward Rae's house when his cell phone rang. He grabbed it from the console without checking the display. "Rae? Any news?"

Witt's chuckle sounded from the speaker. "Sorry, it's just me. But if you're asking about your brother, he's safe at my house."

"Thank the Lord!" Carl slowed to take the Elk Valley exit off I-90. "How'd he end up there?"

Witt described coming upon Ellis at the grocery mart and convincing him to spend the night in their barn loft. "He's getting into some dry clothes and should be down shortly for supper."

"You're a lifesaver, Witt. I'm on my way right now."

"No rush. We'll save you a place at the table."

Now that he knew Ellis was in good hands, his pulse was slowly ramping down, and he could grab a full breath. With reliable Jordy in charge of things at Hope House, the men would be fine until he got back. "Does Rae know Ellis is with you?"

"No," Witt said flatly. "He hasn't said what happened with Rae, but I gather they parted on bad terms."

"There's a lot more to it. I'll fill you in when I get there."

He disconnected and called Rae's number. She answered almost before the phone had a chance to ring. "He's okay," he assured her. "He's at Witt's place."

"Witt's? How?"

He relayed what Witt had just told him. "I'm heading straight there."

"Would you mind picking me up on the way? I'd drive myself, but I don't know where they live."

Five minutes later, he pulled into her driveway. She was waiting on the front porch and ran across the wet grass to jump into his SUV. Latching her seat belt, she whooshed out a sharp breath. "I will *never* forgive my mother for this."

Based on what little Carl knew about Rae's family, he wasn't sure he could forgive the woman either. Which he knew the Lord would be extremely disappointed about, so he'd have to work at it. Eventually.

"*Forgive us our sins as we forgive those who sin against us,*" he murmured, more to himself than aloud.

Rae huffed and crossed her arms. "That is exactly my problem with God. He expects us to forgive other human beings for how they've hurt us. But then He turns around and—and—" A strangled sound cut off her words.

Carl could guess what she was thinking. How could a loving God have allowed her daughter to suffer and die? How could He have looked away when her marriage was falling apart? He wished he could say something to comfort and reassure her, but in her present state of mind, he doubted it would make a difference.

He reached across the console and gave her arm a gentle

squeeze. For the briefest moment, she leaned into his touch, gratitude filling her eyes.

Ahead, his headlights flashed across the sign for Eventide Dog Sanctuary. As he turned up the lane, Rae straightened and swiped at her cheeks. "This is where they live?"

"Maddie's grandparents established the sanctuary several years ago for aging and unadoptable dogs. Maddie took over after her grandparents were both gone, and with Witt's help, she's expanded and turned it into a thriving volunteer operation. Last I heard, they're currently housing close to forty dogs."

"They sound very dedicated."

"You won't find nicer people anywhere." He parked behind Witt's pickup and shut off the engine. "I'm glad you came along so you can meet Maddie. I think you'll really like her."

Rae answered with a shrug and pushed open her door. Her show of indifference—and *show* was exactly how he interpreted it—reinforced his impression that she didn't make close friends easily, and certainly not the kind she could phone at two o'clock in the morning and feel safe pouring her heart out to.

As they climbed from the car, Carl glimpsed his brother coming down the steps from the barn loft. Ellis's uncertain glance darted between him and Rae.

Carl answered the question in his brother's eyes by marching over and pulling him into a hug. "You okay? You really had us worried."

"Yeah, I'm fine."

"You should have called me."

"No time." Ellis looked past Carl's shoulder toward Rae. "I kinda had to leave in a hurry."

"So I heard."

Rae edged closer. "I feel terrible about this, Ellis." Her voice was still ragged with emotion. "My mother had no right to make you leave, and I told her as much. Please, I want you to come back."

He gave his head a weary shake. "I don't know . . ."

"We can figure all this out later." Carl turned his brother toward the house. "Witt said you were about to sit down to supper."

Witt met them at the back door and ushered them through the mudroom. "Just in time. Maddie's about to dish up her famous Irish stew."

"Famous?" Maddie's laughter met them as they entered the kitchen. "That's a bit of an exaggeration."

Carl inhaled the mouthwatering aroma. "If it tastes as good as it smells . . ."

"Count on it." Witt patted his belly. "I've put on a good ten pounds since Maddie and I got married. So don't let her tell you she isn't much of a cook. Wait till you taste her huckleberry pie!"

Rae hesitated near the door. "I shouldn't have intruded."

"Nonsense." Maddie beamed a warm smile. "I always make extra. Besides, when we saw Carl had brought you along, I had Witt shift everything to the dining room. There's room for everybody."

It made Carl absurdly happy to see Rae's incredulous look. He gave her elbow a quick squeeze and leaned close to whisper, "What did I tell you?"

Soon, they'd gathered in the dining room. Witt sat at the head of the long oak table and offered the seats at his right to Carl and Rae. Maddie and Ellis took the chairs directly opposite.

Sidestepping Ranger, Carl gave the dog a quick pat. He'd noticed Ellis keeping his distance from Ranger, not unlike Rae had acted around dogs when he'd first met her. The Newmans probably hadn't been dog people, and from the way Ellis had described them, Carl shouldn't be surprised.

Witt asked everyone to join hands for a prayer, but when Maddie reached for Ellis's hand, she inhaled a quick breath. "Oh, you've gotten your bandage wet. That's not good."

"The rain caught me by surprise."

"We have plenty of supplies in the first aid kit. I'll fix you up right after we eat." Taking him gingerly by the wrist, Maddie nodded for Witt to continue with the blessing.

The stew was every bit as delicious as Witt had promised. Carl made a mental note to get the recipe from Maddie and share it with Jordy. The Hope House guys would appreciate a new addition to the weekly menu.

Maddie apologized that all she had for dessert was the ice cream and store-bought cookies Witt had picked up on his way home from a handyman job.

"That was definitely a God thing," he said. "Otherwise, Ellis and I likely wouldn't have crossed paths."

Maddie scoffed. "Oh, right. I'm sure it was the Holy Spirit and not your ice cream cravings that prompted you to stop at the grocery mart."

"Now, honey, you know the Lord works in mysterious ways His wonders to perform."

Their banter elicited a few laughs, though both Rae's and Ellis's seemed more like forced politeness. With Rae, Carl could understand it, since she'd confided her faith difficulties.

Ellis, on the other hand, had been edgy ever since

Maddie had first mentioned the need to change his bandage. What *was* it that made him so tight-lipped about his injury?

Rae had to agree with Carl—the Wittenbauers were lovely people. From the moment she'd walked into their homey kitchen, they'd welcomed her like a friend. The discomfiture twisting her insides was her own problem, because she'd put off admitting how desperately she needed friends like these. People who didn't judge her every action, every decision, every word that came out of her mouth. People who were comfortable with who they were and the lives they led. People who clearly had a solid relationship with God and were unapologetic about it.

Determined to try harder at this friendship thing, she slid Carl's empty plate atop hers. "Maddie, the dinner was delicious. Let me do the cleanup while you see to Ellis's bandage."

"No, you're our guest," Maddie protested. "The dishes will wait."

"Please, I insist." Rae stood and gathered more plates and flatware.

Witt scooted his chair back. "We can all pitch in. Ellis, go have a seat at the kitchen table. There's more light in there for Maddie to take care of your hand."

Rising, Carl dropped his crumpled napkin at his place. "Maddie, I can help you with the bandage."

"Good idea, Carl." She started through the living room. "Be right back with the first aid kit."

Soon, Rae and Witt had the table cleared, and while he put away leftovers, she stood at the sink rinsing plates. She glanced over to see Maddie selecting various items from a red plastic container about the size of a fishing tackle box. Ellis cradled his injured hand in the crook of the opposite arm while casting wary looks between Maddie and Carl.

"We'll take it slow," Maddie promised, carefully lifting his hand. "Carl, can you start loosening the tape?"

Ellis tried to pull his arm back. "Maybe you should leave it till I see the clinic doctor again."

"That isn't until Friday," Carl said with a hint of impatience. "We need to do this now."

"But—"

Maddie kept a firm but gentle grip on Ellis's wrist. "Carl's right. It can't heal if it's wet, and you certainly don't want to risk infection."

The poor guy probably felt as if they were ganging up on him. Rae grabbed a dishtowel and dried her hands. "Carl, why don't you let me take over. Your bedside manner leaves a lot to be desired."

He scowled at her. "There's nothing wrong with my bedside manner. I'm just trying—"

"Yes, I know." Brows lifted, she gave him a pointed look. It was blatantly obvious to her that his intention was to get an up-close look at his brother's injury. Why did the details matter so much?

"Oh. Oh, my." While they'd bandied words, Maddie had proceeded with unwrapping the bandage. "Ellis, is this from a dog bite?"

Both Rae and Carl jerked their heads around to look. The puncture wounds on the backside and palm of Ellis's right hand couldn't be mistaken for anything but what they were.

"Why didn't you say so in the first place?" Carl demanded. "Did you think—"

Rae placed a restraining grip on his arm. "Not now, Carl." She turned to Ellis. "You don't have to explain."

Ellis cast his brother a sidelong frown. "He won't be satisfied until I do."

"It isn't that." Looking contrite, Carl pulled a chair around and sat facing his brother. "I just want to be here for you, Els. In all the ways I couldn't after they took you away. But if you can't trust me enough to be honest . . ."

"I know." Ellis lowered his head. "I'm sorry."

Carl's use of what must have been Ellis's childhood nickname had drained the tension from both their expressions. Maybe there was real hope for these two after all. Certainly more hope than Rae had for smoother relations within her own family. She was *so* done with them.

Every last one of them.

Hoping the others wouldn't read the indignation in her face and get the wrong idea, she schooled her expression and returned to the sink. Witt had taken over washing dishes, so she asked for a clean towel and began drying.

At the table, Ellis gave a brief description of getting too close to a truck at a construction site and the dog that had lunged at him from the back of the truck.

Maddie clucked her tongue. "That's awful. I hope the owner took responsibility."

"Mmm," was all Ellis said.

Witt handed Rae another plate. "I hold strongly to the opinion that there are no bad dogs, just bad owners. Some people have no business adopting a dog."

Rae slid a stack of plates into the cupboard Witt indicated. "Some people have no business being parents."

He cocked his head. "That sounds mighty personal."

"I suppose it is." She regretted speaking aloud, but Witt had a way of making her feel like he really cared. Under her breath, she added, "I'm just sick about how my mother treated Ellis. Did he tell you what she did?"

When Witt shook his head, Rae quietly filled him in.

Lips pursed, Witt murmured, "Hurt people hurt people, as the saying goes." He rinsed a handful of flatware and dropped the items into the dish drainer. Angling toward Rae, he propped his hip against the sink. "You've had some major hurts in your life, too. Don't let them turn you into someone you don't want to be."

Her eyes welled. The idea of growing as bitter and controlling as her mother made her physically ill. "What if it's already too late?"

"It's never too late, and no one's ever so far gone that God can't turn things around. If you need proof"—he grinned and patted his chest—"you don't have to look any further than me."

"All done," came Maddie's voice from across the room, followed by the click of the first aid kit latches.

Rae laid aside the dishtowel. Nudging her lips into a smile, she turned toward the others. "Thank you so much, Maddie and Witt. For everything. Especially for giving Ellis a place to stay tonight."

"Yes, thank you," Carl echoed. "Ellis, I wish I could let you stay with me."

"Don't worry, I'll be fine here." He lifted his good hand toward Rae. "I don't want you feeling guilty about any of this, okay?"

She nodded. "You have my number. Call if you need anything."

Carl checked the time and said he should get back to Hope House. As they shared a few more thank-yous and goodbyes, Maddie exchanged phone numbers with Rae.

"You don't need an excuse to call," Maddie said,

drawing her close for a quick hug. "And feel free to drop by any old time. I'd love to get better acquainted."

Rae's throat closed. "I'd like that, too."

As Rae and Carl drove away from the Wittenbauers', she recalled Maddie's gracious invitation: *"You don't need an excuse to call. . . . Feel free to drop by any time."*

Could she really imagine doing so? The possibility made her heart beat a little faster.

They hadn't gone far when Carl let out a long sigh. "I should have thought of Witt and Maddie's barn loft sooner. It'll be a great place for Ellis to get his bearings and think about what comes next." He chuckled. "I'm guessing by tomorrow they'll have him earning his keep helping with all those dogs."

Drawn from her musings, Rae cast him an incredulous look. "I can't imagine he'd want to be anywhere near a bunch of dogs quite yet. Being bitten by a vicious guard dog must have been horribly traumatic." She shuddered. "It's no wonder he didn't want to talk about it."

"You're right." Carl gave the steering wheel a slap. "I'm really batting a thousand in the sensitivity department."

She let the remark pass. "It's good he'll be staying at the Wittenbauers', though. Witt will be a positive influence."

They'd arrived at her house. Carl parked in the driveway but left the motor running. He shifted slightly toward Rae. "I need to thank you again."

Her eyes widened. "What for this time?"

"For keeping me accountable. You and Witt both—you have the guts to hold my feet to the fire whenever I go off the rails."

"That's a mixed metaphor if I ever heard one." She snickered. "And it's quite the honor to be mentioned in the same breath as the venerable Mr. Wittenbauer."

Carl's expression warmed, his eyes twinkling with the reflection from the porch light.

She tried to ignore the flutter in her stomach. "Thank *you* for taking me along this evening. I'm glad I got to meet Witt's wife, and it's a gigantic relief to know Ellis is okay." She grasped the door handle. "Well, I should say good night."

"Rae, wait." When Carl reached across the console, the heat of his touch raced up her arm. "Maybe this isn't the time or place, but . . ."

She paused and glanced back at him, afraid of what he was trying to say and yet curious. Her voice a shaky whisper, she asked, "But what?"

His Adam's apple worked. "I feel like everything that's happened lately has brought us closer, and I—I don't know how to say this, or even if I should, but I . . . I think I'm beginning to— "

She held up one hand to silence him. Her pulse was hammering in a way it hadn't since she'd been a starry-eyed twenty-year-old on her first date with Mark Caldwell.

And remember how that turned out.

Staring through the windshield, she said softly, "If you're trying to say what I think you are, then we both know what a terrible idea that would be."

"Why, Rae? Why would it be so terrible?"

"For one thing, we have to work together." That was the practical rationale. "For another, we . . . we're just too different."

He didn't reply right away, then breathed out a humorless chuckle. "I'm sorry I said anything. Can we blame it on the general emotional intensity of late?"

"Yes. Let's." The words were spoken with as much lightheartedness as she could muster. "Don't give it another thought." She pushed open the door and stepped onto the driveway. Bending to cast him a smile, she said another good-night before marching to her front porch.

She didn't look back as he drove away, all the while berating herself for the quick brush-off. Because she *was* beginning to feel something for him. Something too dangerous to risk, for both their sakes.

As she inserted her house key into the lock, her phone buzzed. She fished it from her purse and answered as she let herself inside.

"Hi, Rae. How are you?"

"Mark?" Her ex-husband was the last person she'd expected to hear from. "Is something wrong?"

"No, everything's fine. Holly and the kids and I are in Missoula for a couple of days to celebrate my mom's birthday. We're flying home early tomorrow, but I wanted to call and see how you're doing."

After he'd moved to Texas, he'd married a widow with a young son. Not quite two years later, he and his new wife had welcomed a baby daughter. She should be happy that Mark had been given a second chance to have the family he'd always wanted—the family Kellie's death had deprived them of—but she couldn't quell an unwelcome surge of envy.

"I'm just great," she said a bit too forcefully. "Couldn't be better." Glad he couldn't see her eye roll, she dropped her purse and keys onto the hall table. "Still loving Texas life?"

He released a relaxed sigh. "My life's good now, Rae. The best it's been since . . . well, in too long a time."

"I'm glad for you, Mark. Truly." She made her way to her bedroom and dropped onto the end of the bed. "And Shadow—you still have him?"

"Oh, yeah. He and Davey have a blast romping through the fields. Lindy's walking now, which means it won't be long before she's right on their heels."

The image evoked a shaky laugh. "I can just see Shadow playing with those kids. He must be so happy."

"He is. He really is." Mark softly cleared his throat. "Rae, are *you* happy? Things may be over between us, but I'll always care. I worry about you."

"Please don't—" Her voice broke. She covered her mouth to hold back a sob. "I, um, I have to go. But thanks for calling. Tell your mom happy birthday for me. 'Bye!"

She hit the disconnect button without giving Mark a chance to respond, then flung the phone across the bed and collapsed onto her pillow. The tears flowed freely now, and she gave in to them. Gave in to the grief and anguish and remorse that for years she'd desperately tried to hold inside.

"God, help me. . . . Help me." She could think of no other words to pray. She only knew she could no longer do this life in her own strength.

It was too hard. Too awfully, incredibly, unbearably hard.

Chapter Eighteen

I t was a good thing Carl hadn't needed to meet with anyone at the ministry offices any time soon. After the way they'd left things the other night, running into Rae would have been uncomfortable, to say the least.

Hard to believe how his feelings had changed in the short time since he'd met her. Their early encounters had been downright frosty, to the point that he'd convinced himself working with her would be a nightmare. As for friendship? Forget it.

But as their acquaintance deepened, his heart had proven him wrong on all counts. Now he couldn't get her out of his mind.

He'd better pull it together before tomorrow's dog-training session, because Alton Isaacs had instructed Rae to observe the classes for evaluation purposes.

Today, though, he was picking up Ellis for his follow-up appointment at the free clinic. He arrived at Eventide Dog Sanctuary shortly before nine and found several other vehicles parked near the kennels.

Maddie waved from the attached fenced yard, where she and three volunteers were overseeing the dogs' playtime. "Ellis is in the kennel building with Witt," she called. "He's helping him install a new storage cabinet."

So they'd enlisted his brother to work near the dogs after all. Carl ambled over and spoke to Maddie across the fence. "During our phone conversations, Ellis has sounded pretty content living here. Does it seem to you like he's doing okay?"

"I'd say so. Witt keeps him busy—mindful of the hand, of course—and he's always after us to let him do more, as long as it doesn't involve direct interaction with the dogs." Reaching down to scratch a shaggy-haired mutt behind the ears, she gave a light laugh. "But we're working on that."

The kennel door opened, and Witt came out carrying an aluminum ladder. Ellis followed with a toolbox.

"All done," Witt said, looking their way. "This guy's a keeper. Would have taken me twice as long without him."

Ellis ducked his head, but he couldn't hide a smile. "Be right there, Carl. Just gonna help Witt put stuff away."

"I'm early. We've got time." He turned to Maddie. "Ellis really looks good. Happy, even. I can't tell you what a relief that is."

"He's gradually opening up to us about his life and everything he's been through. It's wonderful you two found each other again."

Carl's mouth twisted. "Wish I could do more. But I'm stretched pretty thin trying to keep things running smoothly at Hope House." There'd been another incident only yesterday, when he'd discovered a newer resident had broken the rule regarding no smoking in the house. "I'm sure Witt told you the board is weighing the possibility of ending the transitional housing program altogether."

"That would be a terrible shame." Maddie gave her head a sad shake, then smiled. "But it'll work out, I'm certain. God always has a plan."

She excused herself to return to the dogs, and Carl went to lean against the door of his SUV while he waited for Ellis. Shortly, his brother emerged from the barn and jogged over. They climbed into the vehicle, and Carl headed toward Missoula.

Breaking a stretch of awkward silence, he asked, "Everything still going okay?"

"Yeah, Witt and Maddie are great. Witt's going to put in a good word for me with the handyman service he works for."

"Sounds promising." Carl cast his brother a quick glance. "Is that the kind of work you'd like to keep doing?"

"For now." The words came out on a tired sigh. "Since I never got my high school diploma, I don't have that many choices."

"Have you thought about getting a GED? That would open a few more doors. You could even work toward a college degree if you wanted to."

"College—me?" Ellis scoffed. "That'd be the day."

"Don't write off the possibility." Carl shot his brother a look fraught with meaning. "You know that whatever you decide, you won't be going it alone."

As he returned his attention to the road, the jumble of emotions he read in Ellis's expression gnawed at his insides. Regret? Guilt? Hope? All of the above? He was only just beginning to comprehend how broken his brother must be, how having the Newmans for parents had crushed his spirit.

At the clinic, Ellis allowed Carl to join him in the exam room, and there he got a closer look at the injured hand.

The dog must have been a big one, but considering how deep the bites were, the doctor said it was healing on schedule. He recommended Ellis begin a few weeks of physical therapy.

Scooting off the exam table, Ellis snorted. "C'mon, Doc, ya think I'd be getting treatment at your free clinic if I had insurance to cover PT?"

"I'm just telling it like it is," the doctor said. "Otherwise, you'll likely never regain full use of your hand, and that will most certainly be an issue for the type of work you were doing previously." He offered Ellis some brochures. "Try one of these providers. They may be willing to work out a discounted rate or payment plan."

When Ellis turned up his nose at the brochures, Carl accepted them. "Thank you. We'll take a look."

At the car, Ellis slumped into his seat. "No way I can afford PT. My hand's a little stiff, but I'm managing okay."

"If you're serious about wanting to work for Witt's handyman service, you'll need to be a hundred percent." Carl started the engine. "Anyway, I can help with the cost. Don't worry about it."

"I don't want you supporting me. I need to pay my own way."

"Okay, then, you can pay me back after you're working again." Carl took a closer look at the brochures. "This one's off Reserve, not far from Hope House. Let's go check it out."

The PT center staff proved accommodating and set Ellis up for four weeks of twice-a-week therapy on a discounted payment plan. A therapist on duty had just had a cancellation and could start Ellis that afternoon, which gave them an hour to grab something for lunch.

Over burgers and fries, Ellis asked how Rae was doing. "Did she ever settle things with her mom?"

Carl couldn't forget how angry and upset Rae had been over her mother's callousness toward Ellis. "I doubt it."

"What—you haven't talked to her?"

"Not since Tuesday night when I took her home."

Ellis skewered him with an incredulous stare. "I thought you guys worked together."

"Not *together*, exactly. Rae oversees several of the Equipped and Empowered programs."

"Well, then, what about the vibes you've both been putting out?"

Keeping his head down, Carl dragged a fry through a puddle of ketchup. "Vibes?"

"It's pretty clear there's something going on between you."

"Uh, no." Carl snorted. "As you pointed out, we just work together. Sort of." He stuffed his mouth with a huge bite of hamburger.

Ellis shrugged and took another gulp from his drink cup. "Right, what would I know? It's not like any woman with half a brain cell would ever go for a loser like me."

"Don't say things like that, Els."

"Hey, it's the truth, and I'm not hiding from it." He pointed at Carl with a soggy fry. "You, on the other hand, are obviously avoiding what's right before your eyes."

"And what would that be, exactly? Because if you're suggesting Rae has feelings for me, you couldn't be more wrong."

Rae dreaded having to make an appearance at Saturday's dog-training class. The past few days had been difficult, no thanks to the reminder that her ex-husband had found a way to move forward into a happier life. She should have asked him to share whatever secret he'd found, because after Kellie died, he'd been even worse an emotional wreck than she.

As if that were possible.

The class was just getting started when she slipped inside the playroom at the Elk Valley Animal Shelter. She sidled over to a bench along the wall and took out her phone and planner. She'd make some notes and snap a few photos, which would then go into her weekly report on the status of the canine project.

Carl noticed her and smiled—if she could call a quick twist of the lips an actual *smile*. He strode over to say he wouldn't have much time to talk. "I'm on my own this morning. Witt got an emergency repair call from the handyman service."

"Then please don't let me keep you."

All business, he marched away. After she'd cut him off the other night, she had no right to feel hurt, but she did.

Trainer Luke Daniels and his dog, Fletch, began the class by demonstrating *down-stay*. The tricolor border collie's watchful demeanor reminded Rae so much of Shadow that it brought an ache to her heart. How well she remembered the patient attentiveness of Kellie's little black service dog, furry ears on alert, gaze trained on his young mistress. Shadow had responded almost instantly to Kellie's every need, sometimes even before she'd asked.

With a mental shake, Rae put aside the memories and returned her attention to the class. Cocoa's and Zippy's handlers were doing a good job of emulating Luke's commands, although more often than they liked, the dogs ignored them to run around and play.

Quite the opposite, blue-eyed Frankie appeared eager to follow instructions, even with the trainer repeatedly reminding Glen how to correctly give the commands and then to praise Frankie for his prompt obedience.

"Glen!" Carl's sharp reprimand startled Rae. "Get control of your dog."

She looked up from her notes to see Frankie running straight toward her. The dog slid to a halt and plopped down on his haunches, his ice-blue gaze colliding with hers.

"Well, hello, there." She laid her planner and phone aside. "If I'm not mistaken, you're supposed to be in class."

Whimpering, Frankie pawed the knee of her jeans.

Carl jogged over and snatched up Frankie's leash. "Sorry, Glen is really falling down on the job today."

"So I noticed."

He tipped his head toward her open planner. "Can you maybe not put that in your report?"

"I know you were hoping the dogs would give the men a sense of responsibility, but if it isn't working . . ."

"It *is* working. The other guys are getting the hang of it. Glen just needs more time." He sounded desperate, scared even.

She hesitated. "I can't *not* mention any problems or concerns. You know that." Glancing past him to where Glen was sulking by the far wall, she pursed her lips. "Okay, I'll do my best to downplay Glen's issues. But if he doesn't show some progress by the next class, I won't have any choice."

"Thank you." With a brusque nod, Carl led Frankie away.

Rae watched for a few moments as Carl gave Glen a

firm talking-to. He handed him Frankie's leash and sent him to rejoin the group but stayed nearby to reinforce the trainer's instructions.

The class ended with an impromptu Frisbee-catching performance by Luke and his talented border collie. That grabbed Glen's interest, and all three men wanted to know if their dogs could learn similar tricks. Luke promised he'd add some Frisbee lessons, but only after the dogs had mastered a few more obedience skills. Maybe that would give Glen enough motivation to get his head in the game.

Gathering up her things, Rae considered making a silent departure, but she was concerned about Ellis and how his clinic appointment had gone. Hopefully, his hand had improved enough that he could look seriously at finding a paying job.

Rae waited near the exit while Carl sent the men and their dogs out to the van and then exchanged a few words with the trainer. Approaching Rae, he slowed. "Was there something else?"

"I wanted to ask how your brother is doing."

"He's doing okay. He started PT yesterday afternoon." Carl held the door for her. "His therapist thinks he could have full use of his hand again in a month or so."

"That's good news. Please give him my best." With a polite nod, she stepped past him and started down the corridor. "Enjoy the rest of your weekend."

"Rae, wait." His tone carried a note of defeat.

Steeling herself, she pivoted to meet his gaze. "Yes?"

"About the other night . . . I apologize for making things awkward."

Tamping down a tumble of emotions, she cast him a stiff smile. "We're both adults. Professionals. I think we can cope with a little awkwardness."

"Of course. You're right." He didn't look any more convinced than she felt. "The guys'll be waiting at the van. I have to go."

"Yes. Well, goodbye." She'd spoken so softly that she doubted he'd even heard. He marched past her without looking back. By the time she reached her car, the van was pulling away.

On her way home, she made a quick stop at the grocery mart to pick up a few things. As she turned up her driveway, she glimpsed her brother's car parked in back beside the travel trailer. If not for the pint of mocha almond fudge ice cream she'd splurged on, she'd have marched straight out to confront him. The time it took to leave her groceries on the counter and put the ice cream in the freezer helped to cool her temper, but only slightly.

She marched out to the trailer and hammered on the door. "Reece? I know you're in there. Open up."

Rustling sounds came from inside. Something metal clattered as it hit the floor. "Okay, okay, I'm coming."

Rae jumped back as her brother stumbled out. Clad in a T-shirt and plaid flannel pajama bottoms, he looked as if she'd awakened him from a sound sleep.

She didn't care. "What are you doing here?"

"Mom said the trailer was empty and that I could move in." His eyes were bloodshot. He pulled a hand down his whiskery cheek.

"The trailer's on *my* property. I get to say who uses it and who doesn't." This was the last straw. The *very* last straw. "For pity's sake, Reece. Go home and work things out with your wife. On second thought, don't. You don't deserve Heather, and she deserves a lot better than the likes of you."

His face became a sneer. "Mom was right. You've turned into an overbearing, self-righteous shrew."

She staggered back, tears stinging her eyes. Her next words were no more than a whisper but spoken with the force of a frigid north wind blowing down from the Rockies. "Leave. Now. And if you *ever* trespass on my property again, I'm calling the sheriff."

Chapter Nineteen

Living at the Wittenbauers', Ellis felt more settled every day. They weren't that much older, maybe by fifteen years, give or take, but the way they'd taken him under their wing . . . if only his adoptive parents had been more like them. They even treated their dogs with more kindness and patience than he'd ever gotten from the Newmans.

Oh, those dogs. The little ones, gray-muzzled and missing a few teeth, weren't so scary. But the big ones—those, he did his best to avoid.

Especially Ranger, who too closely resembled the beast who'd buried his fangs in Ellis's hand.

Witt made sure Ranger gave him space whenever he came to the kitchen for morning and evening meals. But Witt was usually working somewhere over the noon hour, and when Maddie had one or two of the bigger kennel dogs in the house, it was a lot less stressful if Ellis took his lunch upstairs to the loft.

He missed Rae, though. And he had no right to—not in the romantic sense, anyway. For one thing, there was

Carl. His brother could deny it all he wanted, but there was *something* going on between those two.

For another, Rae was light years out of Ellis's league. A blue-collar grunt and a smart, stylish career woman? Fat chance.

About as much chance as Ellis ever getting that college degree Carl hinted at yesterday on their way to the free clinic.

The only thing less likely was getting Ellis inside a church again. Over supper on Saturday, he had to turn down Witt's invitation to go with him and Maddie the next morning. Then, as Maddie dished up banana pudding for dessert, Carl called with almost the same request.

Carrying the phone out to the mudroom, he pinched the bridge of his nose. "Look, Carl, no offense, but . . . I don't do church. I *can't* do church."

Silence. Then, "Because of the Newmans?"

"I decided a long time ago that if the real God is anything like the one Harold Newman claimed, I want no part of Him."

"I get it, Els. But God *isn't* like that, I can promise you. If you'd only—"

"Don't push it, okay?"

"Okay, okay. For now." Carl's tone lightened. "In the meantime, could I talk you into coming over to Hope House later tomorrow? On Sunday afternoons, we usually hang out, toss a football or play board games, throw some burgers on the grill. It'd be a chance for you to meet the guys and also get to know a little more about what I do here."

Over his shoulder, he glimpsed Witt and Maddie starting to clean up the kitchen. They'd scheduled an orientation on Sunday to introduce new volunteers and possible donors to the dog sanctuary. He'd just as soon not be around when that started up.

He exhaled slowly through his nostrils. "That sounds okay, I guess."

"Great. What if I pick you up around three?"

On Sunday afternoon, he was waiting at the end of the Wittenbauers' lane when Carl drove up. He climbed into the passenger seat and buckled in.

Carl cast him a curious grin. "In a hurry or something?"

"Kinda." Ellis glanced in the direction of the kennels. "They're having some kind of meet-and-greet, and all the dogs are out running around in the yard. It was freaking me out a little."

"Uh-oh." Carl turned the SUV around to head back through town. "I did tell you we have three dogs at Hope House, didn't I?"

He sort of remembered that. "Yeah, your dog program or whatever. They're not gonna be loose, though, are they?"

"I'll have the guys keep them on leashes or in their crates." With a laugh, Carl added, "But don't worry. The dogs are all very friendly."

Ellis replied with a snort.

Soon, Carl exited the freeway and drove through a quiet neighborhood in northwest Missoula. They reached a gabled two-story house with a couple of older-model vehicles parked out front. Carl pulled into the driveway, stopping alongside a passenger van that looked like it had seen better days.

"Here we are." Carl switched off the engine and pushed open his door.

Beyond him, Ellis glimpsed three guys in the yard tossing a Frisbee back and forth. A noisy pack of dogs ran in circles around them.

Ellis's hand began to throb. He made no move to exit the car. "Can we just—"

"Hang on. I'll get the dogs secured."

This was a bad idea. A totally awful idea. Worse than running the canine gauntlet would be the weird looks he'd get for being such a wimp. Witt and Maddie had never once shamed him for his fear of dogs. But these guys, supposedly overcoming even worse hardships than he'd faced? How likely were they to sympathize?

"Hey." A lanky guy with a gray ponytail grinned at him through the window. "I'm Jordy. Welcome to Hope House."

Ellis eased open his door. "Thanks. I was, uh . . ."

"I'll take you in through the front door. How's that sound?"

Like he'd already been labeled a coward. That's how it sounded.

Sucking air through his teeth, he decided he wouldn't become their laughingstock. "Forget it," he said, climbing out. He gave the door a good, hard slam and faced this Jordy fellow with a swaggering grin. "I'm a backdoor kind of guy."

Jordy eyed him up and down, then gave a solemn nod. "The back door it is."

He'd stalled just long enough for Carl to get the dogs leashed. As he followed Jordy through the gate, the dogs barked and lunged, but he tried his best not to react. He kept a respectable distance while Carl introduced him to guys whose names he'd never remember in a million years.

Afterward, Carl invited him up to the deck and offered him something to drink.

With an uneasy glance toward the yard, he tucked his injured hand against his ribs. "A beer would hit the spot about now."

Carl frowned. "We don't allow alcohol on the premises."

Man, he was getting judged all over the place. This could turn into a miserably long afternoon. Huffing, he plopped into a deck chair. "Whatever you've got, then."

Carl said he'd be back in a few minutes and went inside.

At the rattle of wheels behind him, he shifted to look. Jordy was rolling a grill across the far end of the deck.

"Need a hand with that?" Ellis waved his left arm. "One is about all I can offer."

"You could get me a bag of charcoal." Jordy nodded toward the garage. "It's in the storage room in back. Ask any of the guys. They can show you."

Great. That meant he'd have to actually approach one of them. It'd have to be whoever had the least scary-looking dog at the end of the leash.

The black-and-white dynamo? Nope, totally out of control.

The floppy-eared brown mutt? Docile as it appeared, that one definitely had the biggest teeth.

Which left the walking fur coat with those creepy blue eyes. This one looked like it should be up in Alaska pulling a sled.

Ellis braved a few steps into the yard. He'd judge his next move by whatever the dogs did. The first two watched him only until a squirrel chattering from a tree branch drew their attention. Then both started yapping like crazy and tugging at their leashes.

Blue Eyes looked up at the squirrel, then seemed to decide the critter wasn't worth the effort. The dog lay down in the grass and rested its chin on its front paws.

Best behaved dog of the bunch, for sure. Ellis swallowed and came closer. "Hey, uh—sorry, I forgot your name."

The guy turned with a grin. "It's Glen."

"Glen. Right. Say, Jordy asked me to get the charcoal for the grill. Said you could tell me where to find it."

"No prob." He dropped the dog's leash and motioned toward the back of the garage. "Right this way."

With a wary glance to make sure the dog stayed put, Ellis followed. Glen led him through a side gate and into a dark, musty toolshed attached to the rear wall of the garage. The lightbulb hanging from the ceiling barely penetrated the gloom.

"Watch for spiders," Glen warned. "The charcoal should be on that shelf over there, next to the lawnmower."

"Thanks. I got it from here." Ellis made his way over to the shelf. Spying the bag, he hefted it with his left arm and turned to leave.

Glen was leaning in the doorway. He grinned and wiggled his brows. "Did I hear you say something about wanting a beer?"

"Uh, yeah. But Carl said it's against the rules."

"Well, what he doesn't know . . ." Quietly closing the door, he edged around some tools toward a stack of boxes in the far corner. After shifting the top crates onto the floor, he pulled back the lid on the next one and drew out two brown bottles. "They're not as cold now that the weather's warming up. But a beer's a beer, right?"

Ellis swallowed over his sandpapery throat. "Not sure this is such a good idea. What if Carl finds out?"

"Aw, he won't. I'm careful." Glen started to toss a

bottle to Ellis but seemed to think better of it. He set down the beers while he rearranged two of the sturdier crates. "Here, take a load off. I'll pop the top for you."

"But Jordy . . . the charcoal."

"By now, that crabby ol' cook'll be too busy getting the burgers prepped to miss you. What's ten more minutes, anyway?"

"Remember, young man, Jesus is always watching."

The voice of the kindly store manager who'd given a little boy a second chance all those years ago drew Ellis up short. He could almost feel the insistent pulsing of that little Ten Commandments card in his wallet.

Of all times, why now?

But it was just a beer. *Just one beer.*

Who was going to know?

Chapter Twenty

Since her confrontation with Reece, Rae had been a total mess. She'd hardly slept, and she'd barely eaten anything—not counting the pint of mocha almond fudge ice cream and an entire bag of salty tortilla chips. By Sunday morning, she was stumbling around in a daze with purple bags the size of water balloons beneath her eyes.

Sometime that afternoon, she emerged from her stupor and decided it was time to do something proactive. If ever Rae needed a phone-a-friend lifeline, today was one of those days.

Bolstering her courage, she found Maddie Wittenbauer's number and placed the call. It rang once and then went straight to voicemail. After waiting twenty minutes, she tried again. Same result.

Shoulders drooping, she let out a whimper. Was she so awful at friendships that she couldn't think of one other person who'd even care what she was going through?

Carl. Carl would care.

If she'd let him.

She started to call, then decided against it. She'd sound too whiny over the phone, too awash in self-pity.

What if she went to his place, just showed up unannounced? If she read anything but welcome into his reaction, she could claim she was making a spur-of-the-moment site inspection. That *was* within her purview of responsibilities, after all.

Before she could talk herself out of the plan, Rae showered, styled her hair, and dressed. Going for a casually professional look, she chose a white shirt tucked into belted black slacks. She reached for her favorite houndstooth blazer to top it off, then remembered she'd worn it the first time she'd met Carl. *Not* one of their more promising encounters.

She opted for the caramel-colored thigh-length cardigan instead. People said it complemented her hair color perfectly.

Why it mattered so much today, well, she'd put a pin in that thought for now.

Soon, she turned onto the street leading to Hope House. Catching a motion near the curb, she did a double-take.

Frankie?

Yes, it was that blue-eyed dog, sitting at the edge of someone's lawn.

She slammed on the brakes and threw the gearshift into Reverse. When she drew even with the dog, he looked straight at her through the side window and yipped.

This couldn't be good. She reached across and shoved open the passenger door. "What are you doing out here all by yourself?"

Frankie barked again, then pranced over and hopped into the seat as though he'd been waiting for her arrival.

"Well. Aren't you presumptuous. I hope your feet are clean." She fingered the dangling leash. "Where'd you leave Glen? Or did *he* abandon *you*?" That seemed more likely, considering how inattentive the guy had been during class yesterday.

Rae got out and jogged around to push the passenger door closed, then buckled back in behind the wheel. A block farther along, she glimpsed two men she recognized from Hope House looking frantically in all directions. Hands cupped around their mouths, they shouted Frankie's name.

"Looks like I got you home none too soon." Rae parked in the driveway, then got out and waved. "He's right here!"

The guys rushed over. The taller of them pulled open Frankie's door and grabbed his leash. "There you are, fella! You had us worried."

"I'll go tell Carl," the other man said as he loped toward the back gate.

The first man stooped to give Frankie a brisk rub behind the ears. "Oh, boy, Glen's in even bigger trouble now. This is probably gonna do it for him."

"What happened?" Rae asked. "How did Frankie get loose?"

Straightening, the man grimaced. "Better if you talk to Carl about it. *If* he ever calms down long enough. In the almost two years I've been here, I've never seen him this mad."

So much for seeking out Carl to confide her troubles in. Apparently, he had plenty of his own—and of the kind he likely *wouldn't* be pleased for her to learn about, considering the transitional housing program's already tenuous state.

Before she made things worse, maybe she should go.

Shouting from the backyard stopped her.

"I can't believe this!" Carl bellowed. He sounded both angry and scared. "I thought you understood. Do you have any idea the position you've put me in—put *all* of us in?"

"I'm sorry, okay? What do you want me to say?" There was no mistaking Ellis's voice, nor the defiance in his tone. "And, hey, I'm not the one you oughta be yelling at—not that you'll ever believe me."

Rae couldn't let this go on. She barged through the gate and up the deck steps, then crossed to where Carl stood nose-to-nose with his brother. "Honestly, you two! This feels like déjà vu all over again."

They whirled around as if ready to turn the attack on her.

She held her ground. Barely aware of the circle of men watching from a safe distance in the yard, she jutted her chin. "I think you'd better tell me exactly what's going on."

Carl's chest rose and fell with each sharp breath. He glanced toward the men in the yard and then back at Rae. "Let's talk inside." With a pointed look at Ellis, and then at Glen, who'd been standing with his head down and arms crossed a few feet away, he added. "All of us."

Rae followed the three men into Carl's office. He indicated the seating area near the front window. Looking morose, Ellis and Glen took opposite ends of the sofa. Rae opted for the padded armchair across from them and folded her hands in her lap.

Carl sat stiffly on the edge of a leather recliner that had seen better days. "You were going to find out sooner or later." He heaved an exhausted sigh. "I found these two in the storage shed drinking beer. Seems Glen's been keeping a stash there practically since he moved in six months ago."

Ellis leaned forward. "Rae, you gotta believe me—"

"Don't." Carl slashed the air with a flattened hand. "Don't you dare try to deny what I saw with my own eyes."

Slouching deeper into the sofa, Glen didn't even look up.

Rae's stomach rolled over. She wished she'd gotten right back in her car and driven away before hearing all this. How could she not report it to the board? Alcohol on the premises was about as serious a rule violation as there was. And how on earth had Ellis gotten involved?

Closing her eyes briefly, she murmured, "Carl, we should speak privately."

He nodded and ushered Glen and Ellis from the room, instructing another resident to escort them to the living room and make sure they didn't leave. Returning to his chair, he fell into it with a thud. "How long do you think the board will give me?"

"I have no idea. But I suspect they won't be very forgiving in this matter."

"I can't just kick the other guys to the street. They don't deserve to pay for Glen's mistakes." Carl's voice broke. "Or mine."

Her heart ached for him. She reached across the space to squeeze his arm. "I know what Hope House means to you. If I can do anything at all—"

He jerked his head up. "What are you even doing here? Did you somehow *know* this was going to happen?"

"What? No! How could I?"

"I don't know. It just seems awfully convenient that you'd show up at this exact moment."

"You are unbelievable." Bad enough her mother and brother had turned on her, but now Carl as well? And just when she'd begun to trust him. Her whole world felt like it was spinning off its axis. Eyes stinging, she stood on wobbly legs. She fumbled for her purse, then remembered she'd left it in the car.

"Rae, wait." Carl stood and blocked her path to the door. "I had no right to say such things. I'm out of my head, obviously. I'm so, so sorry."

"It's all right. Heat of the moment and all." She choked out a bitter laugh.

"It's *not* all right." He gripped her shoulders in a desperate manner that both jarred and thrilled her. "Rae, please. Forget everything else for now. Why *are* you here? There must have been a reason you came over."

She briefly considered her original plan B, to call it a spontaneous site inspection, but something wouldn't let her lie—especially under the present circumstances. Most especially not to him.

After all she'd endured this weekend, the intensely personal wounds she'd come seeking solace for, his warmth and strength beckoned. Her hands crept up between them and pressed against his firm chest. All she had to do was take a single step forward, and she could fall into his arms.

"Rae . . ."

She had no need to take that step herself, because he was moving toward her. His arms slid around her back. He tucked her into the cleft of his shoulder, her head resting beneath his chin. It felt new and scary and yet infinitely familiar.

It felt like coming home.

This is what home feels like.

The unbidden thought made Carl tremble. He wasn't sure how Rae had ended up in his arms, but the scent of her, sweet as a meadow on a sunny day . . . the warmth of her breath against the hollow of his throat . . . nothing had ever felt so right. His fingers found their way into her silky hair, and he suppressed another tremor.

She tipped her head to look up at him, then lowered her gaze and slowly backed away. "I—I'm sorry. I should never have . . ."

Reluctant to let her go, he slid his hands down her arms and gently took hold of her wrists. "Why not, Rae?"

"Because we can't do this." She pivoted and broke free. "*I* can't do this."

He knew his mind should be on how to deal with Glen and Ellis and everything else gone wrong this afternoon, but at the moment, he simply didn't care. "Why won't you let me in?"

She kept her face averted. "I thought I made myself perfectly clear the other night."

"Because we work together? That's a flimsy excuse and you know it." He glanced toward the door and scoffed. "Besides, at the rate things are going, that won't be the case much longer."

"Don't talk like that."

"Why not? It's true." His stomach plummeted all over again as thoughts of this afternoon's discovery intruded. Where had he gone wrong? How had he been so oblivious that Glen could sneak beer onto the premises right under his nose?

Then there was Ellis and his involvement—even after Carl had told him alcohol was expressly prohibited. He'd done his best to get past all the doubts and suspicions about his brother and try to trust him, only to have that trust betrayed.

His entire life felt like one long series of betrayals. The drug-abusing mother who'd abandoned her sons. His terrified little brother torn from his arms. The endless series of foster homes. The struggle against all odds to put himself through school and build a career of helping others.

And standing right in front of him, the first woman in forever to kindle hopes for a future he'd never imagined could be his.

Had he really come this close to losing it all?

God, where are You?

Facing him, Rae adjusted her sweater and squared her shoulders. "All else aside, decisions must be made about Glen. Today."

He gaped at her. How could she revert this quickly from the vulnerable, sensitive woman he'd just held in his arms to this persona of detached professionalism? "You do realize what will happen if he's removed from the program? In a matter of days, he'll be right back where we found him —in and out of shelters, asking for handouts on street corners, or more likely face down under a bridge somewhere in a puddle of his own vomit."

"You know how this works, Carl." She thrust out her arm. "We can't help someone who doesn't want to be helped. It isn't fair to the ones working hard to do better. To *be* better."

Her voice had cracked just the tiniest bit with those last words. The despair in her tone made him ache to hold her again, to bring back the unguarded, open-hearted Rae of moments ago. Something told him her reason for coming here this afternoon had no connection whatsoever with

Ellis or Hope House or any aspect of Equipped and Empowered Ministries.

Something also told him the moment for disclosure was long past.

"Okay," he said roughly. "I'll do what I have to do."

She nodded. "If I can help . . ."

"I don't see how."

"Then I should go." Brushing past him, she quietly left the room. Shortly, the click of the back door confirmed her departure.

Carl had stalled as long as he could. Steeling himself, he strode to the living room. Ellis stood staring out the front windows, while Glen sat in an armchair, his heels tapping out a staccato beat on the wood floor.

Halting across from him, Carl drew a slow breath. "Glen, go pack your things. I'll drive you downtown to a shelter. From there, you're on your own."

Panic filled the man's eyes, the first actual show of remorse he'd exhibited since Carl had found him in the storeroom. "You can't do this to me. Please!"

"You knew the rules when you were admitted to the program. You also signed an agreement acknowledging the penalties for breaking them."

"C'mon, man." Glen shoved up from the chair and grabbed handfuls of Carl's shirt. "Give me another chance —please!"

"Forget it," Ellis stated, still facing the window. "My sanctimonious brother doesn't believe in second chances."

Despite the searing stab wound to his heart, Carl tried not to visibly flinch. "Five minutes, Glen. Get to it." He motioned for one of the older men in the room to make sure Glen followed through. "I'll be waiting at the van."

As he started toward the kitchen, Ellis followed and

snagged his elbow. "You're seriously gonna dump him somewhere and leave him to fend for himself?"

Carl shook off the hold. "Don't you get it? I have no choice. *No choice.* But you—" He shuddered, anger and disappointment surging through him like a tidal wave. "Get in the van. I'll take you back to Witt's after I drop off Glen."

"No."

"*No?*"

"You heard me. I'm going with you. Wherever you dump Glen, that's where you'll be leaving me."

Carl's jaw dropped. "Don't be ridiculous. You don't even know Glen."

"Maybe not. But I know what it's like to feel like you have nothing. No one. No way out." With a brisk shake of his head, Ellis stormed out the back door.

I do, too! Carl wanted to shout. His brother had no idea the pain and inner turmoil he was going through right now. If it were up to him, of course Glen could stay. Carl would do just about anything to keep every single one of these men off the streets, living among caring friends, and on an upward path toward stability and a productive life.

"Excuse me, Carl." Martin came up beside him. "If Glen's out of the program, we need to know what to do with Frankie. You want one of the other guys to take over with him?"

"I don't know yet," he muttered. Eyes squeezed shut, he pinched the bridge of his nose. How much worse trouble would he face if anything had happened to the dog after his escape through the gate Glen had failed to close?

"How about Ramón and I look after him till you figure it out?"

"Thanks. That'd help a lot." He couldn't bring himself

to admit that once Rae reported to the board, they'd likely pull the plug on the canine project immediately.

Backpack hanging from one shoulder, Glen trudged into the kitchen. "I'm ready. Let's get this over with."

Over with. An apt descriptor for Carl's career and everything he'd hoped to accomplish.

Chapter Twenty-One

Monday morning found Carl seated in Alton Isaacs's office, the executive director's massive desk between them. Rae sat in a chair near Carl's, but they had yet to make eye contact. He hoped his sweaty palms wouldn't mar the finish of the armrests he gripped for dear life.

Fingers laced upon the desktop, Mr. Isaacs cleared his throat. "I'm very sorry about this, Carl. I know how much of yourself you've invested in Glen's rehabilitation. But he isn't the first to wash out, and he won't be the last."

"I know, sir." Carl blew out sharply. "But I can't help feeling like I've failed him."

"He failed himself," Mr. Isaacs insisted. "Unfortunately, the board of directors must take this recent incident under consideration, and you're well aware of their ongoing concerns about the transitional housing program."

"Which makes no sense." Gut churning, Carl sat forward. "Why would they shut down the program because of a few setbacks when it's been proven to help so many?"

"Budgets," Rae murmured. "It always comes down to money."

Carl snorted.

"She isn't wrong," Mr. Isaacs said gently. "Some of our outreaches are already operating on a shoestring. The board has to consider the bigger picture, or E and E won't have the wherewithal to help anyone."

A million arguments paraded through Carl's brain, any reason at all he could use to convince the board not to ditch transitional housing. He thought of Witt, who likely never would have escaped homelessness—much less built an amazing life with an amazing woman—if not for his two years at Hope House.

There were countless other success stories as well, and the potential for many more. Jordy was weeks away from completing his two years and moving toward independence. Martin was only a few months behind. And Ramón —the new maturity he'd developed in the two weeks he'd been working with Cocoa was nothing short of miraculous.

The dogs. They'd already formed strong bonds with their handlers. Returning them to the shelter now would be too cruel.

He drew a pained breath. "Could you at least convince the board to let me finish out the full three months of the canine project? At least with Martin and Ramón. They've been doing really well."

Mr. Isaacs skewed his lips. "That much, I can certainly try. Besides, I'm confident the board won't eliminate our transitional homes without implementing some sort of provision for the residents currently in the program."

"What will you do with Frankie?" Rae asked.

He cast her a reluctant sideways glance. "I thought about assigning him to someone else, but he's been listless since yesterday—which seems odd because it isn't like Glen ever really connected with him."

Rae shrugged. "Maybe the connection was the other way around. Dogs sense things about people that humans can miss."

Carl started to say that Frankie must have really misjudged Glen, but before he could, Mr. Isaacs's intercom buzzed.

Their boss excused himself to answer. After exchanging a few words with Kitty, he returned his attention to Carl and Rae. "Apologies, but we'll have to cut this short. I'm needed at home."

Carl stood. "Your wife, sir?"

"Yes, another bad turn, I'm afraid." He was already stuffing things into his briefcase. "Prayers appreciated."

The man bustled out, leaving Carl alone with Rae. He hated being so near to her while this unbridgeable chasm stretched between them.

She started for the door, then turned, her voice hard. "I still can't believe you left Ellis at the shelter with Glen."

"He insisted. What was I supposed to do?"

"How about take a beat and listen to *his* side of the story?" She faced him squarely. "Why are you always ready to believe the worst about your brother?"

"Why do you insist on believing the *best*? Are you—" The idea hit him like a ten-ton boulder. He took a staggering step back. "Why didn't I see it?"

"See what?"

A weak laugh escaped. "You and Ellis. All the time you've spent together. All the ways you've been looking out for him."

"You have got to be kidding me." Her upper lip curled.

Head shaking, she angled away. "No, Carl. You could not be more wrong."

"Then explain it to me, because the signals I've been getting from you are all over the place."

Planner hugged to her chest, she closed her eyes and inhaled slowly through her nostrils. Carl couldn't tell whether she was gearing up for her next verbal assault or about to make a run for it. Either way, he suspected the answers he sought wouldn't be forthcoming.

"All right, you want the truth?" she said, taking him completely by surprise. "The truth is, I have no clue how to deal with what's happening between us. I didn't expect it. I didn't want it. And now that it's a thing, I don't know how to make it go away."

Despite the thunderous beat of his heart, he made himself reply softly, soothingly, afraid she really would run for the hills if given the chance. "Then you're admitting we do have a . . . a *thing* going on?"

Her face crumpled. "I've been trying to protect you, Carl. Don't you get it? I'm damaged material. A relationship with me would only pull you down, and I like and respect you too much to let that happen."

"You think I'm *not* damaged? I've told you my story. I've known so few examples of good relationships that I'm not even sure I'm capable of one." He reached for her. "I only know I want to try."

She stared unmoving at his outstretched hand for so long that he slowly let it drop. "I—I can't. Please understand—"

"Oh! Excuse me." Kitty peeked in from the outer office. "I just came from getting coffee and didn't realize you two were still here."

"We were just leaving." Rae strode quickly past and was gone.

Brows cocked, Kitty cast Carl a concerned frown. "I'm sorry if I interrupted something."

"No problem." He stifled a groan. "Apparently, it was over before it even began."

Thankfully, Rae had no other appointments on her calendar that day. In her current state of mind, not even her practiced façade of professionalism could have masked the emotional storm raging beneath the surface.

As she perused a multi-church tag sale proposal, her thoughts wandered. How could Carl seriously believe she felt anything for Ellis other than friendly concern? She'd only meant to smooth the way for Carl and his brother to reconnect. Apparently, she'd only made things worse.

Talk about failed relationships! She truly took the prize.

"You don't need an excuse to call."

Maybe it was time to try again.

Maddie answered on the first ring. "Rae, hi! I saw you tried to phone yesterday. I had my cell turned off during an event we were hosting at Eventide."

"It's okay. I figured you were busy."

"We heard from Carl about what happened at Hope House yesterday. It's just awful. You were there?"

"I was, yes." She swiveled toward the window. "Is Ellis back yet?"

"No, but Witt spoke with him last evening. He insisted on staying with Glen at the shelter, and we're hoping they're both okay." Maddie harrumphed. "I get that Ellis has a point to make, but I'm not sure he's going about it the right way."

"And Carl isn't listening, either. He's erected a huge wall of distrust where his brother's concerned."

"There's clearly more to the story. Maybe when everyone's calmer, they can clear this up."

"I hope so." Bees buzzed around dandelions just beginning to bloom in the sunny area behind the building. Somehow, the view settled Rae enough to brave her next question. "Asking about Ellis isn't the only reason I called." She took a deep breath. "Any chance we could meet for lunch?"

"I'd love to." Maddie suggested the Smith Family Hometown Café in Frenchtown. "What time?"

"How about twelve thirty? I have a few things to finish up first."

Feeling lighter than she had in days, she quickly worked through the next several items in her inbox. Just before twelve thirty, she squeezed into a parking space in the popular café's nearly full lot. The hostess led her through the restaurant to a booth near the back, where Maddie was already perusing a menu.

Rae slid in across from her. "Thanks for meeting me. I haven't done anything like this in ages."

"Like . . . asking a friend to lunch?" Maddie's smile warmed. "I would have fallen out of the habit, myself, if not for a very persistent friend who refused to let me hide from the world, no matter how badly I wanted to."

"You?" Rae cast her a doubtful look. "But you're so open and approachable."

"Thank you. That wasn't always true, believe me. The combination of losing my grandparents and an extremely ugly breakup with a lying, adulterous boyfriend shoved me deep into a shell of distrust and self-protection. It took my best friend's not giving up on me, and then Witt coming into my life, before I found the courage to open my heart again."

A lump crept into Rae's throat. "I'm afraid my heart is permanently locked down."

"I thoroughly doubt that." Maddie reached across the table for Rae's hand. "We're created to be in relationship. In the Book of Genesis, God makes it clear that being alone isn't good for us. We need Him most of all, but we also need each other."

Stalling while she found a tissue in her purse, Rae debated whether to admit how distant she felt from God. How long could she go on pretending her faith was intact? She'd come frighteningly close to revealing the full extent of her doubts to Carl that day at Five on Black, until the focus conveniently shifted back to him.

But hiding the truth from Maddie, who'd offered her friendship freely—and whom Rae had sought out *because* she so desperately needed a friend—seemed incongruous. Why had she come today if not to risk sharing her true self with someone she hoped would not only empathize but perhaps guide her toward a better, more hopeful way of living?

As she searched for the courage to speak what was on her heart, a blue-jeaned server approached. "Ready to order, ladies?"

Rae was almost grateful for the interruption. "Sorry, I haven't even opened the menu yet." She looked to Maddie. "Any recommendations?"

"The avocado chicken salad on rye is one of my favorites. That's what I'm having. And an iced tea with lemon."

"I'll have the same." Rae smiled and handed the server her menu.

When they were alone again, Maddie said softly, "Ready to talk now?"

She sighed. "I think I am."

Over the next several minutes, she gave Maddie the condensed version of her life story. Growing up as the eldest of six and deciding early on that she never, ever wanted children of her own. Going on a blind date with Mark Caldwell and feeling instantly that she'd met her soul mate. A brief courtship, an even shorter engagement, then marriage, and only five months later unexpectedly finding herself pregnant.

"I was horrified at first and wasn't sure I wanted to go through with it. But having Mark's baby, believing that together we could build the happy, peaceful, harmonious family that my chaotic childhood never came close to . . ." Her throat closed. She took a sip of water.

"I understand," Maddie said. "When our growing-up years were far from ideal, it's easy to question whether we're ready for parenthood." Forearms on the table, she leaned in. "But I have no doubt that you were a great mom. Tell me about your little girl."

It was almost surreal, the way Maddie made it easy to let it all out—the hopes and joys of Kellie's first years, the devastation when they learned of her heart condition, the repeated hospital stays, the unanswered prayers for a donor.

Then the unrelenting grief. The blistering anger. Feeling as if a nuclear bomb had been dropped dead center on her world, with radioactive fallout poisoning everything that remained and breeding a cancer that slowly but methodically devoured her capacity for love.

"Eventually, I stopped feeling anything. Mark wanted

us to talk about Kellie. I just wanted to be numb." She sniffed and dabbed a tear from the corner of her eye. "That's when my marriage fell apart."

Their meals arrived then. Maddie again reached for Rae's hand as she bowed her head to pray. "Dear Lord, thank You for the comfort You offer through the gift of friendship, sisterhood, and shared burdens. Bless and heal Your daughter Rae, and help her to know she is never, ever alone. Amen."

Your daughter.

The words lodged in Rae's heart with a sudden, acute awareness of a love deeper than she'd ever known. A single sob escaped, and then another, and another.

"Oh, honey." Maddie slid into the booth beside her and wrapped her in a sisterly embrace. Speaking soothing words against her ear, she let her cry until the tears and tremors subsided, then pressed a wad of tissues into her hand.

"Th-thank you," Rae mumbled, blowing her nose. Glancing around, she was grateful several of the other diners in their section had already finished and left. "I'm so embarrassed."

"Nonsense. We all need a good cry now and then. Something tells me you were long overdue."

Rae released a sardonic laugh. "I've certainly been crying much more than usual lately."

"That's the Holy Spirit's work. He's opening up your heart again." After giving Rae another quick squeeze, Maddie moved back to her side of the table. "Don't be afraid of the tears. Let them wash away the pain and sorrow so you can finally heal."

"I hope you're right." Twisting the damp tissues she clutched, Rae swallowed hard. "I probably don't have to tell you that faith has been a huge struggle for me."

"Loss and grief can do that to you, as I know all too well. But the farther we feel from God, the closer He draws to us. All we have to do is turn to Him, and He'll be right there with arms wide open."

A smile crept across Rae's lips. "I think I actually felt that while you were praying."

"See? He's never left your side." Beaming, Maddie picked up her sandwich. "And on that note, why don't we get back to lunch?"

Suddenly famished, Rae spread her napkin on her lap. "Let's."

There would be time later to sort through her myriad thoughts and feelings, and many things she had yet to face wouldn't be easy. For now, though, she preferred to enjoy this meal with her new friend and savor today's spiritual hug from the "Daddy-God" she dearly longed to know better.

"Stop staring."

It was no use asking, of course. Nobody escaped Frankie's perceptive ice-blue gaze. The dog had been traipsing after Carl ever since he'd returned to Hope House following the meeting with Alton Isaacs. Now, Frankie sat at Carl's feet, furry muzzle resting on his knee.

Carl pushed away from his desk and bent forward to scratch Frankie behind the ears. "Try to understand. I don't want to return you to the shelter, but I have no idea how much longer there'll even be a Hope House, much less a place here for you and Cocoa and Zippy."

Or me.

If he didn't have the transitional home and his residents

to look after, would Equipped and Empowered Ministries move him into another department? Or would he find himself hitting the pavement to look for a job elsewhere?

Then there was his brother. He slid to the floor as yesterday's disaster played through his mind like a horror movie. "Please, Lord," he prayed aloud, his back pressed against a drawer pull. "Please let there be a way to fix this mess!"

When Frankie squeezed between his legs to lick his face, he couldn't hold back a weak chuckle. "Thanks for the shoulder to cry on, fella."

Frankie barked and trotted to the door, then back again.

"Need to go out already? Okay, okay." Carl pushed to his feet.

But instead of heading for the back door, the dog went to his crate, which Carl had moved into his own room last night. Frankie ducked inside, turned around three times, and then lay down, his chin on the threshold.

Carl heaved a groan. "If you're trying to tell me that you have no intention of going back to the shelter, like I told you, I'm pretty much out of options."

Frankie exited the crate and trotted from the bedroom. Carl followed him to the study, where the dog began sniffing around a chair in the seating area.

"What are you after, boy?" Glimpsing something shiny beneath the cushion Frankie had nudged aside, he bent for a closer look.

It was a gold hoop earring, about as big around as a quarter. Rae had been sitting in that chair yesterday. It could only be hers.

Recalling her cool dismissal earlier made him press his eyes shut in misery and regret.

Frankie's high-pitched yip snapped him to attention.

This time, the dog ran straight for the kitchen. By the time Carl caught up, Frankie was tugging on his leash, which hung on a hook near the back door.

Hearing the commotion, Cocoa and Zippy had emerged from their napping spots, and now all three dogs were barking and prancing around Carl's legs.

"What's up with you guys, anyway?" Apparently, a simple run around the backyard wasn't going to suffice. "Obedience class isn't until Saturday. Where, exactly, do you think we're going?"

Frankie nosed Carl's left front pants pocket, then looked up expectantly.

He'd almost forgotten he'd dropped Rae's earring into his pocket. Realization dawning, he let his jaw drop. "You're kidding, right? No. Absolutely not. I am *not* taking you to see Rae."

Frankie dropped to his belly. Head on his front paws, he rolled those expressive blue eyes toward Carl in what could only be a doggy pout. First Cocoa and then Zippy matched his pose. Now there were three moping dogs.

And one moping human. Because no way was Carl going to subject himself to another encounter with the woman who'd folded, spindled, and mutilated what was left of his increasingly fragile heart.

So how was he supposed to return her earring, which she must have missed by now? Maybe he could leave it with Kitty. Except Kitty would see right through him and most likely order him to deliver the earring himself.

Better idea. When he stopped at the E and E building during his afternoon vanpool run, he'd send one of the guys in with the earring. Easy-peasy. Perfect solution. No harm, no foul.

Frankie whimpered. Actually, it was more of a low growl.

"What—you're a mind reader now?" Glaring, Carl shook his head. "You're not the boss of me, and I am *not* going to be blackmailed by a dog."

It was nearing four o'clock, which meant time to hit the road. Coaxing Cocoa and Zippy into their crates with treats, he soon had them secured. Frankie, however, refused to budge from his spot by the back door.

"Okay, fine. You can ride along. But only because I'm already running late and don't have time to mess with you." Carl snapped on the leash and led the dog out to the van.

Naturally, Frankie wanted to ride shotgun, but Carl nipped that in the bud and told him he'd have to sit on the floor in the passenger row or else stay home.

The first guys Carl picked up from their jobs were happy to find Frankie in the van. The dog mostly ignored them, though, which reconfirmed Carl's opinion that assigning the dog to a new handler at this point might be counterproductive. Better to return him to the shelter and not risk more broken bonds.

At the ministry building, Carl pulled into an empty space near the main doors. He pulled the earring from his pocket, then reached back to hand it to Jordy. "This belongs to Ms. Caldwell. Would you mind running it in for me?"

Admiring the piece of jewelry, Jordy grinned. "Sure you wouldn't rather do it yourself?"

"I should stay in the van with Frankie. He's been a little moody since . . . well, since yesterday."

"Separation anxiety. Yeah, I hear that's going around." The man offered a knowing smile. "Be right back."

"And let the guys inside know we're here."

While the men in back gabbed about their workday, Carl tuned them out and resumed his brooding. He couldn't remember when he'd felt this burdened by the weight of responsibility. How was he supposed to cope? Where were the answers he so desperately needed?

I know You must have a plan, Lord—for me, for these men, for my brother, and for the dogs, too. I just wish You'd let me in on it.

After several minutes, Jordy returned with the men from their counseling appointments. Frankie sniffed each one as they climbed into the van but then resumed his vigil at the window. If he was waiting for Glen, Carl didn't know how to make him understand that Glen wasn't coming back.

He wished someone would help *him* understand why the woman he thought he might be falling in love with refused to even give them a chance.

Chapter Twenty-Two

One night in the homeless shelter was about all Ellis could stomach. Besides, he'd quickly gotten fed up with Glen. Bad enough the jerk had gotten himself kicked out of Hope House, but then he had to go and break more rules at the shelter. Glen was out on his ear before morning and cursing everybody within a hundred miles of Missoula.

Good riddance. Didn't Ellis have enough problems of his own? The last thing he needed was guilt by association. All because of a stupid beer that he'd ended up turning down anyway.

Not that Carl would bother to listen. What was a guy supposed to do when his own flesh and blood would rather believe the worst than give him the benefit of the doubt? Hadn't he been trying hard to turn his life around ever since the brainless decisions that had gotten him to this point in the first place?

Angry enough to do some cursing, himself, Ellis had been wandering around downtown Missoula for most of the day. It wasn't like he had anywhere special to be. He'd briefly considered hiking over to the interstate and hitching a ride as far away as whoever happened to stop for him was headed. What did it matter where he ended up? It wasn't like anybody cared.

Well, maybe Witt and Maddie. And Rae. They'd at least treated him like a real human being. Like somebody worth the effort.

If only he could think of himself that way. Like somebody who mattered. Somebody worth caring about.

Waiting for the walk signal at the next corner, he sniffed and used his thumb to flick away the wetness beneath one eye. How much closer to rock-bottom could a guy get?

Keep this up, loser, and you're gonna find out.

The light changed. Two guys in cowboy hats and quilted vests jostled past him like he was invisible.

"Hey!" he shouted, fists clenched.

The guys kept walking, but the one who'd bumped him gestured with an all-too-recognizable "salute."

"Same to you," Ellis grumbled. He decided to choose a different route.

At the next corner, a familiar dingy white pickup pulled over. Witt waved and rolled down the passenger-side window. "Been driving around lookin' all over for you. How about you hop in and we'll head on home?"

Ellis had to work hard at not looking too relieved to see his new friend. He shrugged and started toward the truck. "Why not?"

Before he could reach for the door handle, Ranger stuck his head out the window and barked.

Ellis jumped back.

"He's just happy we found you," Witt said with a laugh. "He'll make room. Get in."

Sucking air between his teeth, Ellis eased open the door

and edged into the seat. He froze as Ranger greeted him with a wet tongue across his ear.

Witt didn't say much until they were on I-90 heading toward Elk Valley. "So," he began, "sounds like you're back to square one with your brother."

"Huh. What else is new?" Ellis crossed his arms and pressed as close as he could to his side of the truck. He still couldn't escape Ranger's hot breath.

"The Lord'll work things out. Just be patient. With God *and* with Carl."

"I expect they've both washed their hands of me by now."

Witt scoffed. "The good Lord doesn't give up on anyone. Ever. As for Carl? He'll come around, mark my words."

Peering around the dog's snout, Ellis frowned at Witt. "How do you stay positive all the time? I mean, after all the bad stuff you told me you've been through. Losing your job, your family, your whole life basically."

"Yeah, but look how much I've gained." The way he grinned, he could only be thinking about Maddie. "'But one thing I do: Forgetting what is behind and straining toward what is ahead, I press on toward the goal to win the prize for which God has called me heavenward in Christ Jesus.'"

"Another Bible verse—figures." Ellis shook his head. "What does that even mean?"

"It means you've got to quit dwelling on what *was* and start looking ahead. The past is done with. What matters is what you do with the future God's given you." Witt glanced over, a glint in his eyes. "He's calling you to something better. Something more amazing than anything you've yet to imagine."

Ellis did his best to smother the tiny spark of hope that flared in his chest. If he hung around Witt much longer, he might actually start believing this stuff.

And that could be dangerous. Even life-changing.

But you've been wanting to change your life, right?

Sliding his gaze toward Witt, he was struck all over again by the man's air of contentment, of utter and unassailable peace. If Witt's God could do that for him, then He was a whole lot different from the God Harold Newman had tried to cram down Ellis's throat.

What more could he lose by giving Witt's God a chance?

Chapter Twenty-Three

Rae fingered the earring Kitty had just handed her. "Jordy dropped this off yesterday evening?"

"Yes. Curious that Carl didn't come inside to bring it to you himself." Kitty shifted her weight to one hip and crossed her arms. "Or perhaps *not* so curious after all?"

Blowing a strand of hair off her face, Rae leaned back in her desk chair. "It's complicated."

"Does it have to be?" The woman's expression turned sympathetic. "I realize things are tense with the current Hope House situation, but you and Carl seem so—"

"Please. Don't say it." Rae lifted both hands.

"All right, I won't. You're both smart enough to figure this out for yourselves. I just hope you will before it's too late." Kitty turned to go, then tossed a wink and a smile over her shoulder. "I will say, though, that cats are a lot less trouble."

No doubt about that. Rae rolled her eyes as Kitty marched out. She just might have to stop at the animal shelter on the way home and pick out a kitten.

The more she thought about it, the better the idea sounded. Although maybe not a kitten. An adult cat would be calmer, more settled, an easier adjustment for both of them at this point in Rae's life. She could get used to a warm, furry body curled up on her lap every evening while she watched TV or immersed herself in a good book . . . or possibly dusted off the Bible she hadn't cracked open since before Kellie died.

Imagining her precious daughter smiling down from heaven to see Mommy finding her faith again, she released a quiet sigh. Kellie would probably get a laugh, too, over the idea of her pragmatic and punctilious mother adopting a cat.

Maybe it was time to drop the attitude and throw caution to the wind, at least this once. It shouldn't be too hard to come up with an excuse to take the afternoon off. She'd stop at a pet store for the necessary supplies, then visit the Elk Valley Animal Shelter. The rest of the day would be reserved for bonding with her new feline companion.

But first, she had to get through this morning's board meeting. The mere thought made her stomach heave. She'd promised Carl she'd do her best to advocate for the continuation of the transitional housing program. As for the canine project, she feared the worst.

Waiting for board chair Enid Mason to bring up Sunday's incident at Hope House, Rae tried not to fidget as nervous perspiration trickled down her spine. She only hoped the navy blazer she wore over a white blouse would conceal any wetness.

Ms. Mason began the discussion by asking Alton Isaacs to describe for the board exactly what had happened. He kept to the facts but made it clear that, in his mind, the fault did not lie with anything Carl had done or failed to do.

"If any blame is to be assigned," Mr. Isaacs concluded, "it must go to Glen himself if not to our screening process for placing him in transitional housing before he was ready."

There were nods of agreement around the table, including from Enid Mason. "Then it is my recommendation," she stated, "that we suspend the transitional housing program at this time. We can discuss reinstatement if and when the budget allows, and only after a thorough internal housecleaning and staff retraining."

Rae didn't miss the bruised look in her boss's expression as he sank into his chair. "Excuse me." She sat forward, palms pressed against the tabletop. "How can you not see that ending transitional housing outright would be a terrible mistake? It would be a cruel and unforgivable disservice to those who are diligently striving to successfully complete the program."

Ms. Mason turned her unyielding gaze upon Rae. "You're suggesting we continue pouring funds into a broken system and risk another embarrassing and costly disaster like last weekend's?"

Flipping through her planner, Rae found the statistics she'd researched prior to the meeting. "According to reports covering the past five years, our transitional housing program averages an eighty-percent successful completion rate. Furthermore, post-exit follow-ups indicate less than ten percent of program graduates fall back into homelessness." She tapped her pen against the page. "Those are pretty impressive numbers any way you look at them."

"I'm not denying the benefits of the program," Ms. Mason said, "but I've looked at the numbers, too. Homelessness is on the rise, and transitional housing assists a very limited portion of that population. E and E dollars could go a lot farther if we shifted that money toward shelters and food insecurity initiatives."

"In other words, keep the unhoused dependent on handouts rather than offer them a better alternative." Rae slammed her planner shut and pushed back her chair. "How shortsighted can you get?"

"Rae . . ." Mr. Isaacs shot her a warning frown.

A board member at the far end of the table spoke up. "She makes a good point, Enid."

"I agree," said another. "My company has hired at least three program graduates. They're among the best employees we have."

Lips pursed, Enid Mason folded her hands. "Very well. Let's put it to a vote. Would someone like to present a motion?"

In a matter of minutes, the board voted five-to-two to keep the transitional housing program intact, but with the caveat that Alton Isaacs would immediately begin a review of current practices and implement any necessary adjustments and retraining. In the meantime, the board would continue to monitor the program closely.

Rae cleared her throat. "And the canine project? You did promise Carl three months, and in my estimation, the other two dog handlers are doing exceptionally well."

Admitting she couldn't think of an overriding reason to end the experiment, Ms. Mason agreed. "If there is no other business, do I hear a motion to adjourn?"

Rae had never been more grateful for a meeting to end. She tossed her things haphazardly into her leather tote, then sidled past the minglers and out the door.

Mr. Isaacs caught up with her outside her office. "We should chat a bit."

She swallowed hard. "I overstepped badly, didn't I?"

"Just a tad, but . . ." He glanced around, then lowered his voice. "You said exactly what needed to be said."

Blinking in surprise, she drew a quick breath. "Thank you, sir. I just couldn't listen a moment longer to Enid Mason and her faulty arguments."

Her boss nudged open the door and followed her into her office. "Enid can be quite opinionated, but in her defense, she does have the best interests of the ministry at heart." Stuffing his hands into his pants pockets, he released a chuckle. "I have to admit, though, *your* change of heart over the past few weeks has been a pleasant surprise."

A tiny shiver went through her. Setting her tote on the desk, she murmured, "In what way?"

"Despite your many credentials that convinced me to hire you, I'd become concerned that you and Enid may be cut from the same cloth—risk-averse, too firmly focused on the bottom line, caring more about protecting our resources than the people we invest them in."

It pained her to acknowledge how well he'd pegged her. She sincerely hoped—*prayed*—she wasn't that person any longer. "Working here is teaching me a lot. About myself. About what I want from life. About my relationships with others . . . and with God," she added softly.

Mr. Isaacs nodded and offered a fatherly smile. "I see that. I definitely do." He cleared his throat roughly. "I won't keep you any longer. But let's put our heads together soon about overhauling the transitional housing program. It's too important a ministry to abandon."

"Of course. We should bring Carl and the other transitional home counselors into that discussion."

"Good idea." He turned to go.

"Um, sir? It's been kind of a stressful morning." A shaky sigh escaped. "Would you mind if I left a little early?"

"Not at all. Take the whole afternoon." Looking suddenly drained, he let his shoulders droop. "I may do the same."

When he pulled the door closed behind him, she sank into her desk chair and rested her forehead on her clasped hands. A genuine prayer, the first in a long, long time, formed in her mind. *Father God, bless this kind man. Give him strength to care for his wife and the courage to face what comes.*

It was nearing one o'clock when Rae parked at the Elk Valley Animal Shelter. All the way over, she'd waged an internal debate about the wisdom of adopting a cat, but she refused to talk herself out of it. Squaring her shoulders, she marched into the lobby.

"Hi. Can I help you?" Of all people, it had to be Luke, the trainer who'd been teaching the obedience classes for Carl's canine project.

Maybe he wouldn't recognize her. She edged backward toward the door. "Oh, I, um . . ."

"Hey, aren't you the lady who's been at the Saturday classes with those guys from Hope House?"

No escaping now. "That's right." She pasted on a smile. "I didn't realize you also worked here at the shelter."

"It's a side job. What brings you by?"

"Well, I . . . I haven't had a pet in a while, and I've been thinking about getting a cat."

Luke shot her a knowing grin. "Yeah, I was getting lots of not-a-dog-person vibes from you."

"It isn't that." She pressed her lips together. What was the point of trying to explain? "I mean, since I work full-time, a cat would probably be more adaptable to my routine."

"Mm-hmm." Stepping from behind the counter, Luke started for a side door beneath a sign that read *Kitty Korner*. "Okay, let me introduce you to some cats and see if you click with one. Are you thinking kitten, or more mature?"

"Mature, but not too old. How long do cats live, anyway?" Best if she knew what kind of commitment she'd be in for.

"Twelve to fifteen years, typically, although I've heard of some that make it to twenty or even longer." After closing the door behind them, Luke perused the felines meowing from inside their cozy enclosures. He stopped at one and brought out a yellow-and-white shorthaired cat. "Have a seat and see how you and Mr. Peanut get along."

She already didn't like the name, but the cat seemed friendly as Luke set him on the floor near her foot—right up until she tried to pet him and he swiped at her with claws extended.

"Oookay, not this one." Luke scooped up Mr. Peanut and deposited him back in his cage. "Let's try Agatha. She's a bit more docile."

Ignoring Rae, the plump tortoiseshell cat flounced to the other side of the room and began grooming herself.

After equally disappointing results with three more felines, Rae sighed. "Maybe I'm not a cat person after all."

"Don't give up yet. Cats take a little longer to bond. Let's try—" A chime sounded from the lobby, and Luke moved toward the door. "Sorry, I'm the only one here right now. Feel free to visit with the other cats inside their kennels till I get back."

As she made the rounds, kittens showed the most interest, meowing and poking their tiny paws through the grates to bat at her finger. They were cute, yes, but Rae hated to imagine what her house would look like after a playful kitten entertained itself all day while she was at work.

Memories of baby-proofing the house after Kellie started crawling made her press a hand to her chest. She should come back and try this another time. If at all.

Intending to slip out without interrupting Luke and the visitor, she eased open the door to the lobby.

An excited, high-pitched bark bounced off the walls, and a moment later, a dark, furry body nearly mowed her down.

"Frankie, no!" The shout came from Carl. "I'm so sorry —*Rae?*"

She couldn't find her voice at first. It didn't help that the doggy-grinning husky parked at her feet wouldn't take those startling blue eyes off of her. "What are you doing here?"

"That should be obvious." Snatching up the leash, Carl tried to tug the dog a few steps back, but Frankie was having none of it. Carl harrumphed. "I don't know what's gotten into him."

"Pretty clear to me," Luke said with a laugh.

Rae seemed to be the only one in the dark. "Seriously, what is going on?"

With Carl struggling to regain control of the dog, Luke intervened. "Carl was just telling me that things didn't work out with Glen, and now he wants to return Frankie to the shelter. However . . ." He fingered his chin. "I'm thinking there may be a better solution."

Carl's plan had been to drop off the dog and leave. This decision had been hard enough. He didn't need anyone trying to talk him out of it. He cast Luke a doubtful frown. "What are you suggesting?"

"Just look." Luke tipped his head toward Rae.

With hardly a glance at Frankie, she firmly gave the hand signal for *sit*. The dog immediately obeyed. The only part of him still in motion was his tail sweeping the floor as he gazed up at her.

Carl pulled a hand across his face. "So that's what he's been trying to tell me for the past three days."

Looking more annoyed by the second, Rae squared her shoulders. "You're obviously making a joke at my expense. Care to share the punchline with me?"

"No offense intended." Luke waggled his palms. "It's just that you came in today planning to adopt a cat, but the way this guy's acting, he definitely has other ideas."

Her brow furrowed. "Frankie? You mean . . ." Now she was gesturing wildly with both hands. "No, I—I couldn't."

"Boy, was I ever wrong about you," Luke said with a snicker. "You're a natural with dogs."

Exactly what Carl had thought after she'd calmly motioned for Cocoa to sit that day on the Hope House deck. Rae only believed she was through with having dogs in her life. Even Frankie knew it. He'd been angling to be her dog from the first time they were introduced right here at the shelter.

Arms crossed, Rae edged away. "This is ridiculous. Anyway, my trunk is full of the cat supplies I bought on the way over." Her chin shot up as if she refused to notice how Frankie scooted forward with every step she took backward. "I came here for a cat, and I intend to leave with a cat. Period."

Carl choked on something between a laugh and a groan. It killed him that no matter how many times Rae rebuffed his feelings, he was falling harder for her every day.

Which didn't change the fact that Luke was right. Frankie wanted to be Rae's dog, and the blue-eyed glamour boy wasn't taking no for an answer.

"Just think about it, Rae," Carl pleaded. "It's either you or the shelter. You wouldn't really do that to Frankie, would you?"

She glared. "Didn't you bring him here to do exactly that?"

Clearing his throat, Luke stepped between them and took the end of the leash. "Hey, guys, let me look after Frankie while you work this out. The Kitty Korner's private. You're welcome to talk in there."

"Thanks, Luke." Although Carl wasn't sure he could trust Rae to keep her claws sheathed. Possibly one of the cats would come to his defense if things got out of hand.

"I don't know what good you think this will do," Rae grumbled as he held the door for her. "You will *not* change my mind about taking Frankie. Or any other dog, for that matter."

"Okay, I hear you." He let the door click shut, then gestured toward the wooden bench running down the center of the room. After they'd seated themselves—a good three feet apart, Carl couldn't help noticing—he shifted to face her. "If you've got a better idea than turning Frankie over to the shelter, I'm all ears. Believe me, this was never my first choice."

"And you've exhausted all available options, I assume. Including letting another resident take over Frankie's training."

"He shows zero interest in any of them. Since Sunday

afternoon, he's hardly eaten a thing, and all he's done is pout. Until he saw you out front, the only time he showed any signs of life was when he found your earring and then practically dragged me out to the van so we could bring it to you at the ministry center." Carl clicked his tongue. "How he knew you'd be there, I have no idea. When I wouldn't take him inside, he whimpered and whined the whole way back to Hope House."

Surprise, and the faintest hint of a smile, flashed briefly across Rae's expression. Glancing away, she ran her knuckle under one eye.

The cat directly across from Carl poked a paw through the cage door and meowed. He walked over and scratched its chin with a fingertip. A loud purr rumbled from the cat's throat.

"Wow," Rae deadpanned. "I'm certainly not Mr. Peanut's type, but it sounds like he'd *love* to go home with you."

"Well, that is definitely not happening." Releasing a frustrated sigh, Carl returned to the bench. "I half expected you'd be calling after the board meeting to say *all* the dogs had to go."

Rae edged closer and lightly rested her fingertips on his arm. "I should have called you right away. The board agreed to let the canine project continue for the full three months. The transitional housing program is safe, too—for the time being, anyway."

How could he feel both grateful and unsettled in the same moment? With her touch doing crazy things to his pulse, he altered his position just enough for her hand to fall away. "Ramón and Martin will be glad to hear they can continue training their dogs. But what exactly does 'for the time being' mean for Hope House?"

She briefly described what the board had discussed. "No one really wants to see the program end. They only want to ensure fewer problems and more positive outcomes."

"Without straining the budget. I guess I can understand that."

"And you and the other counselors will all be involved in those discussions."

Carl nodded. "That's good. I appreciate that you stuck up for us. It means a lot."

"Of course." Rae plucked at a pet hair on her skirt. Carl couldn't tell if it was from Frankie or one of the cats she'd been visiting with before he arrived. Either way, she was effectively using it as a diversion to keep from making eye contact.

Hearing voices out front, he blew out softly and pushed to his feet. "Sounds like they're about to be busy." It was a convenient excuse to end the torture of being this close to Rae. "I should finish my business with Luke."

As he gripped the doorknob, she released a sharp breath. "Wait."

He turned without speaking.

She stood and wrung her hands. "All right, I'll do it."

"Make sure I know what you're talking about."

"The thought of Frankie stuck here at the shelter . . ." She shuddered. "It's too much to bear."

He did his best to tamp down the giddy relief surging through him. "You're saying you'll adopt him?"

She looked a little queasy, but she nodded firmly. "Yes. I'll adopt him."

"Thank you, Rae. He's going to be one very happy dog." *Unlike me, who's suddenly insanely jealous.*

"I don't have any dog supplies, though."

"No problem. I have his crate and bedding in the back of my SUV. I think the shelter has some starter packs of dog food up front."

"Then it appears I'm fresh out of delaying tactics." Giving a huff, she marched past him and out to the lobby.

For a second, he couldn't seem to get his brain in gear. He'd never expected in a million years that she'd actually agree to take Frankie.

He had to admit she'd seemed different lately. Cracks had begun appearing in her usual stiff and formal façade, as if she had to work harder and harder at keeping it in place. He'd like to know what had changed.

He only hoped it meant she'd eventually open her heart to him.

Chapter Twenty-Four

Much as Rae would have preferred to load Frankie into her little red car and be on her way, the dog crate would never have fit in her trunk. She didn't have much choice but to let Carl follow her home and help her get everything inside.

"The crate can go next to my bed," she told him as he toted it through the front door. "Down the hall and to the left."

Frankie wasted no time jumping onto the sofa and nudging cushions and an afghan around until he'd made himself a comfy nest.

Arms akimbo, Rae glared at the dog. "Looks like we need to start by setting some clear boundaries."

"Good luck with that," Carl said, returning from the bedroom. "Anything else I can do before I go?"

"No, but thank you—I *think*." She skewed her lips. "I must really be going soft."

Making puppy-dog eyes of his own, Carl asked, "Would that be so bad?"

She sank onto the sofa next to Frankie and massaged the

dog's neck. The feel of his silky-soft fur beneath her fingers brought back memories of Kellie's faithful Shadow-dog, and a lump formed in her throat. *Please, God, if You really care, don't let me regret this.*

Carl edged toward the foyer. "Guess I'll head out then."

Rae stood on rubbery legs. Was she ready to be left alone with her new companion? Her emotional state was bumpy enough already. "You could stay a bit longer, make sure Frankie and I get off to a good start. Later, I could make us an early supper. Nothing fancy—just something from the freezer—"

"Best offer I've had in a while, but I can't. I still have to pick up the guys from jobs and counseling and then see that everyone's fed at Hope House."

"Oh. Right."

"Anyway, I got a call from Witt as we left the animal shelter. Ellis is back at his place, and . . ." A shaky breath escaped. "He's pushing me to come over and talk."

"I think that's a good idea. I've been—" Moving closer, she puffed out a sigh. "I've been praying for you two."

He looked at her askance. "Really?"

"Well, trying, anyway." She shrugged and managed a brief smile. "It's a process."

"I'm glad, Rae. I know you've struggled." He reached out as if to take her hand but pulled back at the last moment and stuffed his fingertips into his jeans pocket. "Are you talking to someone? Getting spiritual guidance?"

"Sort of. Maddie and I had lunch yesterday. She's already encouraged me a lot."

"I knew you'd like her."

"I do. Very much."

Carl sidled closer to the door. "Okay, then. Call if I can help at all with Frankie's adjustment." He looked past her toward the living room, and a grin formed. "Although it looks like that isn't going to be an issue."

"For him, maybe. Me, though?" Rae grimaced. "That remains to be seen."

"Something tells me it'll all be fine." He squared his shoulders and pulled open the door. "I'm really going this time. If I put off this meeting with Ellis any longer, Witt will be all over my case."

"As will I." Rae followed him out to the front porch. "Listen to your heart this time, Carl. Ellis is your brother, and no matter what you've both been through, no matter how many mistakes either of you has made, he loves you, and you love him. In the end, that's all that really matters."

Carl halted at the foot of the porch steps and turned toward her slightly, a thoughtful look darkening his expression. "I keep forgetting that, don't I?"

An ache shot through her chest, as if the words she'd just spoken to him had boomeranged and found their mark in her. "I do, too," she murmured. "Maybe we both need to work harder at remembering."

Carl wished he could have tossed aside his other commitments and accepted Rae's invitation to stay longer. She'd seemed more open and genuine than ever—and she was praying!

Which you should be doing more of, yourself, Carl Anderson.

Especially right this minute, as he turned into the lane toward Eventide Dog Sanctuary. He'd been too angry before to listen to Ellis's explanation about what had happened in the storeroom. Too angry and too scared about what it could mean for Hope House's future . . . and his own.

After Rae told him what the board of directors had agreed to, he'd been relieved and at least partially reassured. He might be down one dog and handler, but there was still time for the canine project to prove its merits and hopefully give the board more incentive not to shut down Hope House.

Or . . . what if God had other plans for him? What if Sunday's incident, on top of everything else that had happened recently, was the Lord's way of telling Carl he'd done all he could in this job, that he should think about moving on to something he'd find even more personally fulfilling?

It was yet another thing he'd be wise to keep praying about. For now, though, he needed to face his brother. *Please, Lord, help me listen—really listen—this time.*

Lost in thought, he'd slowed considerably on his way up the lane. Around the next curve, he glimpsed Maddie riding one of her horses in the pasture, three of the sanctuary dogs ambling alongside. When she lifted one hand in greeting, he lowered his window and waved back. Though she was several yards away, the concern in her smile reached him and gave him a measure of encouragement.

As he parked in the driveway and stepped from the SUV, Witt greeted him with a firm handshake and a manly side-hug. "Wasn't sure you'd show up."

Carl choked out a laugh. "You made it pretty clear what you'd do to me if I didn't."

"Like I'd really hogtie you and toss you in the back of my little truck to get you here."

"Wouldn't put it past you."

"If the threat worked, that's all I can ask." Witt tipped his head toward the house. "You ready?"

"No, but does it matter?"

"Not one little bit." Clapping a hand on Carl's shoulder, Witt propelled him up the back steps. "Ellis is in the kitchen. We've been folding Eventide brochures to give out at the next craft fair where Maddie will be doing pet portraits."

"Is he expecting me?"

"Nope. Didn't want to say anything in case you changed your mind."

The door flew open. Ellis stood at the threshold, arms locked across his chest. "I heard you drive up. If you came to give me another earful about what a lousy, good-for-nothing scumbag I am—"

"That isn't why I'm here." Carl braved a step closer, hands extended. "I blew it badly on Sunday. I'm ready to hear your side."

"Oh, yeah? Well, maybe I'm not ready to talk. There's only so many kicks in the gut I can handle from somebody I used to look up to."

"And I don't blame you. I'm out of excuses, Els. All I can do is apologize. Again."

As silence stretched between them, Carl forced himself to breathe. He barely felt Witt's pat on his back before his friend slipped away, leaving him alone with Ellis. He worked down a swallow over the tightness in his throat. "May I come in? I could help you finish folding those brochures."

"Suit yourself." Ellis pivoted and marched through the mudroom.

Following him to the kitchen, Carl paused at the breakfast table. A supply of flat color copies waiting to be folded lay near stacks of rubber-banded brochures. Taking the chair cater-cornered to Ellis's, Carl picked up a sheet. "These get folded in thirds?"

"Should be obvious." Ellis slid a sheet in front of him and deftly made the creases, then tossed it onto a stack of completed ones. "Easy-peasy."

Carl followed suit and added his folded brochure to the pile. "Looks like your hand is doing a lot better. How's it feeling?"

"It hurts some, but it's not as stiff. I'm keeping up my PT exercises. "

"Good. I'm glad." Figuring they both needed breathing space to work up to deeper topics, Carl remained silent while folding a few more brochures. "Guess you've seen some of Maddie's pet sketches. She's pretty good, isn't she?"

"Yep." Another trifold landed on the pile.

Carl added two more. "I just came from Rae's. She sends her best."

Ellis gave a doubtful snort. "You two are actually on speaking terms?"

"One of several bridges I need to rebuild." He laid aside a brochure and sat forward, hands clasped between his knees. "I'd like to work on ours right now, if you'll let me."

Barely looking at him, Ellis continued folding. "Thought that's what we were doing."

"It isn't happening unless we can actually talk. I mean it, Els. I want to hear your side of what happened Sunday. This time, I promise not to jump to my own misguided conclusions."

Ellis pushed back from the table and shifted sideways. "Okay, you want the truth? I did want that beer. Wanted it badly. So I took it, even got the cap off. I was this close to taking a swig." He demonstrated with his thumb and index finger almost touching. His stony gaze meeting Carl's, he continued in a firm but tremulous tone. "Then I remembered Witt telling me about hitting rock-bottom after he lost his job and how alcohol nearly destroyed him. So I said to myself, *Hey, Newman, you're on a better road now. Don't mess it up.*"

Carl's stomach cramped. "And that's when I walked into the storeroom and saw you."

"And lit into me like a house afire." Ellis's eyes filled. He sniffed hard and drew a hand beneath his nose. "Do you have any idea what it feels like to try and try and *try* to do the right thing only to be disbelieved and rejected by the one person you love most in this world?"

"I—I'm sorry," Carl stammered, his voice a mere whisper.

Without warning, a long-buried memory shot to the surface.

"How dare you blame Zeke for stealing from my wallet! He's done nothing but take care of us."

"Mommy, I didn't do it—you have to believe me." Carl had wanted to take the money—even thought about how to sneak into his mother's purse while she slept off another hangover. How else was he going to get his baby brother into a dry diaper and stop his hunger cries?

Instead, Zeke had found the cash. Not an hour later, he'd come home with a six-pack of beer and some kind of pills in a little paper wrapper, then proceeded to get high while Mommy drooled on her pillow and Ellis kept right on crying.

Next chance he had, Carl didn't falter. If his own mother refused to be responsible for them like she was supposed to, what was the point of being a good kid? Better to steal and get punished for it than let his baby brother go hungry.

Shuddering, he went to the cupboard for a glass and filled it at the sink. With his back to Ellis, he gulped down the water in hopes of washing away the bitter taste of humiliation—not so much for what he'd done as a scared, desperate child, but for how he'd treated his scared and desperate adult brother these past few weeks.

Plunking the empty glass onto the counter, he hung his head. His heart was near bursting with everything he needed to say to his little brother, but the words simply wouldn't come. Shoulders heaving, regrets drowning him, he buried his face in his hands while hoping—praying—for Ellis's forgiveness.

For God's mercy.

Chapter Twenty-Five

Seeing his big brother crumbling before his eyes tied Ellis in knots. He'd thought nursing his anger and resentment would protect him from further hurt, but it wasn't working. Had never worked, to tell the truth.

He stood slowly, inhaled, blew out. It was only a few short steps across the kitchen to reach Carl's side, but crossing that distance felt like wading through mud.

His good hand crept up Carl's back and onto his shoulder. He gave it a hard squeeze. "I love you, big bro. Never stopped. Never will. No matter what."

"That goes both ways." Voice ragged, Carl straightened and turned. "Can you forgive me? Can we try to get it right this time?"

Nodding firmly, Ellis pulled his brother into a rough hug. "When we were kids, all I ever wanted was for you to be proud of me. The day the Newmans took me away was the worst day of my life. It sounds silly now, but I think I kept messing up hoping they'd hate me so much that they'd send me back to wherever you were."

"I wish they had." Carl drew away and grabbed a paper

towel to blow his nose. "If we'd found each other sooner, things could have turned out so different."

"Witt's always telling me that God is in control. That He can bring something good out of everything that happens, even the bad stuff." Ellis shrugged. "I kinda want to believe that."

"I do believe it. Mostly." Offering a weak smile, Carl gestured toward the table. They sank heavily into their seats. "It can be nearly impossible to see the good until we're looking back at it, and sometimes it has to be from years down the road. Even then, I wonder sometimes why God doesn't just fix things. Then we wouldn't have to go through the bad stuff in the first place."

Ellis snorted. "Yeah. Wouldn't that be great?"

Silence enveloped them as Ellis let his thoughts drift back through time. Carl's thousand-yard stare said he was doing the same. What if they'd grown up together in a normal family—with a gospel-centered, God-loving mom and dad instead of judgmental, don't-break-the-rules, God-*fearing*-in-a-bad-way parents like the Newmans? What if Ellis had never been without his big brother to cheer him on at Little League games, help him with his homework, teach him how to drive, give him dating advice?

What if . . . what if . . . what if . . .

There was no end to them. And no point in dwelling on what might have been. All they had was the here-and-now and whatever lay ahead.

Blowing out sharply, he scooted up to the table and reached for a flyer to fold. "Witt's taking me for an interview with Happy's Helpers in the morning."

"Super. With Witt in your corner, it's bound to go well." There was a hint of regret in Carl's tone. Not like he didn't wish his brother a good outcome. More like he was missing out on something.

"If they hire me, maybe you and I could go for pizza later to celebrate?"

"Definitely. My treat." Perking up, Carl took another page and resumed folding.

When they'd finished the last brochure, Ellis had Carl help him count out stacks of twenty-five and secure them with rubber bands. After dropping the banded flyers into a cardboard box, Ellis lifted his hand toward his brother for a high-five. "Thanks, man. Teamwork makes the dream work."

"Sure does." Carl ignored the hand and went in for a back-slapping hug instead. "I'll always be on your team, Els."

"Ditto, big bro." In danger of totally losing it, he cleared his throat roughly. "Say, don't you need to hit the road pretty soon?"

Glancing at the kitchen clock, Carl winced. "Yeah, I do. Didn't realize how late it was getting."

"I'll walk you out."

At Carl's SUV, Ellis set a hand on the doorframe. "About those bridges in need of repair?"

"Yeah?"

"Work extra hard on the one between you and Rae."

Blinking, Carl released a nervous laugh. "I'm trying, but I'm not sure she's willing."

"Not yet, maybe, but soon." Ellis's gaze drifted toward the road as he recalled his run-ins with Rae's family. "She has a few damaged bridges of her own to attend to."

"Guess I'll have to be patient and keep praying." Carl slid in behind the wheel. "Praying about Rae and a whole lot of other things," he added with a sigh, then smiled. "At least one of my prayers got answered today."

"Oh yeah?" Figuring he already knew which one, Ellis grinned back.

"Yep, I got my baby brother back, and nothing's ever going to separate us again."

Feeling like his chest could burst, Ellis watched his brother drive away. He could just about believe in a God who'd go to such great lengths to restore a family after so many years and so much heartbreak had come between them.

Next Sunday, when Witt and Maddie asked again if he'd like to go to church with them, he might even say yes.

Chapter Twenty-Six

Rae would need some time to get re-accustomed to having a dog in the house. The first night was like being a mom again and listening for every little rustle of bed covers or sniffles or footsteps in the hall.

Or coughs or labored cries of "Mommy, I can't breathe!"

Or her worst fear, no sound at all.

More than once during the night, she sat up with a start and turned on the bedside lamp to be sure Frankie still rested quietly in his crate. Each time, he lifted his head, those incredible blue eyes shining up at her as if to say, *I'm fine. You're fine. Go back to sleep.*

By morning, her thoughts had turned to what to do with him while she was at work all day. A cat would have been fine with a bowl of water and a litter box. What was a reasonable length of time to leave a full-grown dog alone in the house and not return to find messes to clean up? Such questions had never been an issue with Shadow, because someone had always stayed close by for Kellie, whether at home or during her frequent hospital stays.

"Well, fella, I can think of only one solution—for today, anyway, since I don't have any outside appointments." She stuffed his crate pad, a small plastic bowl for water, and a baggie of dog treats into a canvas tote. "If I get into any trouble at work for bringing you along, well, so be it."

She did garner a few raised eyebrows as she walked Frankie to her office. Once she'd set out his pad and water bowl in the back corner, he settled down quickly, head resting on his forepaws. The way his gaze continually followed her was slightly unnerving at first, but she soon got used to it—even felt comforted by his watching over her, much like Shadow had done with Kellie.

"Now that's quite a sight." Kitty beamed at her from the doorway.

Rae cast the woman a sheepish frown. "I know I should have asked permission, but this all came about rather unexpectedly, and I didn't know what else to do—"

"No need to explain. I can guess what happened." Kitty sidled around the desk to kneel and give Frankie a pat. "My, aren't you a handsome fellow. I've heard many good things about you."

"He is pretty special," Rae said, swiveling her chair around. "I never thought I'd have another dog after . . ."

Kitty straightened and leaned one hip against Rae's desk, a sage smile turning up the corners of her mouth. "God knew it was time."

Rae scoffed. "I don't know about that. But it is rather surprising that no one had adopted Frankie before now."

"Then that confirms it. The Lord was saving him for you."

Rae could only shake her head and shrug. God did seem to be moving in her life and in her heart again . . . or else she was finally appreciating the fact that He'd been with her all along.

An hour or so after Kitty left, Rae's cell phone buzzed. The display showed Carl's name. She took a moment for her pulse rate to settle before answering. "Hi, Carl."

"Sorry if I'm interrupting, but I, ah, wanted to make sure Frankie's doing okay."

At the hesitation in his tone, she almost laughed. "Why? Did you think I might have already returned him to the shelter?"

"Uh, maybe."

"No worries. He's doing great. In fact, we both are." She glanced over to see Frankie sitting on his haunches, head cocked, eyes questioning. Covering the mouthpiece, she whispered, "Yes, I'm talking to Carl." Into the phone, she said, "Want to tell him hi? He's right here."

"Oh. I thought you'd be at the office."

"We are. I declared it an unofficial take-your-dog-to-work day." She put the phone on speaker and held it toward Frankie. "Say hello to Carl. He misses you."

Frankie obeyed with a bark.

Carl's surprised laugh sounded from the speaker. "Hey, Frankie! Cocoa and Zippy are with me, and they miss you, too."

A rumbling woof and then a high-pitched yip sounded from the phone speaker.

After giving Frankie a scratch behind the ears, Rae shifted toward her desk. "Maybe we should get the dogs together for a playdate sometime."

"They'd like that."

She squeezed her eyes shut. *I would, too.*

"You know," Carl went on, "you and Frankie could join us for the Saturday training classes. If you want to, that is."

"I'll have to think about it."

"I hope you will." He paused, exhaling softly. "Well, I'll let you get back to work."

She felt almost as reluctant as he sounded. "I really am glad you called."

"It was nice to hear your voice, too." He chuckled. "And Frankie's."

After they disconnected, a velvety blanket of contentment enveloped her. She couldn't recall when her spirit had felt this light, this . . . hopeful. *God, is that You?*

Before she could process the thought, the office intercom chirped. It was the volunteer manning the reception desk. "You have a visitor, Ms. Caldwell. Should I send him up?"

Her pulse thrummed. *Carl?* Surely not. If he'd been in the building, he'd certainly have come to her office instead of phoning.

Working hard to maintain a professional tone, she asked, "Who is it?"

"Reece Ogden. He says he's your brother?"

Every last ounce of contentment evaporated. What on earth was Reece doing here? More accusations to throw at her? Another batch of nasty names to bestow? Her next thoughts were truly a prayer: *Lord, help! I don't need this. Not today. And certainly not for the entire office to hear.*

"Ms. Caldwell?"

"Yes, I heard you." Sending Reece away would only delay the inevitable, because he'd likely show up at her house later to lambast her with whatever he needed to get off his chest. She drew a long, slow breath. "Please have someone show him to my office."

While she waited, she grabbed a handful of folders from the filing cabinet and rearranged a few items on her desk. If she could make herself look even busier than she actually was, hopefully it would encourage Reece to cut his visit short.

Watching her, Frankie angled his head with a curious expression.

She hiked a brow. "You wouldn't by chance have learned the 'sic 'em' command, would you?"

He tilted his head the other way.

"Mm-hmm, figured as much."

Within minutes, footsteps and voices reached her from the corridor. "Last door on the right, sir."

"Thanks," came Reece's soft-spoken reply. He edged around the doorframe with a worried look, perhaps afraid Rae might throw something. "Hi, sis. Can I come in?"

"May as well, since you're here." She spread open a folder and tried to appear engrossed in the contents. From the corner of her eye, she glimpsed Frankie rise from his crate pad and sniff the air.

"Whoa." Reece backtracked the two steps he'd just taken. "You have a guard dog?"

Rae swallowed a laugh. "I do. He keeps a very close eye on me. Two of them, in fact." She folded her arms atop the open folder and glared at her brother. "Be warned, if you're here to insult me again, this fellow won't take kindly to it. Not to mention, I can summon Security with the touch of a button."

"Not necessary." Reece inched closer but made sure a visitor chair was positioned between him and Frankie. "I'm actually here to apologize."

Rae sat straighter. "Oh?"

"I was totally out of line the other day. I was angry about all kinds of stuff. And scared. And confused. I shouldn't have taken it out on you."

Stunned into silence, she could only stare.

"I know I have a lot to make up for. A lot of growing up to do." Reece eased around the chair and sank onto the seat. Keeping his eyes lowered, he went on, "Heather may never forgive me, but I'm hoping you will. It's killing me to be on the outs with you, Rae. I need my big sister to hold me accountable."

Now she was beyond flabbergasted. "I'm afraid to ask what happened to change your attitude."

He lowered his head to his hands, his next words coming out on a sob. "Heather lost the baby."

"Oh, Reece!" She stumbled around the desk and into the chair next to his, then wrapped her arms around his shaking shoulders. "Reece, I'm so sorry."

"It's my fault. My fault!" He sat up and twisted toward her, his eyes red, his face contorted. "I should have listened to you, Rae. I've been such a brat. A spoiled, selfish brat."

"Yes, you have." She spoke the words firmly but tenderly. "But that's beside the point now. Heather needs you. You need each other."

"She kicked me out, remember? She's done with me."

Frankie's presence as he crept up beside her gave Rae an extra measure of resolve to console and reassure her brother. "It won't be easy, but you've got to start by regaining Heather's trust. More than that, her respect."

"But how?"

"With your ongoing commitment to being the husband she needs you to be, even when she pushes you away."

He looked at her askance. "How do you know that will even work? It sure didn't for you and Mark."

The truth stung. "You're right, it didn't. But our marriage was missing one very important ingredient back then."

"What's that?"

"Faith. After Kellie died, Mark and I both lost touch with God for a while. Without Him, we couldn't find our way back to each other." Reaching for her brother's hands, she drew a slow, purposeful breath. "But it doesn't have to turn out that way for you. You can start right now by inviting God into your heart and into your marriage. Let Him heal you, and pray for Him to heal Heather."

Reece's brow furrowed. "I didn't think you were into that religious stuff."

"I didn't think I was, either. But lately . . ." She glanced at the dog nudging her elbow as if prompting her to keep talking. "I'm changing, Reece. I was closed off for so long, not letting anyone in, not letting *love* in. But I'm beginning to sense God with me in ways I never did before."

"That's too pie-in-the-sky for me." He stood abruptly. "It was dumb of me to come here. I don't know what I was expecting, but it wasn't this."

She snatched his arm before he reached the door and yanked him around to face her. "You came because you needed your big sister—just like you said, to hold you accountable. That's what I've always tried to do, but I realize now I was doing it all wrong. I covered for you when I shouldn't have. I gave you a safe place to land when you messed up. I even lied for you."

"Rae—"

"No, let me finish. When I felt like I couldn't put up with one more thing, I totally turned my back on you. *I* was the one being selfish, and I'm sorry."

He looked at her as if he didn't recognize her. His mouth worked, but only stuttering sounds came out. Giving a loud sniff, he shook off her hold and strode from the office.

Rae followed him to the corridor. "Reece, please! Stay and talk this out with me."

Without turning around, he lifted one hand in a dismissive gesture and walked faster. A moment later, he disappeared around the corner and was gone.

Disappointment combined with grief over her brother's loss formed a dull ache in the pit of her stomach. Shoulders drooping, she returned to her desk and collapsed into the chair. "I don't know how to fix things," she murmured. "What if I've messed up too many times in my relationships and now it's too late?"

Frankie pushed his snout beneath her hand and whimpered.

Stroking his head, she blinked back a tear and stiffened her spine. She would *not* give in to defeat—not with her family, and not with herself. If God really was recreating her, giving her another chance to become the woman He intended for her to be, then she wouldn't refuse the call.

Even with Reece shutting her out, she could still do *something*. She'd start by reaching out to Heather with flowers and a heartfelt note of condolence and ask about visiting soon. In the meantime, she'd pray night and day for the Lord to open Reece's heart to His love and mercy, just as He was doing with Rae.

In the wake of Glen's departure, malaise had set in at Hope House. It seemed to be part despondency over losing one of their own, part simmering anger that Glen had deceived them. Carl couldn't blame the guys. He felt pretty much the same way. Worse, he carried the added burden of waiting for the other shoe to drop—the termination of transitional housing and these men's stepping stone to full and independent lives.

The one bright spot had been the genuine break-through he'd experienced with his brother. For the first time since Ellis's arrival in Missoula, Carl's load of questions, doubts, and lingering regrets had truly begun to ease.

He'd also regained a measure of hope that things could one day be different between him and Rae. During their phone conversation on Wednesday, she'd sounded different somehow. He couldn't describe it exactly, but he sensed a positive change.

It only made sense that Rae's closest relationships needed to heal before she'd be emotionally able to let Carl into her heart. He was only now realizing how *not* ready he'd been for anything deeper than friendship until after he'd resolved things with Ellis and dealt with all the cumbersome baggage he'd been carrying from their troubled childhood.

He was making progress, and that's what counted.

Thursday morning kept him occupied driving around town looking at used cars with Jordy. The man had worked hard to put aside savings from his restaurant job, and the older-model Honda Civic he settled on brought him one step closer to moving out on his own. As with every program graduate, Jordy's departure in a few weeks would mean another bittersweet goodbye for his housemates—most especially for Carl, who became personally invested in every man who passed through the Hope House doors. There were days he wondered how many more such good-byes he had in him.

Even so, it seemed unthinkable that the transitional housing program could one day come to an end. There were similar programs in and around Missoula that could pick up the slack, but in Carl's opinion, Equipped and Empowered Ministries' solid emphasis on faith-centered counseling and accountability was unmatched.

The decision was out of his hands, though. All he could do was to keep doing what he'd been doing. And pray.

Saturday morning's dog-training class went well. Without the distraction of Glen's inattentiveness, Ramón and Martin made much more progress with Cocoa and Zippy. Carl was disappointed that Rae hadn't taken him up on his invitation to bring Frankie to class, but he couldn't blame her. Things between them were still a bit too unclear.

On Sunday, he drove out to Elk Valley to attend church with Witt and Maddie, only to be pleasantly surprised when Ellis tagged along. His brother looked a little on edge sitting in the church pew, but he listened attentively, even cracked open a pew Bible to follow along with the Scripture readings. After the service, he didn't say much, but Carl had the strong sense that God was calling Ellis closer.

He didn't hear from Rae again until she phoned on Tuesday afternoon following the weekly board meeting. There was something about her tone that made him uneasy. Hope House and the transitional housing program had come up for serious discussion yet again, she told him, and now Alton Isaacs wanted Carl to meet with him and Rae for a chat.

Cell phone pressed to his ear, Carl gave his brow a one-finger massage. "That sounds ominous."

Rae didn't respond right away, which only added to his worries. "Just come to Mr. Isaacs's office at nine thirty tomorrow morning. We'll go over everything with you then."

Go over everything? Like his severance package, perhaps? How, exactly, was he supposed to sleep tonight, much less maintain a façade of normalcy with his men? Jordy and a couple of others had already picked up on the fact that something even more upsetting than Glen's departure was keeping him preoccupied these days.

He barely managed to keep his cool throughout the evening and as he saw the guys off to work and counseling the next morning. His last stop was the ministry center, which gave him time for a coffee in the lounge before heading up to the executive director's office.

His palms were sweating as he approached Kitty's desk shortly before nine thirty. "How nervous should I be?"

She cast him a sympathetic smile. "God's got this, Carl. It'll be okay." A non-answer if he ever heard one. "Rae is already here. You can go on in."

Sucking air through his teeth, he strode to the inner door and eased it open.

Mr. Isaacs motioned to him from the small, round conference table near the window. "Please join us, Carl."

He sidled over and took the nearest chair, which placed Rae and the executive director on either side of him. He gave a polite nod but waited for one of them to speak first.

They shared a somber look across the table. Then Mr. Isaacs sat back and said, "I'll let Rae fill you in on what the board concluded during yesterday's meeting."

Rae's planner lay open before her. After glancing at it briefly, she folded her hands atop the pages and cleared her throat. "This isn't entirely bad news, Carl. In fact, after listening to everyone's thoughts yesterday, I truly believe what the board has agreed to will be in everyone's best interests."

He hated it when she spoke so formally, as though he meant nothing more to her than a subordinate in a business arrangement. Which he was, in fact, but it wasn't at all how he wanted things to be between them. He scrubbed his damp palms on his pant legs. "I'm listening."

"As I assured you after last week's meeting, the board has no plans currently to end the transitional housing program. However . . ." She flicked her gaze toward Mr. Isaacs, who dipped his chin in a consenting nod.

Here it came. Gripping the armrests of his chair, Carl steeled himself for the ax to fall.

"However," she repeated, looking once again at her notes, "considering you've been managing Hope House and counseling residents for over ten years now, the board feels a change may be advisable."

He let that sink in. "What kind of change are you talking about?"

Her whole expression softened. She stretched one hand across the table toward him. "We're talking about what's best for *you*, Carl. The board members think—and after talking between ourselves, Alton and I agree we see it, too— that you're getting tired."

The two of them were on a first-name basis now? It made Carl feel even more like an underling being called on the carpet. He bristled. "Are you implying that my—my *fatigue* is to blame for what happened with Glen?"

"Not at all," Mr. Isaacs insisted. "Or at least, not entirely. You're a skilled and gifted counselor, Carl. That has never been in question. But the kind of deeply personal mentoring you've been doing all these years . . . it takes a toll, both emotionally and spiritually."

That much was true. Worse, he could no longer deny the gnawing suspicion that he was perilously close to burnout. How had it crept up on him so insidiously?

He stood and paced to the far side of the room. If he was about to be fired, it wasn't as if he had new employers waiting in the wings to snatch him up. Besides, after living at Hope House all these years, he didn't even have a place of his own to move home to.

Keeping his back to them, he asked, "What happens next? Am I out of a job?"

Chapter Twenty-Seven

Rae held herself motionless while Alton responded to Carl's question.

"Whether you stay or go is entirely up to you," her boss began. "Before you decide, though, please come back and sit down. We'd like to discuss some possibilities."

Trudging to the table as if he'd aged fifty years, he sat down hard and dropped his chin to his chest. "Okay, let's hear it."

Rae's heart clenched at the utter desolation in Carl's posture. If not for fear of breaking professional protocol—or worse, exposing the deepening feelings toward him that she still wrestled with—she'd wrap him in her arms and promise everything would be all right.

She inclined her head toward Alton as a signal for him to take over the discussion.

He obliged. "Transitional housing is only one of many programs Rae currently oversees, and it takes up quite a bit of time that could otherwise be spent furthering development of other areas of our ministry. For that reason, and after much deliberation, I have recommended to the board that we add a new staff position, Director of Transitional Housing."

Carl glanced up, his expression a mixture of doubt and curiosity. "That's in the budget?"

"It will be, what with a sizable grant we've recently been awarded. As I was saying about the position," Alton continued, "this person would administer all aspects of the program—client evaluation, home assignments, counseling and personal development, job training, all the way through graduation and follow-up. A position of this magnitude requires someone with knowledge, experience, and insight."

"And because I'm a relative newcomer to this organization," Rae interjected, "those are areas in which I'm lacking."

Alton cast her a benevolent smile before returning his attention to Carl. "The position would come with a significant increase over what you're currently earning, and would include a private office here in the ministry building." He slid an envelope across the table. "This contains a detailed outline of the terms, responsibilities, and benefits the board has tentatively agreed to for this new position. With their final approval—which I fully expect will be granted at the next meeting—all we will need is your signature on a new employment contract."

Brow furrowed, Carl cocked his head. "You're offering *me* the job?"

"It was designed with you alone in mind." Alton nudged the envelope closer.

Carl stared at it long and hard before gingerly picking it up. Eyes lowered, he tapped it against the edge of the table. "This is a lot to process."

"Of course." Alton pushed back his chair and stood.

"Take as long as necessary to think it over . . . but not too long," he added with a wink. "We need you, Carl. There's no one better equipped to take on this role—this *mission*."

With a distracted nod, Carl rose slowly and accepted Alton's handshake. Rae stood and extended her hand as well. After a few tense moments, he finally took it. She didn't dare let herself dwell on the warmth of his palm against hers. Not now. Not with so much at stake for them both.

When he strode out, she expelled the breath she'd been holding. She followed Alton across the room to his desk. "You've known him much longer than I have. Should we be worried?"

"I've learned worry is a waste of spiritual energy." He sank into his high-backed leather chair. "Either we trust God for our highest good, or we don't."

"Our highest good . . ." Rae repeated softly. "I like the sound of that."

"It's all God ever wants for us, if only we'll submit to His will for our lives and not insist on our own way." Alton looked toward the window, his expression filled with bittersweet longing. Rae could only assume he was thinking about his beloved wife.

She edged closer. "How is Mrs. Isaacs doing, sir?"

"Thank you for asking. A bit better this week, though I expect it won't last."

"But you still trust God." It was more a question than a statement.

"What else can I do?" He cast her a sad smile. "'Though he slay me, yet will I hope in him.'"

"From the Bible?"

"Yes, the words of Job."

She dropped into a visitor chair across from him. "Sir, I have a confession to make. I . . . I lied on my résumé."

His brows shot up, but not in an accusatory way. Then he laughed. "I believe I know what you're going to say. I've suspected it since the day you came for your final interview."

It was her turn to show surprise. "Then why did you hire me?"

"Because I trust the Holy Spirit's guidance. I sensed deep down that God had a plan for you here—not only because of what you could achieve as our program director, but because of how working here could change *your* life." Lips curling into a smile, he tilted his head. "I wasn't wrong about that second part, was I?"

A pleasant shiver rippled through her. "No, sir, you were not."

"And I am definitely not wrong about the first part. You are a welcome addition to our staff, Rae. Which is why I'm counting on your help to encourage Carl to make the right decision."

"I'll do my best." If he'd even give her a chance after the many times she'd pushed him away. "I still can't get over how you convinced the board to consider creating the new position. How can you be sure they won't change their minds and vote it down next week?"

"Because I have faith in their good sense. You've caught the general tenor at recent meetings. The majority lean toward keeping the transitional housing program. How can they argue with a more direct and focused way of managing it?"

The idea made perfect sense to Rae, and she certainly wouldn't object to having some of her workload lifted. Her heart beat a little faster at the possibility of working only a few doors down from Carl every day—and with him as her equal rather than subordinate. It would give her one less reason for holding him at arm's length, especially since, more and more often, she'd begun to imagine herself wrapped securely in those strong, solid arms.

Carl returned to Hope House in a daze. *Director of Transitional Housing?* Could he handle a real desk job in a real office and a forty-hour work week? Or would he miss the 24/7 interaction with his residents, getting to know them, counseling them, becoming a significant and ongoing part of their lives?

On the other hand, a management position opened up a whole new world of opportunities. Starting from day one, he could provide direct input into *every* aspect of their clients' rehabilitation. Plus he'd have a seat, if not a vote, at every board meeting, where he could address matters face-to-face before any given situation threatened the viability of the program.

Seated outside on the deck, Carl mulled over the possibilities while Cocoa and Zippy play-wrestled in the backyard. He'd barely taken two bites of the ham sand-wich he'd slapped together for lunch. The plate sat on the patio table next to the soft drink can he had yet to pop open.

The dogs drew his attention when their heads shot up and they raced to the side gate. Their tails were going a mile a minute, which suggested whoever was on the other side wasn't a stranger.

Then Rae appeared, a hesitant smile turning up her lips. "May we come in?"

"Uh, sure." Carl stood and ambled down the deck steps.

Once Rae got the gate open, Cocoa and Zippy went wild. The reason for their excitement became clear when Frankie trotted through the opening. As soon as Rae unclipped Frankie's leash, all three dogs took off playing chase around the yard.

Rae set her hands on her hips and laughed. It was a musical sound Carl had rarely heard her utter. "Look how much they missed each other."

I missed you, too, he wanted to say, even though he'd seen her less than two hours ago. Pulse thrumming, he tried to keep his voice level. "Did you come over for an impromptu playdate?"

"Not exactly. I went home on my lunch hour to let Frankie out for a bit and then decided we'd just hop in the car and drive over." Chin lowered slightly, she slid her gaze to him. "The truth is, I've been a little worried about you since our meeting."

"Yeah, that." He scraped one hand across the back of his neck. "It's all I've been able to think about."

She gestured toward the deck. "We could sit down and talk more if you want. I can try to answer any questions you've come up with."

One eye narrowed, he asked, "Are you sure Mr. Isaacs didn't send you over to butter me up?"

"I won't deny he asked me to offer gentle encouragement. Which I would anyway," she tossed over her shoulder as she strode passed him and up the deck steps. "Oh, looks like I interrupted your lunch."

By the time he caught up with her, he was breathing heavily, but it had less to do with climbing stairs than Rae's unexpected arrival. "I discovered I wasn't all that hungry."

"Difficult decisions do have a way of stealing your appetite." Lips pulled between her teeth, she lowered herself into a chair, then added softly, "I've had a bit of experience with that, myself."

Her statement piqued his curiosity. He positioned his chair to face hers and sat. "Recently?"

"More like ongoing." She glanced away for a moment, every trace of lightness vanishing. "But I didn't come over to burden you with my issues."

"I wish you would." He longed to reach for her but instead leaned forward, hands folded. "I'd like to help."

"I doubt you can, but thank you." She straightened, her typical stiff smile back in place. "What questions can I answer for you about the new position?"

"I don't care about that, Rae. I mean, of course I do. But I care about you more." This time he did take her hands, first one, then the other. When she tried to pull away, he held on steadily until her fingers relaxed into his. He drew the knuckles of each hand to his lips and gently kissed them. "I care about you more than you can imagine."

"Carl . . ." She shook her head slowly as a tear traced its way down her cheek. "I'm not—I can't—"

"No more excuses, Rae. You've given me a million reasons not to, but no matter how many times you push me away, I can't stop myself. I'm falling hard for you, and I'm not giving up."

"Why?" The word came out on a tremulous exhalation.

He could only laugh. "Why do I love you? That's like asking why the sun rises every day, why the stars come out at night."

"I'm serious, Carl. There is not one lovable thing about me." She jerked one hand free and swiped at the growing flood of tears. "Even my own family can't stand me anymore."

Narrowing one eye, he studied her as pieces began falling into place. "That's the real reason you came to see me the day I found Glen with the beer. You needed to talk about something that afternoon, but with everything exploding like it did, you never got the chance. Tell me now, Rae. Please, tell me now."

Rae didn't know where to begin. "It's true, I did come that day in need of a shoulder to lean on. But when I discovered what you were dealing with, my family squabbles seemed trivial in comparison."

He clung to the hand he still held, his earnest gaze persuasive. "Did something happen?"

Her voice shaking, she told him about returning home after the Saturday dog class to find her brother sleeping off a drunk in the travel trailer, then the ugly scene that followed. She described what a wreck she'd been over the weekend, and how by Sunday afternoon, she'd realized how desperately she needed the friendship Maddie offered. "But when I couldn't reach her, that's when I decided to come over here."

"Aw, Rae, if only things hadn't gone haywire that day."

"You couldn't help what happened. Anyway, I did finally connect with Maddie. We had lunch and talked, and I shed a whole bunch of tears." She paused for a sniffle. "And she prayed with me."

Carl's smile warmed. "I thought I sensed something had changed for you. Changed for the better."

"It's a day-to-day process." She freed her other hand

and fumbled through her purse for some tissues. After blowing her nose, she sat a little straighter and took a shuddering breath. "Which is why I need you to be patient with me, because I—" Digging deep, she sought the courage to speak the words aloud, though she barely squeaked out a whisper. "I think I'm falling in love with you, too."

Carl sat silent, motionless, as if he wasn't sure he'd actually heard her.

Without warning, Frankie tore up the deck steps with Cocoa and Zippy in hot pursuit, all of them yipping and racing madly around the table where Rae and Carl were sitting. They both burst out in surprised laughter.

"Hey, you guys!" Carl got up and shooed the dogs down to the lawn. "Your timing stinks."

The dogs' rowdy diversion had given Rae time to summon a measure of composure. She smothered a giggle as Carl returned to his chair. "I always believed Kellie's little service dog was a mind reader, but Frankie takes it to a whole new level."

"Why?" Carl asked with a grumble. "Because he knew exactly the moment to distract me from pulling you into my arms and asking if I could kiss you?"

Rae blinked. "Th-that's what you were thinking?"

His smile mellowed. His eyes darkened. "I've hardly *not* thought about kissing you since practically the first time I saw you."

Heart racing, she pulled her lower lip between her teeth. "Even as awful as I've been to you?"

"The stiff, starchy persona you wear isn't the real you." He scooted closer, taking her hands once again and holding her with his gaze. "I see you, Rae. I see the woman you are deep inside, the sensitive, compassionate woman you seem so afraid of exposing to the world. That's the woman I'm falling for, more and more every day."

Throat constricted with swallowed tears, she looked away. "I'm not sure I can remember that person . . . if she ever even existed."

"Of course she exists. She's a conscientious career woman dedicated to doing the very best job for the organization she works for. She's a mentor and counselor for her needy siblings. She's a grieving mother who'd give anything to have her child back."

A sob broke free, and she gave a loud sniff.

"The Rae Caldwell I know is a woman with a huge heart and a whole lot of love just waiting to be shared." Carl edged closer still, until she could feel the warmth of his breath against her cheek. "And she's sitting right here with the man who wants more than anything to love her back with every ounce of his being."

Eyes closed, she tried simply to focus on breathing in, breathing out. She'd come over intending only to urge Carl to accept the new position Alton had offered. She'd never anticipated *this.* "I'm scared," she murmured. "My relationship track record is pretty grim."

"I'm scared, too. Mainly because my romance track record is basically nonexistent." His lips grazed her cheek, and she shivered. "But I thought—I'm *hoping*—we can figure this out together."

Every nerve in her body sang. It almost surprised her that Carl didn't seem to hear the melody. Pulse thrumming, she turned her head slightly, her lips seeking his. It seemed like untold eons since she'd felt a man's tender kiss. She hadn't realized how much she'd missed it until he pressed her face between his palms and gently lowered his mouth to hers.

The deck beneath her, the dogs play-wrestling in the yard, the drone of someone's lawnmower nearby . . . it all faded into nothingness. Nothing except this moment, this man, this kiss that she would remember the rest of her days.

A sound intruded, too insistent to ignore—her cell phone jangling from inside her purse. She groaned as Carl ended the kiss and eased away.

Smiling tenderly, he tucked a strand of hair behind her ear. "Do you need to get that?"

It was the last thing she wanted to do. "It's my sister's ringtone. I'm not exactly in the mood to talk right now."

"Maybe you should, though. It might be one of those bridges in need of repair before we can get on with *us*."

"Bridges?" She cast him a puzzled look.

"Something Ellis and I were talking about the other day. About how you and I both need to deal with the pieces of our pasts—and presents—that hold us back from love."

The ringing stopped, and Rae let slip a sigh of relief. Seconds later, the voicemail chime sounded. She couldn't scrape up the emotional energy to listen quite yet. Head bowed, she told Carl, "I know you're right in every way. Much as I want this—want *us*," she stated, grasping his hands, "I won't be ready until I set things straight with my family."

"If there's any way I can help . . ."

"You already have, by compelling me to be honest about my true feelings. Now," she said, standing on legs that felt a little wobbly, "it's time I rose to that same level of honesty with my mother and siblings."

Carl rose with a worried frown. "What are you going to do?"

"Don't worry, my head's in a much better place since the last time I spoke with any of my family." Gathering up her purse and Frankie's leash, she called to the dog, who met her at the bottom of the deck steps and sat obediently at her feet.

Giving a snort, Carl came up beside them. "That dog adores you almost more than I do."

"Guess we were meant for each other all along." She wiggled her brows at Carl before bending to snap on Frankie's leash. "Now I really should go—"

"Not quite yet." Trapping Frankie between them, he reached across to slide his hand beneath her ear. With his other hand supporting her back, he held her steady for another long, meaningful kiss that left her breathless. When they broke apart, he grinned. "I didn't want you leaving with any doubts about who *really* loves you more."

She sighed. "Message received, loud and clear."

Frankie punctuated her reply with a happy bark.

Chapter Twenty-Eight

Since she'd used her lunch hour to see Carl, Rae dropped Frankie back at home, then picked up a salad on her way to the office. She ate at her desk while catching up on a few emails, but getting her brain back into work mode proved problematic, no thanks— actually, all kinds of thanks –to the memory of Carl's kiss. Her lips hadn't stopped tingling, and her pulse sped up just thinking about the man who was rapidly dismantling the walls she'd erected around her heart.

Her recent conversations with both Maddie and Carl had only deepened her conviction that before she could truly move on, she needed to make peace with her family. How, though, after she'd so gracelessly cut them out of her life? Sybil's voicemail, which Rae had finally worked up the nerve to listen to, left no doubt as to her sister's feelings.

"You've broken Mom's heart," Sybil ranted during her minutes-long diatribe. "You have no idea how hard it's been for her since Dad died, and for you to snub her like this? It's just cruel! And let's not even talk about how merciless you've been toward Reece, when you know firsthand what it's like to lose a child—"

At that, Rae pushed the delete button and laid down her phone. Taking a few shuddering breaths, she swiveled toward the window and begged God to ease the constant ache in her chest that Kellie's death had left behind. She felt deeply for Heather and Reece and wished she could reach out, but her brother's abrupt departure after his visit last week had curtailed her hopes of reconciliation. Instead, she'd sent flowers along with a heartfelt note of sympathy.

Neither Heather nor Reece had yet responded, which wasn't surprising. Perhaps with the passage of time . . .

A sudden urge to hear Mark's voice overcame her. Before she could think of a logical reason not to call her ex-husband, she snatched up the phone.

He answered on the second ring. "Rae? You okay?"

"Yes—no—" She gulped down the lump in her throat. "I, um, I was thinking about Kellie, and I . . ."

"I know," he said gently. "I think about her every single day." When she couldn't form the words to reply, he went on, "Did something happen that brought this all up again?"

Sniffling hard, she grabbed a tissue from the box on the credenza. "Oh, so many things," she managed with a sad laugh. "And not all of them bad, although I've certainly made plenty of mistakes."

"Tell me—if you want to, that is. I've turned into a pretty good listener."

When had she forgotten how tender and caring Mark Caldwell could be? She loved him still, though not in the same way. "It's a long, complicated story. Are you sure you have time?"

"I'm sitting here in my truck drinking coffee and doing

paperwork while my crew finishes cleaning up a job site. I'm all ears."

Half an hour later, she'd told him all about her new job with Equipped and Empowered Ministries, meeting Carl and getting off on the wrong foot, Carl's brother's arrival in town, the confrontations that followed with her mother and siblings, Reece and Heather losing their baby . . .

"I handled everything badly," she confessed. "But in the midst of it all—and maybe *because* of it all—I'm finding my way back to God."

"You don't know how happy that makes me." A tremor came into Mark's tone. "I've been praying hard for you."

"Thank you. It means a lot to know how much you still care." She dabbed her eyes, then said shyly, "I have some other news, too."

"Let me guess. You and Carl?"

Her feelings bubbled over then, and while she told Mark all about Carl and how their up-and-down—and now very much *up*—relationship had developed, she had to smile. Mark was no longer merely her former husband and Kellie's dad. He'd become a true friend. Wherever their separate lives took them, she would forever be grateful for the years they'd spent together and the lessons God had taught them through their trials.

The call drew to a close with each of them promising to keep in touch, to which Mark added, "And if there should be a wedding in your future, Holly and I expect an invitation."

Heat raced up Rae's cheeks. "Let's not get ahead of ourselves. This is all still too new, and Carl and I both need to clean up a few more things in our personal lives."

"Then I'll be praying for God's grace to resolve those issues in the best possible way for all involved."

Mark's parting words renewed hope that her family rift could someday heal. Feeling more at peace, she returned her focus to work responsibilities.

By the end of the day, she'd dealt with the most pressing tasks on her agenda, while in the back of her mind, ideas had been forming about how to convene a family conference. If she extended the summons, would her mother or siblings deign to attend?

It was worth a try.

"I've got to tell somebody or I'll explode."

"Sounds serious," Witt replied. Carl had caught his friend as he was finishing up a handyman appointment. "I'm done for the day, but I'm out on Mullan Road west of Frenchtown. Can we meet up at the Smith Family café?"

Twenty minutes later, Carl parked next to Witt's little white pickup. The place wasn't too busy this time of the afternoon, and he quickly found Witt on the dog-friendly al fresco dining porch. Tongue wagging, Ranger sat up and offered his paw as Carl approached.

"Took the liberty of ordering coffee and apple pie à la mode for both of us," Witt said as Carl pulled out a chair. "I've been working on a bathroom remodel the last couple of days, so I've built up quite an appetite."

"Sounds good. I just hope I can settle down enough to enjoy it."

"You did seem kinda keyed up on the phone earlier. Ready to fill me in?"

Carl took a gulp from the water glass at his place, then scraped his palms across the legs of his khakis. "I've been offered a promotion. I think I'm going to accept."

While they waited for their pie and coffee, he gave Witt an abridged version of his meeting with Alton Isaacs and Rae that morning. By the time he finished, a grin had spread across Witt's face.

"I realize it'll mean a huge change for you," Witt said. "But my heart's telling me it's exactly what the Lord's been preparing you for."

Seeing a server striding over with their order, Carl held his reply until she'd left. "I'm getting that feeling, too," he mused as he spread a napkin across his knee. Meeting Witt's gaze, he went on, "But it helps to hear it from the friend whose counsel I've come to trust and rely on."

Witt dipped his chin. "The feeling's mutual. If not for you and all the support and advice you gave me during my time at Hope House, I wouldn't be where I am today. Which is why I'm doubly sure you're the right one to steer the transitional housing program into new and even more promising directions."

While they paused to take a few bites of pie, Carl's thoughts drifted to everything the position would entail. "If I do this, my first order of business would be to appoint my replacement at Hope House. That makes me nervous."

"No doubt." Witt's lips skewed in thought before he took a sip of coffee. "Any ideas?"

"As a matter of fact, I was thinking about Jordy. He's become my right-hand man over the past few months. Whatever's going on, good or bad, I always know I can depend on him."

"I like him. And he's about ready to graduate, isn't he? That could be a win-win solution for him and the ministry."

"Naturally, hiring him would need approval from the board of directors." Carl was warming to the idea more and more. "But I think I could convince them, especially since I'd back him up while he gets the necessary training."

"That sounds like a plan Mr. Isaacs and Rae would support, too."

"Speaking of Rae . . ." Carl didn't even try to keep the silly grin from creeping into his expression.

"You kissed her, didn't you?" Witt slapped the table, rattling their coffee mugs and startling Ranger from his nap. "All I can say is, it's about time."

"Hey, keep it down, okay?" Casting an uneasy glance toward diners at a nearby table, Carl winced.

Witt chuckled and lowered his voice. "Sorry, but I'm just real happy for you."

"I'm happy, too. Happier than I've ever been in my life." He shook his head in disbelief. "I'm in love with her, Witt. So crazy, wildly, head-over-heels in love that I feel like I could burst."

"You're so smart," Rae said that evening as Frankie snuggled next to her on the sofa. "How would *you* handle my family?"

He sat up and slathered her cheek with his wet tongue, then looked at her expectantly with those startling blue eyes.

"I should have known—kisses and treats." Rae laughed and scratched him behind both ears. "Although you could be onto something. It's time I let my mom and siblings know how much I love them." An idea was already taking shape. "I can start by making their favorite family meal."

Too bad she wasn't nearly the cook her mother was, but perhaps that could work in her favor. Marshaling her nerve, she mentally rehearsed her approach, then picked up the phone.

"I see you finally took me off your do-not-call list," Mom answered brusquely. "To what do I owe this dubious honor?"

"Hi, Mom," Rae said as meekly as she could. "You have every right to be cross with me, and I'm sorry. I really want to set things right."

"Humph. About time."

She hadn't expected this would be easy. *Lord, please give me the right words.* "Remember when we were kids, and someone would be having a bad day, and you'd cheer us all up with your homemade chicken pot pie?"

Mom grew silent for a moment. "You kids loved my chicken pot pie." She sniffed. "Your daddy did, too."

"It's still my very favorite comfort food, and nobody can top yours."

Suspicion returning to her tone, Mom asked, "What are you buttering me up for?"

Rae quelled a spontaneous surge of irritation. "Like I told you, Mom, I want things to be better between us. With my brothers and sisters, too."

"Well, of course. We all want that."

"So I was hoping you'd help me arrange a family dinner, the kind we used to have when we were all together at home. I'd like to use it as an opportunity to apologize to everyone, to explain what I personally have been going through, and hopefully move toward the closeness we used to have before . . . well, before everything went so bad."

Silence stretched between them until her mother finally spoke. "Well, I . . . I suppose I could help. When were you thinking?"

"How about Saturday evening? And would you mind

hosting? Because I doubt the kids would accept if I invited them."

Mom scoffed. "Probably not."

"And I'll do the grocery shopping, help with prep and cleanup, whatever you need me to do."

"All right, Saturday evening. I'll text you a shopping list, and then I'll call the kids here in town. Too bad Leo's living in Portland, or I'd invite him, too."

"Maybe we can have him join us on Zoom." It would be good to have all her siblings present in one way or another, because there was so much she wanted them to know and understand. "And maybe you shouldn't mention this was my idea—or that I'm coming at all."

"Don't worry. I get the picture."

After ending the call, Rae breathed a quiet sigh. No matter what the outcome, she'd have to rest in the fact that she'd done her part to make amends. As God was working to change her heart, she could only trust Him to do the same with her mother and siblings, and in His perfect timing.

A snippet from the song "Who Let the Dogs Out" sounded from her phone. It was the ringtone she'd recently assigned to Carl. Grinning, she snapped up the phone, then answered shyly, "Hi."

"Hi, yourself. I've been missing you all afternoon."

"I've missed you, too." She felt like a teenager talking to her first crush.

"I think I've decided to accept the job offer. It feels right."

"Oh, Carl, I'm thrilled. This is going to turn out for the best, I just know it."

He laughed softly. "You're not just saying that because you won't be my direct supervisor anymore, are you?"

"Well, that's definitely a side benefit." Frankie laid his head on her lap, and she absently stroked his fur. "Also, I could really use your prayers about something." She described the plans she was making with her mother.

"I think that's a great idea." Carl's tone mellowed. "Of course I'll be praying. I wish I could be there to support you."

"You'll be there in spirit, and that will give me courage."

"In case you didn't get the message earlier, I love you."

Her throat closed. She touched a finger to her lips before murmuring, "I love you, too."

Saturday arrived much sooner than Rae was ready for. Though work helped to distract her during the day, each evening since Wednesday—and more than one sleepless night—had been spent imagining how the dinner might go, what she would say, how her siblings would respond.

And praying. She hadn't prayed so much or so fervently since the last months of Kellie's life.

She'd learned a lot since then, most of it the hard way. Above all, she was learning to believe again that God loved her and would sustain her no matter how difficult the struggle or how painful the heartache.

When she arrived at her mother's duplex on Saturday afternoon, Mom put her to work dicing carrots, chopping onions, and shredding the precooked chicken breasts that had been marinated in a special mix of savory spices. In the meantime, Mom prepared pie crusts—regular for most of the family, gluten-free for Deena and Dawn.

By shortly after four thirty, the pie crusts were filled and in the oven. Mom asked Rae to set out the good china and silverware upon the lace-trimmed tablecloth Rae's parents had received as a wedding gift and used only on holidays and special occasions. Rae could still pick out the faded spots where one or the other of the kids had dribbled gravy or cranberry sauce.

"Gathering my children together for a family meal again," Mom said as she surveyed the table, "certainly qualifies as a special occasion."

Rae drew her mother into a hug. "Thank you for doing this, Mom. I love you."

As she stepped back, tears sprang into her mother's eyes. Mom sniffed and hurriedly swiped them away. "My gracious, I can't recall the last time I heard those words from you."

The truth stabbed Rae's heart. "Oh, Mom, I do love you, and I'm sorry for . . . for a million things. That's why this dinner is important to me, because I want to apologize in person to you and each of my brothers and sisters."

Her mother studied her as if she couldn't quite make sense of the change in her daughter. She straightened and cleared her throat. "All right, then. I think I just heard Reece's car out front." On her way to the door, she muttered, "Why he refuses to get that muffler fixed, I will never know."

Rae retreated to the kitchen so as not to be seen right away. When she heard Heather's voice, she peeked around the corner. If Reece and his wife had come together, it meant they must be working things out—a promising sign.

Mom drew Heather into her arms. "How are you, honey?"

"Taking it one day at a time." Heather offered a weak shrug, then glanced up at Reece with a smile. "We're doing our best to be there for each other."

Before Rae could duck out of sight, Reece glanced toward the kitchen. The stern look on his face as he strode toward her froze her to the spot. "I wasn't sure you'd be here, too," he said. "But I'm glad you are."

She forced a nervous swallow. "Really?"

His expression softened. "Really. Your tough love is the reason Heather and I are back together. We're getting marriage counseling—grief counseling, too—and things are slowly getting better."

"Oh, Reece, that's wonderful. I've prayed for you both."

"Yeah, that prayer thing. I figure it's worth a try, so I let Heather talk me into going to church with her again."

Before Rae could voice her delight, Sybil and the twins arrived. They weren't nearly as pleased about her presence as Reece and Heather seemed, but Mom shushed their grousing and insisted on their best behavior. She put them to work getting the meal on the table while Rae set up her laptop for the Zoom call with Leo.

When Leo appeared onscreen, he grinned into the camera. "Wow, are you really all there at the same time? Makes me wish I could have made the trip."

"Hey, bro," Sybil said on her way over with a pie. She leaned in for a closer look at the screen. "You need a haircut."

"And you need to get a life," he snapped back with a snort.

Mom set another pie on the table, the delicious aroma filling the kitchen. "Enough, you two. Take your seats."

After everyone had scooted up to the table, Mom took Rae's hand on her right and Reece's on her left. She opened her mouth to speak, only to release a small choking sound. She nodded to Rae to take over.

Tears threatening, Rae almost couldn't push words past her lips. "How about we start with a table blessing?"

Chapter Twenty-Nine

Ever since Carl learned about Rae's plans to talk things out with her family, he'd been praying nonstop. So much depended on the outcome—for Rae's sake, and for his. Because if left unresolved, those lingering issues would continue to claim a chunk of Rae's heart.

And he wanted *all* of her heart, not merely the leftovers.

"Carl? You with me?" Jordy waved a hand in front of Carl's face.

"Yeah. Sorry." For a minute there, he'd forgotten where he was. While the other guys cleaned up the kitchen after supper, Carl had asked Jordy to join him in the study. "Have a seat. I want to talk to you about something."

"Sounds serious."

"It is, but in a good way." Carl settled into the easy chair across from Jordy on the sofa. "Guess you can tell I've been kind of preoccupied lately."

"We've all noticed. I hope you're about to tell me what's

going on so I can dispel a few rumors." With a soft chuckle, Jordy added, "And believe me, they've run the gamut."

"I don't doubt it." Carl sat forward and rested his elbows on his knees. "Before I say anything to the other guys, I want to tell you personally what's going on—and for reasons you'll understand after I explain, some of this needs to remain between us."

Jordy matched Carl's posture. "I'm listening."

"It's no secret that for several months now, the transitional housing program has been under intense scrutiny by the board of directors." At Jordy's nod, he went on, "What the other guys don't need to know is how perilously close the board came to shutting down the program completely."

"Because of Glen, I expect." One hand slapping the sofa arm, Jordy sat back with a huff. "These past two years have been a lifeline for me. I don't know where I'd be today without Hope House."

"It's okay—the program isn't going away. But there will be some changes around here." Inhaling deeply, Carl straightened. "Mr. Isaacs offered me a new position, which I've accepted. I'll be overseeing E and E's entire transitional housing program with the goal of evaluating and refining our practices to make the program even more effective."

Jordy's jaw dropped. "Wow. I guess I'm happy for you, but . . . does that mean you're leaving Hope House?"

"I'm afraid so. But I already have my replacement in mind." Carl allowed a grin to spread across his lips. "And I think you'd be a real asset."

Clearly not catching on, Jordy narrowed one eye. "Sure, I'd be glad to help the new guy settle in. But you know I'll be moving out in a few weeks. Already got my eye on an efficiency apartment in a nice little old lady's basement."

"What if you didn't have to move out?" Carl's grin

widened. "What if you could stay right here at Hope House and continue imparting your wisdom, guidance, and encouragement to the guys—and after they graduate, the new ones who'll eventually come along?"

Jordy's expression grew more puzzled with every word. Shaking his head slowly, he said, "I thought the whole point of me living here was to set me up for making it on my own at the end of my two years."

"It is, and that's exactly what you'll be doing." Carl leaned closer. "But as Hope House's new counselor-in-residence."

Jordy blinked several times. "M-me? You're kidding, right? I'm not trained for anything like this."

"Not yet, maybe, but we'll work on that. In the meantime, you know the routine, and you have the necessary skill sets." Carl had spent the past couple of days digging deeper into Jordy's background. Twelve years ago, he'd been a parttime church pastor while teaching religion classes at an exclusive private school. When he'd failed a student for cheating, the overprotective parents pulled strings to have him fired and then sullied his reputation so badly that no other school would hire him. Thus began his descent into depression, alcoholism, and eventual homelessness.

"Jordy, I mean it." Carl shifted over to the sofa and gripped the man's shoulder. "You're the ideal candidate for the job. Alton Isaacs presented the idea at a special meeting of the board of directors yesterday, and they gave their okay."

It took some convincing and an extra measure of reassurance as Carl methodically listed all the attributes in Jordy's favor, plus the many ways Carl, in his new role, could advise and assist him. E and E would also cover Jordy's enrollment in one or two college classes each semester in counseling, psychology, and other relevant subjects.

Jordy pinched the bridge of his nose and sniffed hard, his shoulder trembling slightly beneath Carl's hand. "I don't know what to say."

"It's easy. Just open your mouth and say yes."

Instead, the man twisted around to seize Carl in a bear hug. "Thank you. Thank you for believing in me. I promise, I'll do my best to make you proud."

"Too late—I'm already proud of you." Carl gave Jordy's back a few hearty thumps before easing away to look him in the eye. "What do you say? Should we go introduce the guys to their soon-to-be new counselor and house manager?"

Jordy laughed through his tears. "All righty, let's do it."

Shortly, with the other men boisterously expressing their approval and mobbing Jordy to bestow congratulatory hugs, Carl slipped away and returned to the study. Things hadn't felt so *right* in a long time, so he spent a few moments with hands folded and eyes lifted to praise God for all He'd done to bring this about.

Excited to call Rae, he picked up the phone, then laid it back down. If her family dinner was going as hoped—or worse, if it wasn't—he shouldn't interrupt. *Please, Lord, soften the hearts of Rae's mother and siblings, just like You did for Ellis and me. You've brought us this far, and I'm trusting the future—our future together—to You.*

Dawn frowned at Rae across the table. "You mean say grace?"

"I do," she answered with a nod. "I realize most of us

have kind of forgotten the habit, but I think it's a good habit, one worth reviving. Do you remember the little song Daddy taught us when we were kids?"

"Oh, yeah, the Johnny Appleseed prayer." Reece furrowed his brow. "I think I still know the words, but you know I can't carry a tune in a bucket."

"Allow me," Leo said from the computer. With a dramatic clear of his throat, he began the song, and soon the others joined in, weakly at first but then with more gusto:

Ohhhhhhhh...
the Lord is good to me.
And, so I thank the Lord,
for giving me the things I need:
the sun and the rain
and the appleseed.
The Lord is good to me.

At the raucous *Amen!* Rae's sisters broke out in self-conscious giggles. "Wow, it's been a minute," Dawn remarked. "Can't believe we still remembered it."

By then, Mom had composed herself. She whispered to Rae, "Let's have dinner while everybody's in a good mood. Afterward, you can have your say."

Forty-five minutes later, with the dishes cleared and the family back at the table with aromatic mugs of hazelnut decaf, Leo spoke from the laptop. "I don't know about the rest of you, but I'm ready to hear from Rae exactly why she called this family meeting."

Sybil angled a look in Rae's direction. "This was *your* idea? I was beginning to wonder."

"Yes, it was my idea." Edging her chair back slightly, she gathered her courage as she looked from her mother to each of her siblings in turn. "This codependent family dynamic we've devolved into isn't healthy."

Deena rolled her eyes. "Enough with the psychobabble already."

"Maybe we should just listen," Heather said, lightly touching Deena's arm.

Rae cast her sister-in-law a smile of gratitude. "What I'm trying to say," she continued, "is that I need things to change. For most of my life, I've tried to be the best big sister I could be—a confidant, a friend in need, an escape plan when the going gets rough. But lately I've gone from one extreme to the other—either all in with a bailout or dishing out lectures before slamming the door in your face."

Murmurs of agreement sounded around the table. Mom tapped her coffee cup with her spoon. "Go on, honey."

"The thing is, as much as I love each one of you, I can't be your rescuer anymore. It's unhelpful for you and emotionally exhausting for me." She paused to note the downward glances and guilty-as-charged looks forming on each face. "I truly regret how badly I've handled this, how bossy or rude or uncaring I may have come across. But I want you to know I'm working on myself, my attitude, my . . . faith."

A thoughtful silence followed. Then from the laptop came Leo's slow applause. "About time, lady. I mean that in the kindest and most heartfelt way. I know I did my fair share of abusing your generosity, but it's because you held my feet to the fire that I now have a good job and actually learned how to balance my checkbook."

Muted laughter circled the table, and one by one, the other siblings muttered apologies for how they'd taken advantage and thanked Rae for the many ways she'd offered help.

Finally, her mother did the same. "How it came to this is more my fault than yours," Mom said as she flicked away a tear. "You were the oldest, and with five other kids to chase after, I depended on you way too much."

Reece took his wife's hand. "It's time for all of us to grow up and learn to stand on our own two feet."

It seemed too good to be true, that her family had actually listened and understood. "I'll still be here for you," she said. "I *want* to be here for you. But with healthy boundaries and—"

"There she goes with the psychobabble again." This time, Deena said it with a teasing grin. "We get it, Rae. So can we be done with the serious talk now? How about a game of Spoons?"

"No fair!" Leo bellowed. "I wanna play, too!"

All Rae could do was smile and silently thank God.

And also make sure to protect her hands from overzealous spoon-grabbers!

It was nearing 11:00 p.m. when Carl's phone rang. On a normal Saturday night, he'd have been sacked out by now, but as intense as the past few days had been, and with so many changes in store, he was too keyed up for sleep.

He tossed aside the C.S. Lewis book he'd been attempting to distract himself with and grabbed the phone off his nightstand. Seeing Rae's name on the display, he stabbed the answer icon. "Hi."

"Hi. Did I wake you?"

"Nope. I was hoping you'd call." He squeezed his eyes shut. "How did it go?"

A contented sigh whispered through the phone. "Good. Really good."

He pumped a fist. *Thank You, Lord!*

"I know things won't get magically better overnight," Rae continued, sounding wistful, "but at least we're all talking now. For the first time in a long time, I felt seen and heard."

"I'm glad for you, Rae. I wish I was there holding you right now."

Her voice softened. "Me, too."

"I could—"

"No. It's late, and I'm wiped out. Let's both try to get some sleep. But tomorrow . . ." she began haltingly. "I was thinking about visiting Witt and Maddie's church. Any chance you'd meet me there?"

"Nothing could keep me away."

They said their goodbyes, and with the sweet combination of gratitude and relief, Carl was finally able to shut down his busy brain and drift off.

At breakfast Sunday morning, when he mentioned he'd be worshiping at Elk Valley Community of Faith, Jordy and two other guys asked about tagging along. He couldn't exactly say no, but he suggested they take separate vehicles. He really hoped to spend some time alone with Rae, maybe take her for a nice lunch and then drive into the mountains and park somewhere with a great view.

Right, like he'd be looking anywhere but at her.

Arriving at the church, he spied a vacant parking spot next to Rae's red Mazda and pulled in next to it. As he came around the building, he caught sight of her walking Frankie on the front lawn. He could only shake his head and laugh.

"What's so funny?" she said with a smirk. "Lots of people bring their dogs to church here. Maddie told me Witt and Ranger started a trend."

"That much is true. But until the last few days, I never would have imagined that you'd be one of them." He chuckled again before leaning in for a quick kiss.

She resisted only slightly, her gaze darting toward the church doors as other worshipers arrived. Cheeks pink, she dipped her chin. "How about we don't make a spectacle of ourselves?"

A glance over his shoulder told him that ship had sailed. Pastor Peters, Witt and Maddie, Ellis, and the guys from Hope House all stood on the front steps and looked their way with mile-wide grins.

"Guess our secret's out." He tucked a strand of hair behind Rae's ear and liked the way she shivered at his touch. "Actually, I don't think it was ever much of a secret. Seems our feelings were obvious to everyone but us."

"I think you're right." Those smiling blue eyes locked with his.

He wiggled his brows and moved nearer. "Want to give them something *really* worth watching?"

She gave a nervous laugh. "Um . . . okay."

Cradling her head with one hand, he slid his other arm around her waist. Holding her so close that he could feel her heart thumping in time to his own, he lowered his lips to hers and savored a long, slow kiss that left him aching for more.

Breathless as they parted, he became aware of the worship song drifting from the open church doors. It was "Mercy," one of his favorites, but this time he heard the lyrics with fresh ears, and something between a laugh and a sob escaped. "God in His mercy really has turned my life upside down."

"Mine, too, in the best way imaginable." Rae pressed his face between her hands, gently thumbing away the moisture slipping down his cheeks while blinking back tears of her own. "How silly we've been. How happy we *could* have been all this time."

When Frankie yipped as if in agreement, Carl scoffed. "Always suspected he was smarter than both of us put together."

"Hey, you two—er, three," came Witt's call. "Church is starting. Planning on joining us or not?"

"Be right there," Carl answered with a flick of his hand. "Save us a seat."

Once they were alone, he pulled Rae close again. He wished he could spend the rest of his life in the depths of those beautiful blue eyes.

Rae tilted her head back and arched a brow. "It's my first time back at church in forever, and you're making us late."

"I know. Sorry. One more kiss first?"

"Well, since you insist." With a wink, she added, "It'll have to last me at least an hour, though, so make it a good one."

He did.

Epilogue

Five months later

Five months later

Carl kept one eye on the elevator doors as he paced the waiting area outside the conference room. In more ways than one, his life was about to change. Again. Was he ready for whatever came next?

"Carl. Take a breath and sit down, will you?" Witt patted the chair next to his. "It's gonna be okay."

No longer a volunteer but a paid part-time transitional housing assistant, Witt was now Carl's right-hand man as well as his best friend.

"Good thing I've got you to help me keep it together." Carl stepped around Ranger, stretched out on the floor at Witt's feet, and collapsed onto the chair. If only he could will himself to be as calm and unruffled as the dog.

Seconds later, the elevator chimed. Carl leapt to his feet as Rae breezed toward them, Frankie trotting alongside. Much as with Witt and Ranger, the dog went just about everywhere with her these days. The dogs greeted each other with tail wags and sniffs.

"You're late," Carl said, interlacing his fingers with Rae's. "I was getting worried."

She smirked before brushing his cheek with a light kiss. "You worry too much. Has the meeting started yet?"

"I think so. Kitty told us to wait out here until the board had time to go over their findings."

"I expected as much. But I have every confidence it'll be good news."

Witt stood. "That's what I've been trying to tell him. He's been nervous for nothing."

The conference room door eased open, and Kitty peered out. "The board is ready for you, Carl."

Drawing a shaky breath, he slid a glance toward Rae. "Not sure I'm ready for *them*."

"Oh ye of little faith." Rae clucked her tongue and seized him by the elbow. "Let's go, fella. Time to face the music."

"But what if they're not willing to dance?"

"Then we'll fire the band."

Carl had no idea what either of them was even talking about anymore. Rae's grip was strong, and before he knew it, she'd propelled him through the door.

All eyes turned toward them. It took Carl a moment to register that they were all smiling.

Even Enid Mason, who initiated a patter of applause. "Bravo, Carl. We were just discussing the wonderful job you and Witt have done with the canine program. According to reports from the second trial, it was even more successful than the first. For the next round, how would you feel about expanding to include two more transitional homes?"

"The . . . the *next* round?" Hardly able to push the words out, he could only gape.

Rae discreetly poked him in the side. "I told you there

was no reason to worry." She tucked her arm through his. "That's great news, Enid. I'm sure Witt can get things rolling. Remember, after Saturday, Carl and I will be away on our honeymoon for the next two weeks."

The reminder brought a bubble of anticipation to Carl's chest. He still could hardly believe they were getting married this weekend.

"Oh, yes," Enid said, a gleam in her eye. "We're all very happy for you both."

"Hear, hear!" Alton raised his coffee mug in their direction, and the others around the table did the same.

Face warming, Carl dipped his chin. "Thank you. Thank you all, especially for your support during the changes we've been incorporating."

Enid invited them to take their seats, and the meeting continued with more weekly reports and discussion.

When they adjourned an hour later, Carl was breathing much more easily. Good thing, since he and Rae had a two o'clock appointment for their final premarital counseling session with Pastor Peters. Instead of brooding over a negative response from the board, now he could put those concerns behind him and give the pastor and his bride-to-be his undivided attention.

Talk about life-changing events! Six months ago, he could never have anticipated what his future would hold – reconnecting with his long lost brother, stepping into a new and even more rewarding position with the ministry, meeting the woman who would not only steal his heart but freely give him hers in return.

God was good. So very, very good.

Dressed and ready but needing some alone time, Rae sat before the mirror in the Elk Valley Community of Faith bride's room. There was one person's voice she really needed to hear before she stepped into her future.

Mark answered right away. "Hi, Rae. I'm sorry we couldn't make the trip to be there for you today."

"I understand. You have a family of your own to think about."

"I've been thanking the Lord every day that you've found the happiness I've always wanted for you." He paused, then added softly. "And Kellie would be so happy for her mom."

"I believe she would." When she sniffed back a tear, Frankie edged closer and rested his chin on her knee, those ice-blue eyes speaking his loyalty and affection.

A light tap sounded on the door. Maddie called softly, "Rae? It's almost time."

She said goodbye to Mark, then checked her reflection and adjusted the sapphire pendant Carl had given her as a wedding gift.

As a harpist and flautist played "Oh Happy Day," Frankie proudly escorted her down the aisle, where she took the hand of the man who'd pried open her heart and taken up permanent residence. Vows were spoken, laughter and kisses shared, wedding guests greeted, and bouquet tossed.

With the festivities coming to an end, Rae sent Frankie home with Witt and Maddie, where he'd spend the next two weeks hanging out with Ranger. The two dogs had even won over Ellis, who'd made a comfortable home for himself in the Wittenbauers' barn loft and split his time between assisting in the kennel and working for Happy's Helpers.

At long last, it was just the newlyweds. Carl aimed his

SUV up I-90 toward Spokane, where he'd secured reservations at a classy hotel. Tomorrow, they'd continue on to Astoria for several days exploring the Oregon coast.

He reached across the console for her hand and drew it to his lips. "Happy?"

"Extremely. Are you?"

His besotted smile said she hadn't needed to ask. "If I'm dreaming, I never want to wake up."

"Same here. In fact, I was thinking—"

"That sounds dangerous."

She punched his arm.

He flinched. "Ow!"

"Fine. I won't tell you my idea." Nose in the air, she crossed her arms. "And it'll be your loss."

"Then I insist. Tell me what's on your mind."

She waited long enough to make sure his curiosity was thoroughly piqued, then cast him a sideways glance. "We passed a sign awhile back for a cozy riverside motel. The exit's coming up." Her tone silky and inviting, she continued, "Would it throw a huge wrench in your plans if we didn't make it all the way to Spokane tonight?"

Carl's eyes darkened as he looked her way. "Sweetheart, that would be a mercy."

Looking for other books in the Montana Mercies series?
Read Witt and Maddie's story in the first book,
A Steadfast Companion

Followed by Julia and Lane's story in book two,
His Unexpected Grandchild

If you enjoyed *One Glance of Your Eyes*, please spread the
word among your reader friends and wherever you share

about books on Facebook, Goodreads, Instagram, or other social media.

Reviews are always deeply appreciated. A review doesn't have to be lengthy or eloquent, just a few brief words sharing your honest impressions. Reviews and personal recommendations are the best ways to help authors get discovered by new readers.

To receive regular updates about Myra Johnson's books and special events, subscribe to her newsletter using the signup form on her website:

www.MyraJohnson.com

With gratitude . . .

I spend hours a day in my (relatively) quite home office with my computer on my lap and looking like I got dressed in the dark. In the meantime, my sweet husband makes supermarket runs, keeps the lawn trimmed, starts the washing machine, makes sure the car is in good repair, and even (sometimes!) makes supper. When we're in social situations but I'm too introverted to mention I'm a writer, he jumps right in to brag about me and share which of my novels are his favorites. Best supportive spouse ever!

I'm also incredibly grateful for the local writers I hang out with and the encouragement and advice they provide: Joyce, Bruce, Lori, Vannetta, Robin, Wendi, Rhonda, Brenda, Kayla, Karen, Mary Pat, Cathy, Sheri—and especially Teresa Lynn, my insightful editor!

None of my success as an author would be possible without my Heavenly Father, Who always seems to provide just what I need at exactly the right time, and in ways I couldn't have imagined. Thank You, Lord, for making me a writer and blessing the work of my hands!

About the Author

After a five-year sojourn in Oklahoma, then eight years in the beautiful Carolinas, native Texan Myra Johnson and her husband are happy to be home once again in the Lone Star State enjoying wildflowers, Tex-Mex, and real Texas barbecue! Myra has been writing stories for as long as she can remember. Her published novels have garnered many awards, including top honors in Christian Retailing's Best for historical fiction and the National Excellence in Romance Fiction Awards. Her books have also earned acclaim in the ACFW Carol Awards, Georgia Romance Writers Maggie Awards, Selah Awards, HOLT Medallion, and Faith, Hope and Love Christian Writers Reader's Choice Awards.

Married for 50-plus years, Myra and her husband have two beautiful daughters married to wonderful Christian men, plus seven amazing grandchildren and a beautiful great-granddaughter. The Johnsons share their home with two pampered rescue dogs and a snobby but lovable cat who thinks he's the boss of everyone.

To receive regular updates about Myra's books and other news, be sure to subscribe to her newsletter (signup form on website).

Find Myra online:
www.myrajohnson.com

facebook.com/MyraJohnsonAuthor

instagram.com/mjwrites

bookbub.com/authors/myra-johnson

goodreads.com/MyraJohnsonAuthor

pinterest.com/mjwrites

x.com/MyraJohnson

Novels by Myra Johnson

Find the complete list at Myra's website,
www.MyraJohnson.com

MISSOURI LOVE STORIES

Autumn Rains

Romance by the Book

Where the Dogwoods Bloom

HORSEMEN OF CROSS ROADS FARM

A Horseman's Heart

A Horseman's Gift

A Horseman's Hope

WEST TEXAS SWEETHEARTS

Rancher for the Holidays

Worth the Risk

HILL COUNTRY HAVEN

Her Hill Country Cowboy

Hill Country Reunion

The Rancher's Redemption

Their Christmas Prayer

THE RANCHERS OF GABRIEL BEND
The Rancher's Family Secret
The Rebel's Return
The Rancher's Family Legacy

MONTANA MERCIES
A Steadfast Companion
His Unexpected Grandchild
One Glance of Your Eyes

FLOWERS OF EDEN HISTORICAL SERIES
The Sweetest Rain
Castles in the Clouds
A Rose So Fair

TILL WE MEET AGAIN HISTORICAL SERIES
When the Clouds Roll By
Whisper Goodbye
Every Tear a Memory

CONTEMPORARY WOMEN'S FICTION
All She Sought
One Imperfect Christmas
The Soft Whisper of Roses

NOVELLAS
The Oregon Trail Romance Collection: Settled Hearts
Designs on Love
Lifetime Investment

Made in the USA
Middletown, DE
25 November 2025